T0365133

DEFENDER OF THE TEXAS FRONTIER

A Historical Novel

DAVID R. GROSS

DEFENDER OF THE TEXAS FRONTIER
A HISTORICAL NOVEL

iUniverse books may be ordered through booksellers or by contacting:

iUniverse
1663 Liberty Drive
Bloomington, IN 47403
www.iuniverse.com
1-800-Authors (1-800-288-4677)

ISBN: 978-1-5320-7156-0 (sc)
ISBN: 978-1-5320-7190-4 (e)

Library of Congress Control Number: 2019903621

Print information available on the last page.

iUniverse rev. date: 07/09/2019

AUTHOR'S NOTE

This novel describes the life and adventures of John Coffee Hays. Many of the characters depicted are so much a part of Texas history that counties have been named for them. Almost all of the characters were real people who participated in the events described. The historical details presented are as accurate as I was able to research, but I have taken literary license by presuming to put my words into the mouths and minds of the characters.

To Rosalie, my wife for almost fifty-four years.
I think of you and miss you every day.

This is John Caperton's hand-drawn map of Texas as it existed in 1836.

CHAPTER 1

MY NAME IS John Caperton. I have known and been a friend of Jack Hays since we were young boys teaching ourselves how to hunt and fish and live rough in the forests of Tennessee. I am six months younger than Jack. I followed him, and now I leave a record of his story.

We arrived in Nacogdoches thirsty and decided to have a beer. Jack stood at the end of the ten-foot bar sipping at the mug of beer he held in his left hand. I was leaning against the far wall, no more than six or seven feet away. Jack was then nineteen, but he appeared to be maybe fourteen or fifteen years old. He's still slight and is an inch or two shorter than most of the men in any room. His complexion is fair, his nose slightly aquiline. His mouth is firm with thin lips. His chin is square. His beard struggled to be noticed. He didn't move his head, but his deep-set hazel eyes moved continuously, taking in everyone and everything in the room.

All the men in the room, with the exception of the bartender, were dressed roughly. Their wool pants were baggy and dirty with constant use, their shirts dirty and frayed at their collars and cuffs. The men's coats were a variety of styles, including some uniform coats from 1812. Almost all the men wore wide leather belts with one or two pistols jammed in between belt and coat. Some held rifles. Most had large knives in sheaths hanging from their belts. All wore battered hats of indeterminate style and age.

Jack was also wearing wool pants, but his were less baggy. The collar of his homespun shirt was stained but not frayed, and his coat was a heavy wool with a tight weave. His hat was beaver felt, the crown crushed flat, the brim drooping. He had two pistols jammed in his wide belt, the heavy grips facing each other. His bowie knife resided in a sheath close to his right hand. A Tennessee long rifle was slung by a leather strap over his left shoulder.

The continuous murmur of men in quiet conversation pervaded the cramped room. Occasionally, the sound of chairs and boots scraping on the wide-plank pinewood floor penetrated the hum. The floor planks, apparently nailed down while green, were twisted. Men often stumbled while making their way to the bar, not always the result of having imbibed too much alcohol. Every time a newcomer entered the room, there was a shout of greeting. Adding to the ambiance was the sharp sound of playing cards slapped with enthusiasm onto the three rickety tables crowding the space. All the sounds were punctuated by the noise of shot glasses and beer mugs set down on the bar and tables. Chunks of thick, sticky Nacogdoches mud dried in the warm closeness of the room and fell in clumps from the boots of the men who were in the bar longest. This was all accompanied by the stench of stale beer, rough whiskey, cigar smoke, and the stink, rising like steam, from the filthy clothing of unwashed males.

Jack watched as some men left and others arrived, crowding past one another through the narrow doorway. The single room of the rough board cabin that served as the bar filled as more men crowded in.

"Shut the damn door!" someone yelled.

It was late April 1836. Wind and rain pounded the town of Nacogdoches in the new Republic of Texas.

The door crashed open again, and a very large man pushed through. This time nobody shouted a greeting. He shoved men aside to claim a place at the bar.

"Whiskey, damn it, George," he shouted at the harried bartender, who, after glancing to identify the speaker, stopped pouring beer into the three mugs he held in one hand. He set the mugs down and poured a shot of whiskey, sliding it through the spilled beer lubricating the bar top.

The big man took up the glass, turned to survey the room, and then drank the cheap whiskey in a gulp. He returned the shot glass to the bar without turning.

"Hit me again, and keep them coming, George. Don't just stand there with your thumb up your ass."

I leaned in toward the man standing next to me and whispered, "Who is that guy?"

2

"The local bully," he whispered back. "Before long, he'll taunt somebody and wave one of those fists in his victim's face."

I noticed all the men in the bar did their best to avoid looking at him, except for Jack, who didn't take his eyes from the huge fellow.

The man standing next to me whispered again. "I noticed you came in with that young man at the bar. If he's your friend, you best tell him not to do anything to provoke. After a couple shots of that rotgut, Big Al will try to pick a fight with someone, and if that youngster doesn't stop staring at him, he'll be the one."

Jack kept his place at the bar and continued to gaze at the bully.

The big man quickly consumed three more shots of whiskey and then suddenly shoved the man standing next to him. "Back off, shithead. Don't crowd me, or I'll beat the crap out of you."

The man backed away, gulped what was left of the beer in his hand, put the mug down on a table, and ran from the bar.

The bully smiled, pleased with the reaction he forced. Then he noticed Jack looking at him. "What you smilin' about, twerp?" he shouted, pushing past three men to stand very close to Jack.

I left my place at the wall to move closer.

The bully was a full head taller and at least ninety pounds heavier than Jack. His broad shoulders tapered into a thick neck. Although I was three feet away, I could smell his rotted teeth. Jack did not back away from the stench. The bully clenched his fists.

"Wipe that smile off your face, shithead, or would you rather I wipe it off for you?" The bully raised his right fist and waved it in front of Jack's face. "I said to wipe off that smile, or I'll wipe it off for you."

Jack continued to smile while gently placing his mug on the bar. The bully pulled back his fist. The pistol on Jack's left side was in his right hand. The fist started forward, a cap exploded, and the coat over the big man's heart burst into flames. He fell straight back, stiff as a felled tree. He was dead when the back of his head hit the floor, pushing his hat over his still snarling face.

Jack pushed his pistol back through his belt and then swept his eyes around the room. "Anybody think that man was not about to hit me?" he asked.

One man pushed his chair back from the table where he sat. The feet of the chair screeched and then caught on a twisted board. The man stood, pushing the chair over backward.

"That son of a bitch beat me near to death three weeks ago, and others in this room have suffered at those fists. Thanks, young man. We are well rid of that scum."

Several other men in the room voiced their agreement.

"Is there a lawman in this town?" asked Jack. "I suppose I'm in deep shit for killing this man, but I wasn't going to allow him to hit me."

"It was self-defense. We all saw it," said the man as he extricated his feet from the turned-over chair on the floor.

The door slammed open, hitting the wall on the hinge side. A gray-haired man with a four-day-old beard, his potbelly hanging over his gun belt, entered with a pistol in his hand and a badge pinned to his coat.

"I heard a shot. What the hell has Big Al Cranston done now?"

Jack motioned at the body on the floor with his chin. "Is that Cranston?"

One of the men in the room spoke up. "It was completely justified, Sheriff. Couldn't expect the young man to wait until that asshole hit him. I want to buy our hero a drink."

I finally found my voice. "I can verify that man on the floor was about to hit him, sir."

Several men shouted at the bartender to pour Jack a drink.

Jack waved a hand in the air. "Thanks, gents. I've had all the alcohol I need. Maybe another time. We're just passing through." He grabbed my right arm above the elbow. "Believe we'll be on our way, unless there is something else, Sheriff."

"I'll need you and your friend to come to my office and sign a statement, young man. You too, Sam, and anyone else who agrees Big Al was asking for it. I'll have to file a report with the judge whenever he comes around again. What's your name, youngster?"

"John Coffee Hays, sir," Jack answered.

"Any relation to Harmond Hays of Tennessee?"

"Yes, sir. He's my daddy."

"How's he doing?"

"He and my ma both died of the cholera about four years ago."

"Sorry to hear that. I served with him in 1812 under General Jackson. Didn't one of your uncles marry Andrew Jackson's sister?"

"Yes, sir. She's my great-aunt Cage, my ma's side."

"Well, boys, the tree this lad sprouted from is one tough giant of the US of A. Let me shake your hand, John Coffee Hays. Nobody in this town is likely to weep over the loss of Big Al. Some of you boys haul his carcass out of here. Leave him on the porch of my office until I can order a coffin, but wrap him up in a tarp first. No sense in spreading his blood all over town. George, looks like you'll have a mess to clean up."

The bartender replied. "He rarely paid for what he consumed, so no great loss. A bucket of water sloshed on the floor will get most of it. The rest will just mix with the dirt."

As we followed the sheriff to his office, Jack whispered, "So that's how it feels to kill a man. Glad I didn't take the time to think about what I was doing. Just a reflex. Still, I'm glad I'm not in trouble. Wonder if Big Al has family who will mourn him?"

Four weeks prior to arriving in Nacogdoches, I rode to Jack's uncle's plantation to tell Jack about the slaughter at the Alamo. I knew Jack had returned to the plantation the previous evening after completing a land survey working with his cousin.

News of the Texans' struggle to rid themselves of Mexico reached Tennessee daily, and many, including Davey Crockett, had already made their way south to offer aid. The possibility for adventure had a strong pull on me, Jack, and our friends. We talked about joining the fight. Jack told me he took the step of accumulating letters of introduction from relatives and family friends who were personally acquainted with some of the leaders of the Texas insurrection. The letters included one from Gen. Andrew Jackson, whose sister was married to one of Jack's uncles on his mother's side. The hermitage was close to the plantation at Little Cedar Lick, Tennessee, where Jack was born. As a child, he spent many hours absorbing knowledge of horse breeding, military strategy, and, of course, politics from the childless Jackson.

"I'm on my way to New Orleans, Jack," I told him. "A company of volunteers is forming. I hear men from Kentucky, Tennessee, Louisiana, and Mississippi are gathering there. Word is all we need to join up is a pistol, a knife, a rifle, and a good horse. As soon as enough men arrive, we're on our way to Texas. We'll make them Mexicans pay for what they done to the heroes of the Alamo. You in? I'm sure not going to miss out on this."

"I'm in, John. Give me some time to rustle up some supplies and gear, and I'll catch up to you on the road. I have to say goodbye to my family. Any of the other boys going?"

"Just me and you, so far, but I'm on my way to talk to Rory and Ian."

"It won't take me long to catch up. We're finally in for some excitement."

After a short talk with his aunt, uncle, sister, and little brother, Jack gathered some cans of beans and a cloth bag full of beef jerky. He packed the food in one of his saddlebags along with an extra shirt and his letters of introduction sealed in a waterproof pouch. He rolled up a heavy wool blanket and his rain slicker inside a canvas ground cloth and tied them behind his saddle. Caps for his rifle and pistols, along with gunpowder and shot, extra lead, and his shot mold, went into the opposite saddlebag. He took a gunnysack, half-full of a mixture of cracked corn and rolled oats, tied the opening of the sack with a leather thong, and hung the sack over his saddle horn.

He was barely fifteen when his father and mother died within a few weeks of each other. Their deaths left Jack's older brother, William; two younger sisters; and three younger brothers orphans. Jack, his sister Sarah, and his brother Robert, then only five years old, were sent to live with their mother's brother, Robert Cage. His uncle and aunt were kind people but already had a large family of their own. Jack soon decided he was a burden. His large extended family included a cousin who was a professional surveyor. Jack signed on as a chain boy. Within a few months, he had mastered the intricacies and math necessary to survey land and was running his own crew on subcontracts from his cousin.

Jack, Ian Fleming, Rory McCloud, and I were all born within six months of each other, lived in the same area, and were schoolmates. We arrived in New Orleans and found the company of volunteers headed for Texas. When the enlistments reached ninety, the company departed New Orleans, traveling on two steamboats up the Mississippi River and then overland to Nacogdoches. It wasn't until after we arrived that we learned of the Texans' victory at San Jacinto.

Because there was no fighting for us to do, most of the volunteers returned home. Jack and I decided to stay an extra day in Nacogdoches to talk about what to do next. Ian and Rory decided to return home, but Jack wanted to see more of Texas and I decided to stick with him. We saddled our horses and traveled to Washington-on-the-Brazos.

"This is the place where Texas declared its independence," said Jack.

"If you say so," I replied.

"I want to visit a man by the name of Isaac Donohoe. He's an old friend of my uncle Abner Cage. Lives not far from here on Clear Creek. We'll ask someone how to get there."

A gray-bearded man, his skin darkened by many years of exposure to the elements, was sitting on a straight-backed chair on the porch. He was leaning back against unpainted vertical lapboard siding, the front legs of the chair a full six inches off the rough wood floor.

"Mr. Donohoe, I'm John Coffee Hays. I have some letters for you from my relatives, including your old friend my uncle Abner, and from my grandpa. This here is my friend John Caperton."

The old man leaned forward, and the front legs of the chair hit the porch floor with a bang.

"Well, you boys get down from those horses and come inside. You're one of Elizabeth's boys, aren't you? Sorry to hear about your folks." He stood up but remained slightly bent over. He shuffled his legs to shake out the stiffness in his knees. "Come up, come up."

Donohoe looked back over his left shoulder at the open door to the house. "Sarah, have we got any lemonade left to serve these young men?"

"I'll make some fresh. You'll have to come inside for it, though. I'm not going to serve it to you."

Jack smiled at the exchange, dismounted, removed his battered hat, and ran his fingers over his matted-down hair. "My aunt told me you came here with Stephen F. Austin."

"Yep, that's God's truth. Texas has been good to me and mine. Why are you here, John Coffee?"

"My grandpa Hays nicknamed me Jack. That's mostly what I answer to."

"All, right, Jack it is. What brings you this far west?"

"I had hoped to kill some Mexicans, but it appears they are already beat—no army left to join."

"Not so, Jack. Gen. Tom Rusk is chasing the Mexican Army back to Mexico. Santa Anna got himself captured by Sam Houston, and I hear Rusk is now somewhere northeast of Goliad. If you find him, I'm sure he will welcome you."

"That's an interesting possibility," said Jack.

"Well, we'll find you both a bed for the night and some grub. You can rest your horses in the barn, and there's grain for them. You can stay as long as you like, but I expect you'll want to be off at first light."

"Yes, sir. Thank you for your hospitality. We'll go take care of our horses."

"You do that, boys. I'm going to catch up with my old friends from these letters you brought me."

He sat back down, leaned back in the chair, and opened the letter on top of the pile Jack handed him.

We rode into the main camp of the Army of the Republic of Texas in late May. After we explained we wanted to volunteer and had letters of introduction to General Rusk, we were escorted to the general's tent. We waited patiently outside until several officers exited, and then a sergeant showed us in.

The general was reading some documents. He did not rise or look up.

"General Rusk, my name is John Coffee Hays, and this is John Caperton. I have letters of introduction from Isaac Donohoe and Gen. Andrew Jackson."

Still without looking up or speaking, Rusk held out his left hand. Jack placed the two letters in his hand. Rusk leaned back in his canvas camp chair and unfolded the letters. He read through them quickly and then more slowly.

"Well, Mr. Hays, you seem to be quite an accomplished young man. According to these letters, an exceptional horseman, a crack shot with both rifle and pistol, and not afraid of a fight. I can use a man of your talents in my spy company. Mr. Caperton, do you have some letters?"

"No, sir."

"He's as good as me in everything," Jack spoke up.

"How old are you boys?"

"We are both nineteen, sir. What's a spy company?" asked Jack.

"Spies are scouts for the main army. They patrol our flanks to prevent attacks and range ahead of the army to keep track of the enemy and gauge potential weaknesses or indications they will turn and fight. They are frequently on their own or in small groups and need to be comfortable with that. You both think you are up to doing that job?"

"Yes, sir. We can do that," both of us said at the same time.

"Good. The sergeant outside will sign you up and take you to where the spies are camped. Here are your letters back, Mr. Hays. You both just follow orders, and you'll do fine. Dismissed."

It was early in June. Jack and I were among thirty spies who rode into Goliad in advance of General Rusk's army. We spread out through the streets and alleys, on the watch for any enemy soldiers. There were none. The next morning Jack and I, along with two other men, were walking along the Bexar Road.

"Do you believe what Jack Shackelford told the major?" asked Jack. "He told him the Mexicans marched somewhere between four hundred twenty-five and four hundred forty-five of our men along this road and along the San Patricio and the Victoria roads. There were Mexican soldiers lined up on each side of all three roads, and they shot our men from only feet away. Them that didn't die right off were clubbed or knifed to death. All this while we had that son of a bitch Santa Anna as a prisoner."

"Yeah, Herm Ehrenberg told me the same story," answered Sean McAffey, removing his hat and scratching his scalp through a thick mat of black hair. "He and Shackelford were both wounded in the Battle of Coleto. Shackelford was saved by a Señorita Francita Alvarez, and Herm played dead until the Mesicans pulled out."

The other man with us called himself John Smith. He was taller than any of us, skinny with slopping shoulders. He always seemed hunched over, as if trying to avoid attention. His fingernails were broken and black with dirt. Although his posture seemed to indicate that he remained unnoticed, he was unable to avoid adding his thoughts and opinions to any conversation. Jack told me he suspected Smith was running from the law.

"I heard General Fannin was the last to be killed," said Smith. "He had a bad leg wound and the Mesicans sat him in a chair 'cause he couldn't walk. Then they made him watch his men being massacred. Afterward, they dragged him, still on the chair, to the courtyard in front of the church and blindfolded him. As a matter of courtesy, he asked them to send his personal possessions to his family, to be shot in the heart and not in the face, and to be given a Christian burial. The bastards took all his stuff, shot him in the face, and burned his body, along with all the others. His body was somewhere in that stinking pile of souls we found yesterday."

Jack stopped walking. "Well, let's get back," he said. "We're supposed to continue digging that huge grave just off the road between Goliad and the Presidio la Bahia. General Rusk wants a formal military funeral tomorrow morning. If it was up to me, I'd bring Santa Anna here and slit his throat on top of that mass grave. He's the one who gave the order to kill all prisoners. I would also like to get my hands on the Mexican commander who followed that order. I'd make him dig a hole with his bare hands, beat the shit out of him, then slit his throat. What kind of slimy bastard would do such a thing?"

Jack stripped off his shirt as we walked back. He tied the sleeves of the shirt around his waist.

"Damn, digging is gonna be hot work today."

The rest of that summer, General Rusk's army harried the forces of Gen. José de Urrea as the Mexican army withdrew. We pursued them south to Refugio and then southwest to San Patricio on the Nueces River. After crossing the Nueces, General Urrea believed his army was back in Mexico. General Rusk did not. We spies kept close track of all of the dispersed units of Urrea's army. Whenever a unit made a stand, Rusk sent whole companies to attack in force. Rusk forced the Mexicans across the Rio Grande where they stopped to build up the fortifications around the town of Matamoros.

The Army of the Republic of Texas camped along the Rio Grande. Our job was done, and we waited for the strapped-for-cash Texas government to raise enough funds to pay us and discharge us.

Jack and I sat with Sean McAffey and John Smith, huddled close to our campfire. The chilled winds and rains of early October blew from the northwest. Even as far south as we were, watching Matamoros, it was damned uncomfortable.

Sean held out his hands full of Spanish and Mexican silver coins.

"I joined up in early March, seven months ago. I reckon it was two hundred and fifteen days. Supposed to get a dollar a day, but what's this shit? How do I know this shit is real and worth the two-hundred-plus I got comin'?"

"I don't think Texas would cheat you, Sean," said Jack. "I hear the government is struggling to come up with cash. Those coins will spend—I'm sure. Let's see them. Yeah." He picked out ten coins. "See, these are worth ten pesos each, probably over a hundred dollars in American money. Besides, you get a land grant too."

Sean shook his head.

"Yeah, I guess, but then I have to pay for a survey to register the land. What did they give you, Smith?"

"Crap." John Smith held out his hand to show us what he got.

"I was only in a hundred and fifty days, and they gave me paper money from Mississippi, Kentucky, and North Carolina, and then these goddamned shinplasters from some private company I never heard tell of. Who will take this crap in exchange for anything? And what the hell can I do with three hundred acres of land someplace outside Gonzales? Shit, I never even been to Gonzales. What did they try to pay you two off with?"

"We haven't talked to them yet. John and I are still hoping we can find something to do here in Texas."

CHAPTER 2

IN THE MIDDLE of November, Jack and I, along with ten other newly discharged comrades, were riding back along the same route we had taken south with General Rusk. We were living off the land. We hunted deer, rabbits, whatever we could find. Jack shot a young buffalo cow standing two hundred yards away, and we took the rest of the day to harvest the meat. We cooked most of it that same night. Some we roasted to eat, and then we hung thin strips overnight in the smoke from green mesquite twigs and leaves thrown on smoldering campfires. We also took strips of the thin hide inside the back legs. It made the best wadding for rifle and pistol balls.

We spent two days in San Patricio where we were able to trade some of our shinplasters for black powder, two boxes of caps, some feed for our horses, coffee, and cornmeal. At Goliad, the whole group of us visited the mass grave and paid our respects to the victims.

"I will never forget you," whispered Jack under his breath. "The bastards will pay for this."

The next morning, the group of men dispersed, most returning home. Jack and I rode to Victoria, across open country east to the Colorado River, and from there northeast to the capital of the Republic, by then located on the Brazos River at Columbia.

The town, if one could call it that, was a collection of clapboard buildings and log cabins, muddy tracks that belied being called roads, and a ragtag collection of roughly dressed men presumably doing the business of the Republic of Texas. The weather was rainy with a cold wind pushing in from the northwest. We road past fallow fields of mud.

"What do you suppose they grow here?" I asked.

"Cotton would be my guess," answered Jack.

After seeing to our horses at the large shack that served as a stable, we made our way to a clapboard building under construction with a sign identifying it as Kelsey's store. Our clothing, by then, was patched with whatever had come to hand, threadbare, and filthy. We learned the store was under construction because Mr. Kelsey's original clapboard building, built in 1833, had been requisitioned as offices for the president, vice president, and secretary of state. The only other government building was the former residence of Capt. H. S. Brown. Most of the government officials shared log cabins scattered around the two government buildings.

We checked into the building called a hotel for a room, a bath, and a haircut. Jack still lacked enough whiskers to warrant a shave, but the hot lather on my face was luxurious.

The following morning Jack presented himself at the Kelsey Building, introducing himself to a clerk. I went with him but found a stool to wait on in the clerk's room. Jack explained that he had letters of introduction from Andrew Jackson and others.

"I would really appreciate it if President Houston could find some time to talk to me."

"I'll check," said the clerk, passing through a door and closing it.

We could hear the murmur of voices, and then the clerk reappeared.

"President Houston asks that you leave your letters then return an hour after lunch. He'll see you then."

Jack handed over his packet of letters, still in their waterproof pouch.

"Thank you, sir. I will return this afternoon." The clerk took the pouch and nodded.

When we returned, the same clerk gestured at the open door to the office behind his desk. He didn't look up from the paper he was writing on.

Later that day, Jack told me that the room he entered was barely ten feet square. There was no window. In one corner was a small desk with thin, tapered legs. It didn't appear to be sturdy enough to support the piles of documents stacked on it. A straight-backed wood chair stood in front of the desk. An oak cask stood next to the desk. On the cask was a lit kerosene lamp that gave off a strong smell and weak light. In the far corner was a narrow bed on which Sam Houston lay propped up on several pillows. His left leg was resting on two additional pillows. On the floor next to the bed and within easy reach was a bottle of whiskey.

Houston's high forehead and the bald top of his head were framed by gray hair that stuck out at all angles and fell over his ears. His eyes were deep set and close to the narrow bridge of his nose. Two deep clefts worked their way down in a straight line vertically from the inner corner of each dark eyebrow.

"Take the chair, Mr. Hays. Your letters are in your pouch on the desk. You can take them when you leave. I have known General Jackson for many years, and although we have always disagreed about our country's treatment of the Indians, he has been a good friend and mentor. He supported my election as a congressman from Tennessee and my term as governor. I know many of your relatives and served with both your father and grandfather. As long as I have known General Jackson, he has been stingy with praise, but both he and his sister have lavished praise on you and your family. I wish the old man thought as highly of me, but that's a different issue."

Houston reached for the bottle on the floor and took a long swig. Then he held out the bottle.

"No thank you, sir. I'm not opposed, but I don't drink much myself."

"It's this damn ankle. Stray bullet at San Jacinto near took it off. Hasn't healed, and the sawbones tell me it's not likely to any more than the Creek arrowhead in my groin or the goddamned Brit lead balls in my shoulder and arm. Anyhow, Hays, I presume you're looking for employment, same as everyone else who comes through that door."

"Yes, sir, in a way. I understand the Republic is strapped for funds and the army is being disbanded, but in my time with General Rusk's spies, I learned there is considerable danger on the frontier from the Comanche, as well as Mexican banditos. How do you plan to protect your citizens?"

"Well, Mr. Hays, our treatment of the Indians continues to be disgraceful. The Comanche are doing exactly what you or I would do in their place—protecting their lands. You know, I lived with the Cherokee and speak their language. My second wife was Cherokee."

"Yes, Sir. My grandpa told me."

"I'll bet he did. Damn fine soldier. He was one of Jackson's favorites."

Jack continued. "The fact remains, sir, that the Comanche are raiding your settlements, killing the men in most cruel manner, and raping and killing the women they don't take as hostages or slaves. What is done to the women and children they take as slaves I don't want to imagine. I want to do everything I can to protect them."

"Yes, I'm well aware, Hays. Don't get on a soapbox with me. Earlier today I spoke with some of your officers and others from Rusk's command. Most of them know of you. They told me you are a natural leader of men and command great respect. I understand your compadres in the spies wanted to elect you sergeant, but you refused."

"Yes, sir. I don't know enough about soldiering to be in charge of other men."

"Well, I have the solution for that. I'm giving you a letter to carry to the best scout who ever served me, Erastus Smith. I have commissioned him to recruit a ranging company that will be responsible for protecting our western and southern frontiers. He's in San Antonio now. I want you to go there and volunteer. How does that sound to you?"

"Good, sir. My friend John Caperton served with me in the spies, and he is with me and can do everything I can. I can vouch for him and his skills. Will there be a place for him?"

"No doubt. I'm certain Smith can find a use for both of you."

He groaned and shifted his raised leg before reaching again for the bottle.

"He was hitting the bottle of whiskey the whole time I was in there with him," Jack told me later. "But I guess all those wounds really give him a lot of pain. He's been through plenty, I suppose, and if the booze helps, why not?"

It was mid-December 1836 when we arrived in San Antonio after a cold, wet journey. He was still riding the same spirited bay mare that tried her best to buck him off every morning. My gelding was calm, steady, and reliable. Before we left Columbia, Jack purchased a set of Mexican spurs. He brought the bay under control each morning by sinking the sharp points of the spurs into the mare's abdomen.

Jack presented the letter from President Houston to Erastus Smith that identified us and recommended that Smith sign us into his ranging company. Smith, in his early fifties, stood only an inch or two taller than Jack. His long arms and legs didn't seem to fit his compact body. While

Jack was explaining why we were there, he never took his eyes away from Jack's face.

That same afternoon we were sworn into the company that Smith called his scouts, his spies, or his rangers, depending on his mood. After we took the oath for a twelve-month enlistment, Smith waved us away. He wasn't a man to waste time on nonessential conversation. Once outside, we were at a loss for what to do next. We removed our saddles from our horses and started to rub them down with a scrap of gunnysack.

A big man dressed in buckskin clothing and moccasins approached with his right hand extended. "Jack Hays?" he asked.

Jack stood up straighter but was still a full head shorter than the big man. "Yep."

They shook hands.

"You John Caperton?" He extended his hand to me.

"Yes."

"I'm William Wallace. Deef said I should attach myself to you boys and show you the ropes."

"Deef?"

"Yeah, Captain Smith. You did notice he's mostly deaf?"

"I did," I answered.

"Yeah, well you need to stand directly in front of him if you want to talk. He can't hear much, but he can read your lips if you talk slow enough. Even Sam Houston calls him Deaf Smith. Most everyone I know calls him Deef, but not to his face unless you want your hide removed. To his face, we call him Cap or Captain."

"Got it. So, what's your story Mr. Wallace?" I asked.

"Who the hell is Mr. Wallace? I'm Bill." His smile included his whole face. He grabbed Jack's hand again and continued to hold it in his powerful grip.

I reckoned the man weighed at least 240, none of it fat. His hand was callused with coagulated blood in deep cracks in the skin of his fingers. Jack extracted his hand and then glanced at the big man's feet.

"My God, those are the biggest feet I believe I've ever been this close to. I suppose your nickname is Bigfoot?"

The big man laughed with delight. "I like it. From now on, I'm Bigfoot Wallace."

Jack joined him laughing.

The two men laughed, and I could feel the bond forming between them. That evening the three of us shared a campfire on the banks of the San Antonio River.

"So, you now know all there is to know about John and me," Jack said. "What's your story, Bigfoot?"

"I was born in 1817 in Lexington, Virginia."

"We're all about the same age then."

"I guess, but I'm from royal stock."

"No shit? Do tell."

"Yep, I'm a direct descendent from both William Wallace and Robert Bruce."

"Another damn Scotsman," Jack joked. "We're everywhere."

"Yeah, Scotland must be a crappy place 'cause there's a shitload of us that made it to the colonies. Anyhow, when I learned both my brother and my cousin were among the ones murdered at Goliad, I hightailed it over to Texas. Got here too late to kill some Mexicans right off, but Deef says there's a damn good opportunity to kill some with this outfit."

"Well, I am happy to hear that. We helped bury those men at Goliad. I'm sorry you lost kin there, but I'm ready to seek vengeance for them even though the pay stinks, especially since Texas is broke and probably won't be able to pay us anyhow. Does the government really supply keep for us and our horses?" Jack questioned.

"We'll be living rough. Mostly outside in whatever weather presents itself. Deef does get ammunition for us, though," Bigfoot noted.

"That's good news. I'd hate to give up my dollar a day to buy my own caps, powder, and lead."

"Deef says the country we'll be patrolling still has lots of game." He patted the stock of his Kentucky long rifle. "This relic shoots pretty straight. I reckon anything within two or three hundred yards will serve to keep us from starvin'."

"Three hundred yards ... No shit, Bigfoot?"

"Don't mean to brag, but she hasn't failed me yet."

Jack smiled and punched the big man in the arm. "We'll see, we'll see. Now tell me what you know about our captain. Just how old do you reckon he is?"

"Dunno, at least fifty I'd say. Maybe more. Been here in Texas a long time. Married a widow lady from San Antonio with three girls, and they've had three more girls of their own. Heard tell he had a son, name of Travis, but the boy died of the cholera in 1833, only six years old."

"That's hard."

"Yeah, the way I heard it, Deef first couldn't make up his mind between the Mexicans and the Texans, being married to a Tejano and all. He even converted Catholic to marry her and became a citizen of Mexico. Bought him a ranch about four miles south of where we're sittin' now. His place is nearby the Mission of San Jose. When the Mexicans were laying siege to San Antonio, he came back from his ranch one night, and they wouldn't let him back into town to his family. Pissed him off so bad he went straight to find Houston and volunteered."

"I'd say that's pretty pissed off," Jack said. "So, what did he do after he joined up?"

"Well, he already had quite the reputation in Texas. He brought in muley cattle from Louisiana to upgrade his herd of longhorns. Most everybody knows he's an expert tracker and pathfinder. Reckon he knows more trails and landmarks in Texas than about anyone. He is a crack shot with rifle and pistol and also has a reputation as a considerable killer of Comanche. Sam Houston knew him, and the first thing Houston done was to send him back to San Antonio to find out what happened. He speaks Mexican like a Tejano. He managed to bring out a Mrs. Dickinson and her daughter who were eyewitness to what happened at the Alamo. Her husband was one of them killed."

Jack looked up as several young men walked over to join the group. He nodded his welcome. Bigfoot introduced each man by name, and we stood to shake hands. Six young men were then gathered around the campfire listening to the story of the living legend who was their leader.

"So, did Deef fight at San Jacinto too?" asked Jack.

"Oh yeah. After he returned with Mrs. Dickinson, he was assigned to Captain Karnes's cavalry company of the First Regiment of Volunteers. He was put in command of new recruits and trained them by taking them with him while he gathered intelligence. He taught them how to ride hard and fast, live off the land, and avoid detection."

"San Jacinto?"

"God you're impatient. I'm getting to it. Houston kept retreating so he could recruit more volunteers, but those he already had wanted to fight. He was finally forced into fighting at San Jacinto when some of the units told him they were going to bring it to the Mexicans with or without him. Deef told Houston he could destroy Vince's Bridge to prevent Santa Anna from retreating or getting reinforcements. Houston told him to get on it, so Deef took ten of his recruits with him, snuck behind the Mexican army, and destroyed that bridge. They first tried to burn it but couldn't get a fire going hot enough to get the job done, so they took it down with axes and still got back in time to join the fight."

"That took some balls."

"Yeah, but he wasn't done. Managed to capture General Cos all on his own. Then after Santa Anna was a prisoner, he was the one who carried that son of a bitch's orders to the rest of the Mexicans, telling them to retreat back to Mexico."

"Well, boys," murmured Jack, "sounds as though old Deef is the one to lead us to glory."

There were a few chuckles, but nobody actually laughed at his joke.

CHAPTER 3

MY FAMILY'S HOME is on the corner of Presa and Nueces streets in San Antonio. My guess is that most folks just know it as my house, Deef Smith's house. I know they call me that, but I don't allow it to my face. Every morning I'm up before dawn. While I'm sitting on the edge of our bed, my wife, Guadalupe, pounds on my back. It seems to ease my coughing and helps me breathe easier. She prepares coffee, and then we take some alone time, just sitting on the front porch, sipping coffee, sharing the moment together, and watching the sky lighten in the east.

This morning I walked around to the shed in back of our adobe house and saddled one of the three horses I keep there. I covered the four miles to where my company was camped at an easy lope. It is a pace any of my three horses can maintain for hours, if necessary.

The topography of the lands bordering the Balcones Escarpment is covered by savannahs of live oak. During spring, there are broad meadows ablaze with wild flowers, especially bluebonnets. It is easy to hunt buffalo, bear, deer, antelope, wild turkey, Sandhill cranes, coyotes, and wolves in this country—not too many people yet. As the sun rose above the eastern horizon, I arrived at the campsite. Each day I spend time drilling the men. Their horses are staked out to graze during the night, so they had to learn to bring them in quickly and efficiently. Then I have them practice saddling and mounting the horses, faster each day. Those skills are just a small portion that I have to teach—skills that might save their lives. This morning the company managed to go from their bedrolls to their saddles within minutes.

The next drill was riding at a fast gallop while moving from side to side and from erect to a low crouch. The idea is to make themselves a more difficult target. More hours are spent firing their muzzle-loading pistols and rifles from a moving horse then and reloading while the horse is moving, even at a lope or gallop. Significant time is also spent in target practice and reloading drills while dismounted. I also train the men to fire their weapons in volleys, dividing them into platoons of five or ten. The first platoon fires and then remains in place to reload while the next platoon steps forward to fire. I teach them to pick and call out their targets so none of the targets are left uncovered and no targets are hit by more than one man. They practice at distances from twenty-five to over one hundred yards.

I have identified three of my young recruits: Bigfoot Wallace, Jack Hays, and a twenty-year-old from Kentucky named George Dolson, as my sharpshooters. The three take extra practice with their long rifles at targets up to 250 yards away, none of the targets bigger than a man's head. Bigfoot can routinely hit those targets at three hundred yards. He is the best shot with a rifle in the company—even better than me, and I'm deadly accurate at anything under two hundred yards. Jack Hays routinely scores best of all the men with pistols.

I teach my men how to estimate the number of horses that passed through a location and how long ago they passed. I teach them about edible roots, berries, and plants and which poisonous plants to avoid themselves and keep away from their horses.

"In cold weather, it is often only the poisonous plants that are green. Mules know better, but horses will go right for 'em. Got to watch out for that," I explained.

Instruction is conducted with a minimum of verbiage, a lot of pointing, and frequent interruptions by my coughing. Not infrequently a more severe bout of coughing results in me hacking up blood-tinged sputum. I am both disgusted and irritated by it, but nothing I can do to stop it.

The men make certain to talk slowly and loudly and to stand directly in front of me when they have something to communicate. All of the recruits are experienced hunters. That means they almost always have meat of some kind to keep them going. When the Republic manages to get funds to me, I am able to purchase hardtack, salt, parched and ground corn, bacon, sugar, dried beans, rice, and, when available, dried fruit and coffee. The men are often without some or all of those luxuries.

The company's campsite has to be moved every few days as their horses consume the available forage. When funds are available, they have corn, oats, bran, and sometimes barley to supplement the diet of their animals. This supplementation is especially important when we are covering long distances on a daily basis.

The men are not supplied with any kind of uniforms or clothing. They wear what they have. Most have something to offer protection against wind and rain, a gum slicker, a buffalo robe, or a heavy, close-knit, long wool coat. Shirts are of buckskin, cotton, or wool. Most have wool or heavy cotton pants. Some prefer buckskin. All of them have long, cotton underwear. Hats are of every style imaginable from coonskin caps to Mexican sombreros. The sombrero that I wear is dirty, frayed, and greasy. Jack and several others have low-crowned, wide-brimmed felt hats that in high winds have to be tied to their heads with bandannas. The only time any of them bathe is when they cross a river or are given leave to go to town, on which occasions their clothing is also subject to water, sometimes even to soap.

Mid-February I moved the camp to the Medina River to find more grass for the horses. The company continued their daily training, but I arrived later in the day since the camp was more distant from my home. On the evening of March 6, a Tejano compadre of mine rode into the camp on a lathered horse.

"Two of you unsaddle that horse, rub him down, and give him two handfuls of corn," I instructed. "What news do you bring, Esteban?"

The man spoke loudly and slowly in Spanish. I leaned forward to concentrate on his lips.

"Señor, the Mexicans are gathering an army outside Laredo. They are planning to invade Texas again."

"Bueno, Esteban. Thank you for bringing me this news. When your horse is breathing normally again, please ride back to my home and tell Guadalupe and the girls I love them all but am off to do my duty. Tell them I will return as soon as I can to them. Bueno?"

"Si, señor, of course. Go with God."

Then I turned to address my men, all of whom had gathered around to find out what was happening.

"The Mesicans are forming up an army at Laredo. Saddle up. We're leaving now. It's a long way to go, and we need to travel cross-country. We'll stay away from the roads so they don't learn we're coming."

That same night we rode at a trot for three hours. I led the company along game trails and other landmarks I knew. Much of the time I used the stars to take us in the direction I wanted. We rested for no more than an hour, while our horses found whatever they could to consume. After two days of riding for three or four hours and then resting for only a short time, the men usually fell asleep immediately once they stretched out on the ground.

During the third day, things got ugly. A cold wind from the northeast brought driving, cold rain. All of us hunched in our saddles in a vain attempt to make ourselves smaller, hoping for less exposure to the chilling rain, shivering, noses dripping, and me coughing without respite. Then it got worse—sleet mixed with the rain, and we ran out of grain for the horses. We also used up the last of our parched corn, sugar, and bacon rations. The men reused coffee grounds, but after the third brewing, we were drinking little more than brown-tinged water. While the company continued on at a steady pace, I sent out four men at a time to hunt, but there was little to be found. Bigfoot brought down a lean, pregnant doe, and we managed to make the meat from both the doe and unborn fetus last for two days. An occasional squirrel or rabbit provided a minimum of sustenance—poor fare at best. A stray cow encountered on day six of the journey provided fresh meat for two days and smoked jerky for another two. Feeding twenty-one hungry men was a constant concern.

We finally arrived at the old San Ygnacio Ranch on the Arroyo Chacon after nine days. The owner is an old friend and welcomed me, but he had very little by way of food or supplies that he could spare. It had been a very hard winter, and he had no grain for the horses. He did supply a sack of dried beans for the men. I wrote him a note on a scrap of paper.

"You can submit that note to the Republic of Texas. They will pay you for the beans."

My friend took the note, glanced at it, smiled, and shrugged.

I moved the company about a mile from the hacienda. The men were unsaddling their horses preparing to make camp when a group of five Mexican soldiers, well mounted, appeared over a small rise. As soon as the Mexicans saw us, they turned and put their horses into a dead run, headed in the direction of Laredo. Jack Hay's bay was already unsaddled, but he jumped on her back and shouted for those who had not yet unsaddled their horses to give chase. Seven men joined him, me among them, with a smile on my face. All of our horses were exhausted from the long-forced march and lack of food, so we were unable to gain on the Mexicans. Our horses soon started to struggle, and Jack reigned up holding his right hand in the air.

"No use, boys. Our horses are just too beat. Let's get back to camp."

I entered the following in my written report after returning to San Antonio:

Early the next morning, March 17, took Hays with me to view the road to Laredo and, if possible, take a prisoner to ascertain the force of the enemy station in the town. I found the trail of some cavalry sent out to intercept us, so returned to camp and prepared for their reception.

We waited until afternoon, but no Mexicans showed so we retreated a few miles to find grass for our horses. On our way, I rode ahead to scout and spotted the enemy less than a mile away.

Intended to make a stand in a dry riverbed, but before we were able to get there, I seen some of my men about to be cut off by forty of the cavalry from Laredo. Spotted a mesquite thicket off to the east, hollered to ride hard, and after we all made it told the men to tie up the horses.

We had scarcely prepared for battle when the enemy commenced firing from both the right and left flanks about 150 yards away. A portion of them also were advancing from our rear. I ordered the men to hold fire until the Mexicans were within fifty yards then ordered them to fire in their five-man platoons, as we had practiced. Told them to make certain of their individual targets then fall back and reload. The fight lasted for about forty-five minutes, then the enemy retreated leaving ten dead and taking ten wounded with them. Privates Peter Conrad and George Dolson sustained wounds but were able to travel.

Private Hays's cool and intrepid conduct afforded great encouragement and example to my young soldiers.

Captured twenty enemy horses, but our own horses were in too poor condition to give chase to the enemy. Returned to San Antonio. Only ten of my men had ever been in a battle previous to this. All men behaved well and fought hard. The trip home, taking the roads, was easier but still little forage for horses and the weather turned mild.

April finally arrived with nutritious spring grass. There was also a most welcome infusion of funds from the Texas government. This time the funds were in Mexican silver coins that storeowners were happy to accept. Men and horses were well fed. I split the company into four equal ranging units. Each was responsible for traveling through a huge area of the frontier with instructions to be on the lookout for Comanche, banditos, or the Mexican army. Their orders were to observe and report, not to engage unless forced into it.

I designated Hays to lead the four other men in his group. They were happy he was the one with the responsibility and willingly followed his lead. It isn't clear to me what Jack does to merit so much respect of his peers. He is modest, rarely gives orders, only makes suggestions. The men seem to realize he would never ask someone to do something he wouldn't do himself. He is a natural leader, and somehow the other young men sense that and follow him willingly into any situation. I believe Caperton recognized those leadership traits when they were both young and has been following him for a long time.

Late in April, I sent Hays and his men out to reconnoiter. What follows is, more or less, what Jack told me when he returned, with a Lipan Apache in tow.

As the sun was about to set, Jack led his men up and over a small hill. They found a lone Indian roasting a venison haunch over a small fire. The Indian's horse was hobbled nearby, chomping grass, ignoring the new horses and their riders. The Indian stood as they approached but made no move to reach for the rifle or the bow and arrows lying on the ground near the fire. He was bare-chested, extremely muscular, and obviously powerful.

He wore buckskin leggings and a loincloth. A buffalo robe lay rolled up next to his weapons. He thumped his chest with the palm of his right hand.

"I called Flaco," he said.

"Pleased to meet you, Mr. Flaco," Jack said with a smile.

"You hunt Comanche?"

"Well, not hunt, but we're looking out for Comanche or banditos or Mexican soldiers."

"You hunt Comanche, I join you. Can help."

Jack dismounted but indicated with a wave of his hand for his group to stay on their horses. He squatted next to the fire, and the Indian squatted next to him, turning his back on Jack's platoon.

"Well, Mr. Flaco."

"Not mister, just Flaco."

"All right, Flaco. How can you help, and why do you want to?"

"I follow you two days. You not know I there. Can show how do this and much more. I Lipan Apache. Comanche kill most my peoples, destroy tribe. I want kill Comanche. Can help."

"Flaco means skinny in Spanish, I think," said Jack. "You don't look very skinny to me." He reached over and poked Flaco's well-muscled upper arm.

Flaco smiled and squeezed Jack's arm. "You skinny, but hard, strong. I think we be friends. Help each other."

"Sounds good to me. We've got some salt to put on that haunch. You willing to share?"

"Yes, I like salt on meat."

"Good, I think we've got some coffee and sugar on the packhorse too."

Flaco's smile broadened. "That be good, we share everything."

Jack turned to his men. "You boys climb down. Looks as though we got us a new recruit and some fresh meat for dinner. Reckon this will be a good spot to rest tonight." He walked over to the packhorse and started to untie the packs.

The following day the six men were spread out over a quarter of a mile, riding two abreast. Flaco rode next to Jack. It was sunny and warm, the prairie a perfusion of tall, green grass and colorful wild flowers. A gentle breeze moved the plants, creating gentle waves in a sea of grass.

"You look for sign?"

"Yeah, our job is to range over all the land for ten days' ride north and another ten south of where we are now. Other groups of men are doing the same north and south of us. We are to watch out for sign of large groups of invaders. If we find a small group, we try to catch up and find out what they are doing. If it's a large group, we send a man back to San Antonio to report, and then we follow to keep track of the intruders until help arrives."

"You learn to track how?"

"Well, our Capt. Deef Smith taught me some, but I learned mostly from the Delaware that were near my home at Cedar Lick in Tennessee."

"Not know this place Tennessee, but some Delaware in this country. They be my friends. Comanche also destroy them people."

"I'm sorry, Flaco. The Comanche are mean sons a bitches. I can understand why you want to get even with them."

"Yes, they are dogs but very good warriors. Can do anything with horses. They fight while riding horses, something my peoples not know. Apache use horse to travel but hunt and fight on ground. Comanche learn to ride and hunt from back of horse, start when very young. Ride horse before can run on ground, even women and girls. Very good fighters, Apache, and maybe twenty other tribes pay tribute to them. Too many and too good to fight."

"So, you have some Delaware friends. I would like to meet them. Maybe we can go on a hunting trip with them. We normally patrol for about thirty days then return to San Antonio for supplies and to rest up for a week or so. That might be a good time for a hunting trip."

"Like idea. Wait … stop. You no see that?" He pointed directly west to where a line of trees marked a streambed.

"You see something move over there?"

"No, but something watching. Maybe animal, maybe Comanche."

Jack spread his lips with his thumb and first finger and pushed out a shrill whistle. John Caperton and his other three companions put their horses into a gallop to join him.

"Flaco thinks there could be something in that creek bed yonder watching us. Let's spread out and get over there in a hurry."

They put their horses into a run toward the line of trees. When they were about fifty yards away, Jack looked over at Flaco and raised his eyebrows.

Flaco shook his head and then pointed at a spot just off to his right. They approached the indicated clump of trees and bushes slowly, their rifles cocked, held across their laps. Flaco slid from his horse and disappeared into the brush, moving silently. After a few minutes, he stood up and waved, indicating for the others to join him.

He pointed at an almost invisible impression on the ground.

"He here, one knee, watch us."

The Apache then made his way down a bank to the stream, indicating for them to follow. He stopped and pointed to horse tracks in the mud.

"Leave horse here. Horse not tied, trained to stay and wait. One man here." He pointed at a moccasin print. "Leave fast."

"How long ago?" asked Jack.

"Soon as we start to come."

"Just one man? You sure?"

"Yes, one man."

"Can we follow him? Maybe catch him?"

Flaco looked at each man and then at their horses. All of their horses were breathing hard after the relatively short run.

"No. With packhorse and you horses, cannot catch. You see you horses breathing hard, me pony no. Me pony I take from Comanche I kill. They ponies, much better. No catch this one before he get back to friends. Probably hunting party not far away."

Jack smiled. "Well, Flaco, I can sure see we have much to learn. Explain to me how you knew someone was watching us and how the hell you've deduced it was only one Comanche and that he didn't hightail it out until we started for him."

Jack's instruction began that same afternoon. Before long, with constant practice, he learned to observe everything happening around him. He developed an acute awareness of his surroundings and how to interpret indicators that something was not normal.

Two weeks later they arrived in San Antonio. Jack made his report to me. Other than the one encounter, they had no contact with Comanche or Mexicans. However, during the trip, they visited three extended family settlements—pioneers determined to make a new life for themselves no matter the risk. They found all three to be doing well, but Jack warned them about how far and fast the Comanche could travel. He told them they were occupying land the Comanche consider theirs, and they need to be watchful, armed, and vigilant at all times if they expected to survive. He explained that the ranging companies were here to provide protection but were only a few men with a huge territory to protect. It was impossible for us to be everywhere at the same time. Settling the frontier was a hazardous undertaking. Some of the pioneers would likely be killed, and the Comanche made killing last a long time.

Early the following summer Deef promoted Jack to sergeant. He also appointed him assistant quartermaster. He was officially leading patrols, as well as making certain the company was adequately supplied. The additional duties raised his pay twenty-five cents a day. The rest of the summer of 1837, and through the early fall, Jack, his four-man squad, including me, and Flaco taking our turn ranging over our assigned territory. Deef had to explain that Flaco could not be enrolled on the payroll, but he agreed to look away when Jack made certain the Apache obtained a fair share of whatever supplies were issued. During one deployment, our platoon was enhanced by six members of a band of Delaware Flaco invited to join us.

Jack continued to learn and hone skills second nature for our native friends. How to find food when there was none. How to preserve food when abundant. How to survive in harsh weather conditions with an absolute minimum of protection from the elements. How to start a fire when everything that could burn was water soaked. Most important of all was situational awareness.

In return, Jack and I taught our native friends how to care for and repair their firearms. They practiced their shooting skills and the skills essential for hand-to-hand fighting. Although he was always the slightest in stature, Jack's muscle structure was long and lean rather than bunched, and he was significantly stronger than he appeared. His speed and endurance in foot races was the subject of many campfire stories told by his ranger and Indian friends.

It was mid-September before the long-delayed hunting trip with Flaco and the Delaware braves finally took place. Jack, me, Flaco, and seven Delaware warriors camped on a small tributary of the Pedernales River, north and west of Austin. We were busy butchering the seven deer we had killed and field dressed earlier in the day. The hides were removed, scraped clean, salted, and rolled up to be processed by the wives and female relatives of the Indians after they returned home. Each of us had a riding horse and a pack animal; three of the latter were mules. Two-inch thick venison steaks were slowly roasting over coals after being seared in open flames. A large kettle of water was moved to the side of the fire after it boiled. Ground coffee and two handfuls of sugar were added and stirred using Jack's bowie knife. The smell of coffee, roasted meat, and mesquite smoke mingled, to engulf us.

"We'll let the coffee seep awhile until the grounds settle. We'll have a feast tonight, Flaco." Explained Jack.

"Yes, Señor Jack, I think so. This has been a good trip, no? You learn more Delaware speak too."

"Yeah, I've got a few more words of Delaware, but when are you going to teach me Apache?"

"Too hard, better I learn talk more white man. Better me."

"Better for you," Jack corrected.

Long before dawn, all of us were asleep. Our blankets, or buffalo robes, were folded over so we slept inside the fold. Most of us were using our saddles for pillows. Three of the Delaware were curled into a fetal position, their heads covered. All of us had weapons within easy reach. Suddenly, Comanche war whoops and muskets fired into the air brought all of us to our feet, rifles in hand. The crashing of our stampeded animals and the yelling of the Comanche warriors caused chaos. We seemed surrounded.

"Spread out and find cover. Don't shoot at anything unless you know for certain it isn't one of us," Jack shouted while diving behind one of the logs we had drug close.

It became very quiet. Flaco materialized at Jack's side.

"They have the horses."

"Do you know how many they are?"

"Four or five, no more. They very good at stealing horses."

"Damn sure did it fast enough. I'm going after them. You and our friends with me?"

Flaco spoke a few words to the Delaware who had all reappeared in the clearing. All of them silently began to make small packs of cooked meat, gunpowder, lead balls, scraps of soft leather, percussion caps, and rolled-up bedding. The Delaware also took up their quivers of arrows and their bows. Jack looked around to make certain everyone was ready, and then we all took up our rifles.

"Let's spread out and cut their trail. Whoever finds it, give a shout, and we'll get after them. They'll push hard for a while, but I don't think they'll believe we'd follow them on foot. Go."

A few minutes later, one of the Delaware warriors shouted. We all gathered around where he pointed at the tracks. Flaco bent down and studied the tracks for a few minutes and then wandered off in the direction they had taken.

"Our twenty plus four Comanche ponies. That way." He pointed.

Jack took off trotting in the direction indicated, and we all followed. We followed the tracks for three days, alternately trotting and walking. We rested for less than ten minutes after each hour or so and only slept for two or three hours in the middle of the night. We ate the cooked venison while walking. Along the way, we found some berries, and our companions killed some rabbits with bow and arrow to avoid gunshots. We discovered three camps made by the horse thieves. Each time we arrived closer to the time when the camp was left. As the sun began to set on the fourth day, Flaco was leading with Jack close on his heels. The Apache suddenly stopped, and Jack almost trotted into him. The rest of us came up slowly, bent over, gasping.

Flaco pointed. "There, off in that direction. You see it?"

Jack removed his hat and shielded his eyes with his hand. "What am I looking for?"

"Smoke, not much, thin line. They make camp, small fire. They no believe we follow, like you say."

"Good. Let's get closer, make our own camp, and rest up—no fire. Will you take one Delaware with you and find them? Mark the location, but don't let them know you're there. Who do you want with you?"

"Black Bear. He can move most silent. I leave a mark where you should camp and come back after they sleep."

"Good. Go. We'll see how they like to be jumped in the middle of the night."

Four hours later, Flaco and Black Bear slipped silently into the campsite where Jack and the rest of us were stretched out on the ground, our rifles in our hands.

"They not so far away. Three sleep; one watch ponies."

"Let's get going," said Jack.

A half hour later we huddled, well hidden. The Comanche camp was next to a small creek. The horses and mules were all hobbled in a grassy meadow no more than two hundred yards from where four horse thieves slept on their buffalo robes, close to a smoldering fire. The young warrior given the responsibility of guarding the horses had a long rawhide rope tied around the neck of one of the horses. The other end of the rope was looped around his wrist. He was seated, leaning against a tree but slumped over, dozing. His head jerked up from time to time and then slumped again, his chin on his chest. The hobbled horses were all busy grazing, but the mules had sensed our presence. They apparently recognized us, and did not bray a warning.

Jack smiled.

"Bless those mules. They know we've come to save 'em," he whispered. "Flaco, you and Black Bear take care of that one who is supposed to be minding the animals. The rest of us will surround the camp. Once you take out the sentry, hoot like an owl. All of us will unload on them. Flaco interpreted, and the Delaware warriors all nodded and then slipped off into the darkness.

Flaco crawled up to the dozing sentry, while Black Bear hung back, an arrow notched in his drawn bow. The sentry never knew what happened. Flaco's razor-sharp knife almost decapitated him; his slit windpipe prevented any sound other than a gush of surprised air. Black Bear hooted. Jack aimed and fired his rifle into one of the sleeping Comanche. The rest of our rifles erupted almost simultaneously. Two of the bodies jerked as the balls hit, but one of the thieves jumped to his feet and rushed into the woods. We had all taken aim at only two of the sleeping warriors. The Delaware were quick in pursuit amid much crashing through the woods and underbrush along the creek. A few minutes later, Jack heard the death song of the Comanche, cut off by the exuberant celebratory shouting of the Delaware.

Flaco and Black Bear, already having one scalp, were busy harvesting the scalps of the two killed while they slept. When the warriors returned, Screeching Owl held up the dripping scalp of the one who tried to escape.

"I don't think I want to spend the rest of the night with the smell from these corpses filling my nostrils," said Jack. "Let's round up the animals and go back to the spot where we waited. We'll rest up there then head back to collect our gear. Do you think there are any more of those rascals around to try to avenge them we took out, Flaco?"

"No, not close enough to hear. This small raiding party, all less than eighteen summers. They just want steal horses."

"Well, this has been some hunting trip. Right, boys?" More than any of us bargained for. Good fun."

Flaco interpreted, and the Delaware warriors broke into an impromptu victory dance with a lot of shrieking and whooping.

CHAPTER 4

AFTER RETURNING FROM the hunting trip, Jack and I, and Captain
Deaf Smith went to visit our commander Maj. Henry Karnes. We were in
Karnes's office in Austin. Karnes and Smith sat slouched in tipped-back
chairs, their feet resting on the battered table that served as Karnes's desk.
Jack and I both sat upright on two other chairs. The four chairs and the
table were the only furnishings in the small room built off from the main
room of the new general store in which Karnes was a part owner.

"If we're going to fight Comanche, John and I need to know more
about 'em," Jack said.

Karnes and Smith both smiled and agreed that anyone needs to know
more about their enemies than their friends.

"I think your Apache friend can tell you a lot more about the culture
and behavior of the various tribes, including the Comanche, than either of
us," Karnes said, "but I'm happy to share what I know about them."

He then continued to explain that when land speculators and
entrepreneurs from the United States first started bringing settlers into
Texas, there were between twenty thousand and thirty thousand Comanche
roaming over the plains, ranging all along the eastern slopes of the Rocky
Mountains from north of the Arkansas River south to the Rio Grande,
following the rivers east to the Gulf Coast. They were always at war and
either dominated or formed alliances with the tribes on their borders. They
still considered all the lands, about a quarter of a million square miles,
theirs. Their territory is crossed by nine major rivers, all making their way to

the Gulf: the Arkansas, Cimarron, Canadian, Washita, Red, Pease, Brazos, Colorado, and Pecos and all their tributaries.

Long before the Texas settlers arrived, the Spanish came in and made several attempts to bring the Comanche under control. In the 1740s a Colonel Parrilla was appointed to establish two missions and a fort on the banks of the San Saba River. The Spaniards thought the Apache, with whom they'd had a lot of problems, controlled the area. They had no idea the Apache tribes were subservient to the Comanche.

The Apache pretended to be interested in converting to the Catholic faith and supporting the Spanish missions. What they really wanted was to lure the Spaniards farther north and, by doing so, convince the Comanche they were being invaded. The Spaniards weren't even aware they were being maneuvered into declaring war on the Comanche. The Apache were counting on the Spanish superiority in arms and military tactics to defeat the Comanche.

"I wouldn't have thought they would be that clever and devious," murmured Jack, "although I don't know why I'm surprised. Flaco has plenty of both."

"That's the first lesson, boy," shouted Deef. "You need to get a better idea about the intellect of these savages. They survived and prospered for a long time in this country before any Europeans showed their faces."

Karnes continued his narrative, explaining that by the spring of 1758 two missions and a presidio were mostly finished on the San Saba River. About the middle of March some two thousand Comanche warriors showed up. They accepted gifts from the head honcho of the missions, a Father Terreros. Then the Comanche war chief who had accepted the proffered gifts tossed them into the dirt to show his disdain. That action was the signal for his warriors. Father Terreros and four other priests were stripped, tortured, killed, and mutilated. One of the priests was decapitated. The Comanche plundered the storerooms, taking what they wanted and destroying the rest. They killed many cattle and, in general, destroyed everything they couldn't take with them before setting fire to the missions.

Two weeks before all this happened, Colonel Parrilla was informed that a large contingent of Comanche was on the way. He tried to convince the padres to abandon the missions and come to his presidio for protection. They refused, trusting in God to protect them.

"There's lesson two for you boys. Don't trust for God to protect you or anyone else," chimed in Deef.

Karnes continued telling us that Parrilla had about three hundred people, most of them the families of his soldiers, holed up in the presidio. When he learned of the attack on the missions, he sent out a small patrol to evaluate the situation. They barely cleared the fort when they were attacked. Two were killed immediately, and the rest, wounded by musket fire, arrows, and lances, managed to make it back to the protection of the fort.

"So Parrilla holed up in the fort so he could protect the families of the soldiers?" I asked.

Deef removed his feet from the table and brought his chair upright. He leaned forward, straining to follow the conversation, then shouted: "I heard that little ruckus caused a panic in about all the Mexican communities in New Mexico and Texas. Some old timers in San Antonio told me that folks from all the outlying ranchos forted up there, leaving their cattle and horses untended. Everyone was scared shitless."

After a three-day orgy of killing and destruction, the Comanche suddenly departed. Colonel Parrilla investigated and then reported to his superiors. He requested relief and reinforcements from the commanders of all the forts within a week's ride away. Nothing happened. He followed up with a formal request to the viceroy in Mexico City. That worthy did send orders, on three separate occasions, to various forts in northern Mexico. One commander sent a handful of soldiers to Parrilla, but all the others just offered excuses.

Parrilla complained, and the viceroy lost patience with his subordinates and their excuses. He raised a force of six hundred Spanish regulars and several hundred Indian auxiliaries. He was tired of being embarrassed by the savages and was determined to bring them to heel. The Indian auxiliaries included many Apache who were still hoping for a Spanish victory to set them free.

In August 1759, Parrilla set out with his new army to hunt Comanche. He was smart enough, and experienced enough, to not attempt a battle on the open plains. The cavalry skills of the Comanche, and their ability to bring superior numbers to a battle, were already well documented. Parrilla was not about to start anything that would lead to certain defeat. He made his way east, staying in the timbered country bordering the Comanche-dominated plains.

He eventually found his savages. Unfortunately, they were Tonkawa, subservient but longtime enemies of the Comanche. Parrilla surrounded the Tonkawa village, attacked and killed seventy-five warriors, and took a hundred and fifty women and children back to San Antonio.

"Yeah, they forced all them innocent folks to convert. Many of 'em are related to the Tonkawa you see in town now. A pretty sad lot," shouted Deef.

After that debacle, the colonel turned north. He was near the Red River that October when he came upon several thousand Comanche, Wichita, Osage, Red River Caddoans, and some other tribes—all united in their hatred of the Spanish, and all determined to protect their territories. These alliances of convenience were, and still are, part of the diplomatic genius of the Comanche. They were able, and willing to form alliances with enemies when it was mutually convenient.

Jack, tired of sitting, got to his feet and paced the small room. Karnes continued his history lesson.

The Indians were well deployed and built up earthen breastworks. Parrilla's forces were facing extermination, but he was full of Spanish pride, believing in the superiority of his men. He ordered an attack. His Spanish regulars charged on command, but his Indian allies recognized and understood the odds. They dispersed. Once his regulars felt the magnitude and ferocity of the Indians' defense, they started to pull back. Their retreat quickly deteriorated into a panic-driven rout.

Karnes rubbed his forehead with his right hand and then pushed a lock of red hair hanging over his eye back over his head, smoothing it down. "The Comanche and their allies were quite satisfied to capture all of the provisions and supplies of the Spanish Army," he said. "They burned the wagons, took all the horses and mules that were still living, and divided the spoils. Parrilla's forces only sustained a few casualties, a fact that made it difficult for him to justify his actions to his superiors."

"What happened to him?" asked Jack.

"I don't know for certain but suspect he was tried for something other than stupidity and ended up a broke and bitter man."

"So, did the Spanish ever have any successes fighting the Comanche?" I still had questions.

"Well there was one man: Don Juan Bautista de Ansa."

De Ansa was the governor of New Mexico from 1777 to 1787. He was the first to launch a successful war with the Comanche. He was probably the most experienced and brilliant Indian fighter New Spain produced after the conquest of Mexico.

Deef got to his feet and paced the room. Karnes continued to talk, so

Deef maneuvered himself to stand in front of him to better catch what the commander was saying.

One of the most notorious Comanche war chiefs was known as Cuerno Verde, or Green Horn, of the Kotosoteka band. De Ansa gathered an army of nearly 350 regulars and about 250 Indian allies and then set off to find Green Horn. He crossed the front range of the Rockies and then traveled northeast onto the high plains bordering the Arkansas River. He found Green Horn's village, but the chief and most of his warriors were off stealing horses.

"Let me guess. He attacked the village and killed women and children," murmured Jack.

"Of course. His men killed eighteen old men, along with several young boys and women. He captured thirty women, thirty-four children, and more than five hundred horses. He tortured a young boy until the boy's mother told him Green Horn was expected back soon, so he set an ambush. When Green Horn and his warriors returned, the Spanish trapped and killed the war chief and almost all of the warriors. He stayed in the field and launched other attacks on other bands as he moved south, but those actions were less successful. This was the first time any Comanche were forced to defend their homeland from a major invader."

Then de Ansa showed his true brilliance. He was able to entice all the war chiefs of the various Comanche bands to come in for peace talks. He made a very good impression on the chiefs by treating them as equals, which was a new concept for the Spaniards. He told them he wasn't interested in bringing in settlers to threaten their hunting grounds or making any attempt to convert them, extract tribute, or extend Spanish rule over them. He offered peace and trade. He offered to trade manufactured European goods for horses and captives. He convinced the Comanche to sign a peace treaty. He also convinced them to form an alliance with their traditional enemies the Ute, so they could combine and subjugate the Apache and Navajo.

"I thought the Comanche and Ute were bitter enemies," said Jack.

"The alliance between the Ute and Comanche didn't last long, but it was long enough to reduce the threat to New Spain from both the Apache and Navajo. The peace between the Spanish and the Comanche held, and as you know, the Mexicans and Comanche still get along," replied Karnes.

Jack stopped pacing and sat down. "I understand why they don't want us here, but still. They are brutes when they attack our people who just want to be left alone to make a living from all this unoccupied country. We've all witnessed what they do to both the women and men when they raid an isolated homestead. The Comanche will have to learn to adopt our ways and make their livelihood off of much less land. Their culture of following the buffalo and making claim to so much empty land can't survive. Our people are land hungry, and there's a lot of empty land here."

"Well, you'll have a face-to-face with some of them soon enough," shouted Deef. "Try to convince them."

CHAPTER 5

SERGEANT HAYS, ALONG with me and the rest of his platoon, were riding south from San Antonio through meadows still green with grass. We rode past grazing cattle, buffalo, and deer, the later always on the fringes, near the protection of thickets of live oak. We skirted the trees, staying on open ground, always alert to everything in our surroundings. We were on the way to make certain a group of outlying settlers were still alive. If they were still occupying their property, Jack wanted to put them on guard to watch for Comanche raiders or Mexican bandits. The settlers were often the first to report seeing signs of activity off in the distance. The settlement we were headed for reported a sighting the previous week.

This time, Jack and I were accompanied by four other Rangers: Bigfoot Wallace, Perry Alsbury, Ben McCulloch, and Mathew Caldwell. All of us were still in our early twenties. All of us were driven, wanting to avenge the horrors visited on members of our families or on innocent settlers. We were all looking for action to satisfy our need for an adrenalin rush. We appeared to be anything but a disciplined militia unit. Each one of us was dressed in his own style, or, rather, lack thereof. I suppose we were a ragtag-looking outfit, but we all carried muzzle-loading, percussion-cap, rifles and pistols, and we could all use them to good effect. We were all well mounted on fit horses that could keep going for long distances on a minimum of feed and rest. Each of us was leading a spare horse, another custom borrowed from the Comanche. Two pack mules kept pace, carrying all we needed for a monthlong patrol. With us were six Apache warriors, including Flaco. They were along hoping for the opportunity to kill Comanche.

"So, Sergeant Jack, I have new medicine, more power," said Flaco.

"Indeed … Is that why these warriors are with us?"

"Yes, I now war chief. Warriors think I have good medicine and plenty power when you and I together, so these men choose to follow me. Maybe we kill many Comanche."

"Are you pleased to have these men follow you?"

"Yes."

"So, Flaco, I need to know more about our common enemy, the Comanche. What can you tell me about them?"

I rode up alongside as Flaco related his story of the Comanche. He explained that they call themselves *Nermernuh*, meaning "the people." The Utes call them *Koh-mats*, sometimes *Komantcia*, meaning "some people always my enemy." The Spanish changed it to *Comanche*.

"So, they consider themselves the only people of importance?"

"I think yes. Apache think same. You no think same?"

"I guess we give that impression." Jack smiled as he looked back over his shoulder and shouted. "You boys all believe the white man is superior and should rule this country?"

"Damn right," answered Perry Alsbury, standing in his stirrups.

He was about the same height as the rest of us, except Bigfoot, who towered over the group. Perry was lean and mean with a reputation for finishing fights. His black hair was long and unruly. His brown eyes could see farther than anyone else in the group.

"What the hell are you goin' on about, Jack?" laughed Bigfoot.

Jack looked over at Flaco, who continued his narrative.

He explained that there are five bands of the people called Comanche. The Yamparika are the most north. Moving south are the Kotsoteka, Penateka, Nokoni, and Quahadi. They all speak dialects of the same language. They are all superior fighters from horseback. The only time they fight on the ground is if they get knocked off their horses. Before they tamed horses, maybe five generations ago, they hunted buffalo on foot, but once they had horses, they learned to hunt from horseback and became much more efficient and successful. They are the only native people who know how to breed horses, a skill probably learned from the Spanish. Horses are their measure of wealth and prestige, and some war chiefs can have more than a thousand horses. They also have learned how to break and train wild horses, and their horses are all very well trained. They teach their children to ride before they can walk, both girls and boys. Their woman all ride and some even hunt and fight.

Jack then asked Flaco the question we all wondered about. "So, tell me, Flaco, why are the Comanche so brutal to their captives? They beat and rape the women they capture, both Indian and white, and do unspeakable things to them. They torture the men they capture until they die. I've seen men who were obviously tortured for days before they died. Do the Apache do this as well?"

"Of course. Must make enemy fear warriors, fear to be captured, stay away from our land. We learn to do this when young."

"But some women they keep, both white and Indian. They don't kill or sell all of them to the Mexicans or other tribes as slaves. They also adopt some young girls and boys. Why do they do that?"

"They women no have many babies. Many women lose babies early, maybe because always riding horses. Some Comanche women never born live babies. Captive women born many babies. Also, better if babies not from same band."

I decided to change the subject. "Do you know their secret for breaking horses? I hear it's brutal."

"I never see myself, but once we get back, Lipan man captured when young and adopted into Kotsoteka tribe. He tell me they throw lariat and catch horse around neck. Pull on lariat until horse choke from no air and fall. When horse almost dead, they loosen lariat. Horse struggle to feet covered in sweat, shaking. Comanche then very gentle stroke nose, ears, forehead, then blow air into horse nose. Finally put thong around bottom jaw, jump up and ride. I try to do this with wild horse, but horse throw me off. Better to kill Comanche, take horse, already all trained."

I turned to Jack.

"Well, that's useful information. I guess I need to capture me a Comanche pony."

"Sounds like a good idea to me."

By 1838, San Antonio was swarming with new colonists. Many were veterans from the militia and from the War of Independence, as well as veterans from the ranging companies. Many of these men held land claims.

The population of the town grew from about thirty thousand to close to forty-five thousand in a little over two years. The various land grants all had to be surveyed and platted before they could be registered. Most of the claims were located close to or adjoining a consistent supply of water. In many instances, this meant claiming land along remote streams pushing the frontier ever farther west. Because of the intrusions into Comanche lands, attacks on both survey crews and the more remote settlers' cabins were more common. The Comanche rightly resented the survey crews. They knew what those crews were doing and why they were doing it.

Jack's surveying skills were in great demand, but not just his expertise as a surveyor. His growing reputation as a fearless fighter almost guaranteed the survey would be completed. His friends from the ranging companies, myself included, were always up for a fight. We were happy to sign on for the good wages Jack offered. It was a dangerous business but offered the excitement we all craved, in addition to twice the pay we sometimes received, but was often delayed, from the Republic of Texas.

President Sam Houston faced a continuous financial crisis. He disbanded the militia and allowed funding for the ranging companies to lapse. He was doing his best to keep the Republic solvent.

Deef Smith's health worsened. He was increasingly discouraged by the lack of financial support for his Rangers. During the summer of 1837, Smith turned his command over to Capt. Nicholas Dawson, sold his house in San Antonio, sold his ranch, and moved his family to Fort Bend County. His new ranch was almost two hundred miles east and north of San Antonio, less than fifty miles from the San Jacinto battleground. His tuberculosis continued to worsen.

Sam Houston's sympathy for the plight of the Indians was well known. He wrote, "Everything will be gained by peace, but nothing will be gained by war." He continued to reduce support for all the various military units and disbanded most of them. He believed he could reduce the deprivations by the Comanche by appointing three Indian commissioners to treat fairly with them. His goal was to entice them to make peace with gifts and promises, a less costly strategy than maintaining an armed militia.

In April 1837, Henry Karnes was appointed an Indian commissioner. In May, Karnes and the other two commissioners met with a band of about 150 Kotosoteka Comanche at a location not far from San Antonio. Two war chiefs, Essomanny and Essowakkenny, were happy to accept the proffered gifts. Essomanny promised he would appear before the Congress of Texas to continue the peace talks and establish boundaries. Subsequently, Karnes convinced another band of about one hundred Nokoni Comanche, led by the war chiefs Muguara, Muestyah, and Muby, to visit the Texas Congress for official talks as well. The three Nokoni war chiefs and their followers met with the politicians in late May 1838. The Comanche left the talks in high spirits and with many gifts, including gunpowder.

Within a week, various bands of Comanche stole many Texas horses. One band lured three Texans into their camp by telling them they wanted to trade buffalo hides and horses for ammunition and manufactured goods. The bodies of the three were found after a week of rotting in the sun. Word soon reached San Antonio that the Kotsoteka were killing settlers and stealing their horses and cattle.

Sam Houston had to respond. He recommissioned Karnes as a colonel and instructed him to form a ranging company of militia. Jack and I, along with many of our friends, were subject to being called to serve in the militia when a threat was verified. Information reached Colonel Karnes that a large group of Comanche were following the Medina, a major tributary of the San Antonio River, toward the settlements along its course.

In June, Karnes, the stocky, fiery redhead, was determined as never before. He led twenty-one men, including Jack, Jack's cousin Benjamin Cage, and me, out of San Antonio. After some days of travel, we were resting our horses just west of the Medina. Suddenly, we were attacked by about two hundred Kotsoteka Comanche led by Essowakkenny. Jack's reaction was to spur his horse forward, aiming directly at the war chief. He leveled his rifle, and with his horse at a full run, he shot the war chief in the head.

The rest of us, momentarily surprised by Jack's sudden aggressive action, responded within seconds. We urged our horses forward to join him, rifles and pistols blazing. Jack, holding his rifle in his left hand along with his reins, pulled his pistol and discharged it into the chest of a warrior. While his horse was still at a full gallop, he shoved the empty pistol into his belt and pulled out his second pistol. The Comanche, once they realized their war chief was dead, retreated to gather themselves.

Karnes stood in his stirrups as he shouted instructions. We pulled back to a ravine filled with chaparral. Colonel Karnes dismounted and stood atop the bank of the ravine, directing his men into defense positions. I saw an arrow hit and lodge itself in his left thigh. He reached down and broke off the shaft, leaving the arrowhead buried in the muscle. The wound had to hurt like hell, but Karnes didn't acknowledge it. We lost several horses in that first melee but no men. The Comanche launched two more separate but disorganized attacks. Several warriors were vying to assume the mantel of war chief, so there was confusion, as well as disorganization in the attacks. After being repulsed the second time, the Indians departed. They carried with them twenty dead and an equal number of wounded warriors. Many of their horses were either killed or wounded too severely to be ridden.

Jack's decision to directly attack the war chief was instinctive but not ill considered. He learned from Flaco that warriors decide to follow a warrior and do what he says when he has strong medicine—power that leads to success in battle. If he was defeated or killed, it was a sign his power was gone.

While the Comanche fought only from horseback, the Texans they had encountered previously usually dismounted to be more accurate with their rifles and pistols. The Comanche were surprised by the mounted attack launched by the Jack and the rest of us. The change in tactics also contributed to our success against odds of ten-to-one. We returned to San Antonio with a different mindset on how to fight the Comanche.

When the militia was not called up to protect a town or settlers in the region, there was little for us to do but spend the wages we had accumulated, providing the Republic had the funds to pay us. Some found odd jobs, and some found steadier work on the ranches and farms in the area. Most of the men had plenty of time to haunt the bars and look for trouble. They drank and brawled. Most of the citizens of San Antonio were happy to see us go away on patrol.

When Jack wasn't on active service with the militia or taking care of his quartermaster duties, he sought and accepted survey jobs. He was soon appointed deputy county surveyor, working out of a small one-room log cabin he purchased in the heart of San Antonio and that he allowed me to share with him. The table that served as his desk was situated so he could look out of the open door of the cabin. He liked to be able to view activity on the street and around the partially reconstructed Alamo only two blocks away.

The challenge of going to the far reaches of where men wanted to settle had special appeal to Jack. During that summer and fall, many survey crews were attacked, and some men were killed. Jack knew which men were most attracted to that level of danger and excitement. When he put together a crew for a job, or a series of jobs, it took him only a short time to gather a group of heavily armed and experienced fighters.

Jack was out with me, Albert Drinkwater, Jacob Humphrey, Joseph Miller, Robert Patton, and Bigfoot Wallace. Bigfoot and I had the job of riding around the crew in opposite directions while they worked. We were responsible for making certain the crew was not surprised or interrupted by Comanche or banditos. We were surveying four adjacent land claims along the Pedernales River in the hill country north and west of San Antonio.

Drinkwater and Humphrey were the chainmen. There were two chains. One, when stretched tight, extended to exactly twenty yards, the other to exactly thirty yards. The chains were constructed of four-inch links with a tog or ring on each end joined to the next link.

Jack stood by his tripod, adjusting it with a plumb bob placed over the corner marker he had just built. The corner marker that day was determined with chain distance and compass readings from a huge rock that was unlikely to move. Jack used his sextant, compass, his surveyor's watch to identify the longitude and latitude of the landmark rock. He built the corner marker by piling up stones in a shallow hole he dug at the spot. His transit consisted of a five-inch metal tube with an eyepiece attached to one end of the tube. Within the eyepiece were vertical and horizontal hairlines. One inch from the opposite end of the tube a mirror was imbedded at a forty-five-degree angle from an opening in the side of the tube. Over the mirror was a carpenter's level.

While Jack leveled the transit, Drinkwater held one end of the long chain at the middle of the corner marker, while Humphrey stretched the unwieldy chain out horizontally. They maneuvered the chain to remove several kinks and then laid it flat on the ground in the direction Jack indicated by pointing. They repeated this process from the end of one chain measurement to the next.

Joseph Miller and Bob Patton manned ranging poles, two perfectly straight, six-foot-long poles with an iron shoe that prevented the tip of the pole from breaking off or wearing down. The poles were painted with alternate white and red stripes, exactly an inch wide. They used a plumb bob to make certain their poles were held exactly vertical. Miller stood with one of the poles at the end of the chain. Jack sighted through the transit and indicated with thumb up or down where Miller should slide the red rag on his pole to mark the height of the horizontal line established from the transit to the pole location.

Once the reading was determined, the chain was moved, and Bob Patton stood with his pole at the first mark while Miller moved to the end of the chain. Jack looked through the tube and gave hand signals to Joe Miller to move to his right or left while stretching the chain and holding the rod vertically until the two rods were lined up with the vertical hair of the transit. The horizontal hair, with the bubble centered, was used to mark the difference in vertical distance on the ranging pole with reference to the position of the transit.

Patton was the follower. After Jack made certain the two poles were aligned, Patton pushed stiff wire arrows with a strip of red cloth tied to a loop on the end of the wires into the spot, thus marking the number of chains along the line. Patton also carried hardwood pegs two inches square and sixteen inches long. He pounded them into the ground to mark where the line of traverse changed direction. When the vertical change was steep, a half chain or quarter chain was used.

The crew came to another creek bed cutting into the land. Jack looked at the topography and then at his compass.

"Let's move off to the southwest here," he said, pointing in the direction he wanted. "You'll have to fix the ranging poles end to end to reach high enough, and it'll take both of you to hold it plumb."

Jack made the readings and then used a hard pencil to make notes in his field notebook, recording the number of chains on a line and the elevation relative to his corner marker at the end of each chain. He would use this data after returning to San Antonio to construct a contour map and a plot of the property.

Bigfoot and I rode in opposite directions in a big circle, as much as a quarter to a half mile away, keeping ears, eyes, and noses open for any sign of danger.

On the fourth day, instead of continuing his circuit around the working crew, Bigfoot doubled back in a rush and discovered five young Comanche warriors who had been watching both him and me and Jack's crew. The five waited, sitting on their horses with insolent smiles. Bigfoot stopped a hundred yards away from them and whistled two short blasts.

I put my horse into a run to join the crew and saw Jack look up and order:

"Something's up. Lay everything down and gather up the horses. Be sharp. Watch for any movement."

We rode up to Bigfoot. He glanced over and pointed his chin at the five warriors. The warriors slowly turned their horses and walked them off to the north. We didn't take the bait.

"What's the deal, Bigfoot?" asked Jack.

"Five warriors wearing shit-eating grins," answered the big man. "Rode off north, inviting us to follow. Expect there's more of 'em hid, waiting for us to do somethin' stupid."

"Expect you're right. Let's just mosey back to our stuff. All of you make certain you've got fresh caps and your weapons are loaded. We'll continue the survey, but let's be ready. Keep your horses tethered to your wrist while we're working, and keep one eye watching. Bigfoot, you and John stay with us, stay mounted, keep close watch, and keep a good hold on the halter ropes of the pack animals. They will, no doubt, first try to run off our horses."

We returned to where the crew had abandoned their equipment, and they went back to work. Bigfoot and I kept a sharp lookout. At noon, we all stopped and lunched on hardtack and smoked buffalo jerky washed down with water. We were in a small clearing, a few steps from a creek that emptied into the Pedernales less than a mile away. The clearing bordered an open area of grassland, but growing along the creek were stately cedars with straight trunks, twenty to twenty-five feet tall. We all sat with our backs to each other, keeping a sharp watch.

Jack spoke up. "This would be a damned fine place to build a cabin with all those straight-trunked trees."

The thicket of trees included live oak, as well as a considerable number of juniper trees. There was an occasional mesquite scattered on the prairie. The thick underbrush among the trees consisted of young dogwoods with their green twigs, four-inch leaves, and clumps of blossoms dying at the ends of the branches. There were plentiful and diverse varieties of sumac, their pungent, earthy odor permeating the still air. Jack, watching everything, noticed a lone arbutus tree with its red, pealing bark, but what most captured his attention was the silence. No birds, no insects, no normal sounds.

"You see the one over to your left, about sixty yards out, behind that dogwood, Bigfoot?"

"Yep, I see him. There's at least two more behind that one. Reckon they're just tryin' to get their power up and decide how to go about it."

"Reckon you're correct," said Jack. "You think you can plunk that one from here and help 'em make up their minds?"

"Oh, yeah. I can manage that."

"Okay, boys. Here's the plan," whispered Jack. "Once Bigfoot drops that smart-ass, the rest of us mount up in a hurry. It'll take 'em a minute or two, but I expect they'll jump on their horses and charge us. When they do, each of you pick a man and ride directly for him. When you get a shot, take it. They'll expect us to fort up and fight on foot, not take it to 'em. Anytime, Bigfoot."

Wallace slowly got up to one knee, and then in one motion, swung his rifle to his shoulder, took quick aim, and fired. The warrior who thought himself hidden grunted once and fell back, partially held in view by the sumac he fell on. There was a huge gaping wound in his throat.

"Shit," Bigfoot exclaimed. "I was aiming for his forehead."

The six of us jumped to our feet and leaped into our saddles without touching a stirrup. The Comanche warriors were indeed surprised. After a moment's delay, one of them shouted instructions. In less than a minute, ten warriors were crashing through the underbrush, weaving around trees, coming at us from three directions.

Jack identified the man shouting orders. "I got the one with the eagle feather, long braids, and big mouth. Remember their shields will deflect a ball. Aim where they're not protected by the shield."

Jack hollered, "Alamo," and spurred his horse into a run, directly at the warrior who was shouting instructions.

All of the warriors charging us were experienced fighters, despite their youth. They knew that when a white man with a rifle took a shot, they were able to shoot ten or more arrows while he reloaded.

We presented a very different scenario than what these warriors expected. We were riding directly at them while hunched over in our saddles and bobbing from side to side. We fired our rifles, holding them in one hand, while still out of range of the Comanche bows. Two of the rifle balls connected with flesh. One of the warriors was hit in the left shoulder. He was unable to hold his two-foot-diameter shield in position to protect his body. The shot almost knocked him off his horse, but he was able to regain his balance after dropping his lance. The second warrior was hit in the right thigh. Two rifle balls bounced off buffalo hide shields. After firing our rifles, we jammed them into the holsters hanging from our saddles and drew a pistol from our belts.

Despite his warning, Jack's rifle ball bounced off the leader's shield. When the distance between him and Jack was about thirty yards, the war chief slid off to the side of his horse and launched an arrow at Jack. Jack managed to dodge it. By this time, all of the combatants were clear of the trees and brush along the creek, out in the open grassland. Most of the Indians, confused by our tactics, turned north, their shields held behind their backs for protection. Jack's target tried to turn his horse away from Jack's charge, but Jack reined the gelding he was on and spurred him to collide with the smaller Indian pony.

At impact, the pony stumbled. The warrior managed to pull himself upright while trying to control the pony. Jack continued to spur his horse forward, maintaining contact, keeping both the warrior and the pony off balance. He fired his pistol from only a foot away, but the warrior got his shield in position and managed to deflect that ball also. However, the power of the blast from the pistol was enough to catch fire to the decorated buckskin cover of the shield while pushing it and the warrior's arm off to the side, twisting the man off balance. As the warrior struggled to regain balance and grab his war club, Jack flipped his empty pistol in the air, grabbed it by the muzzle, and clubbed the warrior with the butt of the ten-pound weapon. It connected with the warrior's left temple, knocking him unconscious and off the back of his pony.

There were two warriors on the ground, wounded. The rest, not hurt, were urging their ponies away, legs flailing at the animals' flanks. We reloaded our weapons while giving chase. After five minutes, Jack held up his left hand and hollered, "Whoa."

We all brought our horses to a walk.

Jack took a deep breath. "I think those boys had enough for today. They won't bother us for a bit. Let's head back and make certain those down won't ever bother us."

Upon returning to the meadow, we found one dead warrior, his horse nowhere to be seen. Jack's victim and his horse were gone.

"I reckon he woke up and skedaddled, but he'll have one hell of a headache," said Bigfoot. "I saw you knock him cold with your pistol butt, Jack. I've got to practice that trick of flipping it."

"What the hell were you doin' watching me? I thought you were supposed to be fighting."

"Shit, Jack. That one layin' there is mine, and I can count that one in the bushes back yonder too. Had to leave some of 'em for the rest of you."

Jack smiled. "All right, guess you're right. You didn't want to hog all the fun. You planning to collect some scalps?"

"Shit, Jack. What the *F*? You think I'm a damned barbarian? I don't need no stinkin' scalps for trophies. I reckon I can remember them I killed."

"Well, I'm having trouble remembering all I've killed, and they seem to be adding up," said Jack.

CHAPTER 6

IT WAS PLENTY hot and plenty humid. Our horses were lathered with sweat, and the homespun shirts all of us wore were sticking to our bodies and arms. We had just begun a monthlong patrol heading to the headwaters of the Pedernales. We intercepted a small party of warriors driving a dozen stolen horses. After a short, quick skirmish two warriors were down but the rest escaped. We dismounted to make certain the two warriors were dead and then collected their weapons.

Albert Drinkwater pulled the shield off the right arm of the warrior his rifle ball had hit in the head. He stood up to his full five feet, ten inches, turning the shield over and back while shaking his head. "Look at this thing, Jack. How could anything this light stop a rifle ball?"

Jack came over to stand next to Albert. Both looked much younger than they were. Jack's dark hair was dirty and sprung from his head in unruly clumps when he took off his hat to wipe his forehead with his left upper arm. Drinkwater, an inch or two taller than Jack, was of the same slight build. His hair was light brown, straight, and shoulder-length. His dark brown, deep-set eyes were penetrating with long-sighted acuity. He repeated his question, determined to know the answer.

"Flaco told me about these shields," replied Jack. "He says they use buffalo hide from the shoulders and neck of bulls 'cause the hide is thickest there. They cut out a circle and stretch it over a wood frame. Then they heat the chunk of hide over a fire, let it cool, and continue doing that until the hide is thick and hard. They repeat the process several times, adding several layers. The diameter of the shield is pretty much determined by how big a hide they have to work with, as well as the strength and preference of the warrior who will use it. They're usually about two to three feet in diameter. The bigger it is, the harder it is to manipulate to ward off arrows or balls. You can see how they've lashed several layers of hide to the frame and packed something between the layers to make the front concave. It's the shape that deflects an arrow or lead ball."

"What do they stuff it with?" Drinkwater asked?

"Something light, feathers, maybe hair. Flaco says since we arrived, they prefer paper."

"Really? Paper?"

"Yeah, let's see what this one is stuffed with."

Jack unsheathed his bowie knife and, after some jabbing and poking, managed to stick the tip of the knife between two of the laces on the edge of the shield. With considerable effort, he was able to saw through about ten inches of laces and separate some layers of the hardened rawhide.

"They smeared glue over the laces. That's why they're so tough to cut," observed Bigfoot, who had come over with the others to observe the dissection.

They peeled away the outer layer of rawhide, along with the painted buckskin cover, and exposed pages of printed material. Jacob Humphreys wiped his hands on the front of his shirt and extracted several pages.

"What is it?" asked Joe Miller.

Bob Patton reached over and took one of the pages Jacob was holding, studying it with a puzzled expression on his face.

"This one is from a Bible," Bob exclaimed.

Joe Miller peeled another layer back and extracted more pages. "These are from a Bible too."

The men took turns cutting the laces with their knives and peeled off six layers of rawhide. They collected the pages and piled them up by page number on the loincloth stripped from one of the dead warriors. Each of them held a small stack of pages, calling out the page numbers so they could pile them in order.

"Son of a bitch," exclaimed Drinkwater.

"What is it?" asked Jack.

"I've got the front page. It's the family Bible of the McVains. That's the family we came on a few months ago with their cabin burned to the ground." He frowned, remembering the awful scene. "Jim McVain was staked out with coals on his genitals, his wife with her belly split open, her innards spilled out and her breasts hacked off, and the little baby girl, her head bashed in."

All of the men shuddered, shaking their heads.

"They had two young sons and a teenaged daughter. The Comanche took all three. The trail was at least a week old, no point in trying to catch up. All we could do was bury those folks and the baby. Son of a bitch!"

Drinkwater's tears left streaks through the dirt on his face under his eyes and dripped off his thick, brown beard.

Jack broke the silence. "Let's put as much of their Bible as we have back in order. When we get back to San Antonio, I'll have a sealed box made. We'll eventually get out to the McVains' place and bury their Bible with them. Anybody think that's a bad idea?"

All of the men shook their heads and then wandered off in different directions with their own memories and thoughts.

After about thirty minutes, Joe gathered the Comanche bows. "There are two different kinds," he announced.

"Really?" said Jacob. "Let me see."

All of the men gathered around again.

Joe held up one of the bows. "This one looks to be made out of wood; the other looks like bone."

I learned about Comanche bow and arrow construction from Flaco. The wood ones can take many months to make and are the most valuable. They only use the wood from the hedge apple tree. The heartwood from that tree is super hard. The wood is bright orange when first exposed to the air and then turns brown after it dries out. They look for the straightest sapling they can find. Then they hack it down and chip away until they have the length and thickness of heartwood they need. It requires many days of carving and then scraping it with lava rock until they get it into the shape they're after. Then, they rub it with buffalo fat and brains and set it in a warm spot to season. They repeat the rubbing and curing until the bow maker is satisfied everything is right.

The skill that separates the true craftsman is getting both the upper and lower limbs of the bow to release with even pressure. That can take months to achieve. Finally, they smear glue on it and then wrap it with fresh sinew from buffalo or deer. When it dries, the sinew contracts. The result is a powerful bow. Because they fight from horseback, the bows can't be near as long as those of the eastern tribes who fight on foot.

They use the horns from buffalo, elk, or mountain sheep to make the horn bows. The mountain sheep horn bows are probably the best and most rugged. They soak the horns in warm water until they're flexible. Then they cut, straighten, and flatten the horn material before cutting it into strips. Next, they cut and shape the strips and overlay them with glue made from hooves and horns until the bow is the length and thickness they want. Then they carve it and smooth it until they get the desired balance and shape. Finally, they bind the joints with sinew and cover everything with glue. It will take an experienced bow maker several weeks to construct the horn bows. Most of the Comanche carry the horn bow because it cost them fewer horses to purchase from the bow maker.

"Flaco told me a really well-made wood bow can cost a warrior anywhere from six to ten horses," Jack said.

I also learned about arrows from our Lipan Apache friend. Before they were able to acquire iron, they used flint or bone heads, but the iron is much better and easier to work. They heat sheets in hot coals until the metal is red-hot and then pound it into the arrowheads. Those without barbs are used for hunting, as they are easier to withdraw and reuse. The war heads have barbs and will pull off easily. If a war head hits someone, he can't just pull the arrow out because the head comes off. If it's not dug out, it will usually fester. Sometimes they dip 'em in manure or some dead, rotting animal to make matters worse. Some of the heads are mounted vertically and some horizontally. The vertically mounted heads are used for hunting to go through the rib cage of a four-legged beast. The horizontal for war, to penetrate between the ribs of an upright man. The horizontally mounted are the ones with barbs, and the heads pull off easy.

They prefer dogwood for the shafts of their arrows because those shoots are usually the straightest, but they'll use straight shoots of ash, wild cherry, hackberry, or mulberry. Usually the warriors too old to fight turn to making arrows. They have to season the wood for a couple of weeks or more and then shape them until they are perfectly straight. They prefer wild turkey feathers for the fletching but sometimes will use owl or vulture. Eagle or hawk feathers are too easily damaged. Sometimes they only use two feathers, but three feathers are better. Some arrows have two grooves along their length. Without the grooves, the arrow will staunch blood flow. The grooves keep the bleeding going, so they can track the animal or man until it bleeds to death or they catch up. The Apache use four grooves in their arrows.

"We gonna haul all this crap back to San Antonio or build us a fire?" asked Bigfoot.

Jack replied. "I think we ought to take it with us. Some young boys will have some fun playing with them, once they get strong enough to pull these bows. Any of you tried it?"

We all shook our heads and then took turns. Each notched an arrow and then pulled the sinew bow string the full length of the arrow and shot it at a tree stump about twenty yards away. Not one arrow hit the stump. Most sailed far over it.

"That takes considerable strength and practice," observed Albert.

We left the clearing, leaving the two dead warriors to rot. We rode, each of us leading one or more of the stolen horses, until the shadows from the trees along the Pedernales cast long shadows to the east. We continued scouting our assigned area. One evening after stopping, we unsaddled our riding horses and removed the packs from the pack animals. Then we hobbled all the animals and turned them loose to graze. We made a fire, cooked some rice and beans, and then roasted some venison steaks from a doe Bigfoot brought down at dusk. We were sitting on our buffalo robes, leaning back on our saddles and drinking boiled coffee.

"So, Jacob," said Bigfoot. "Were you and Joe with old Deef at San Jacinto?"

"For certain. Right, Joe? That was somethin' else."

"Deef was still trainin' us, hadn't been with him more than a couple of weeks," chimed in Joe.

"Deef went to see Sam Houston early in the morning. Houston was all dressed up for the battle in that Cherokee coat he wore and a buckskin vest and silver spurs on his boots. He was pacing in front of his tent, agitated, when we got there. Me and Joe and four others didn't want to lose old Deef. He had a habit of just takin' off and leavin' us new recruits, so we followed him everywhere. We hung back some when we saw him just walk up to the general."

Joe added to the story. "Deef shouted at Houston, tellin' him he reckoned any reinforcements for Santa Anna coming down the wagon road would have to cross Vince's Bayou over the bridge. He told him he and his boys could take down that bridge, and reinforcements would have to get around the flooded Bayou some other way."

"And when we whip them Mexicans," said Deef, "they'll play hell runnin' through the Bayou to get clear of us."

"Get her done," said Houston. "But you won't have much time to get back if you want to get in on this fight. We ain't gonna wait for you."

On the way back to where their horses were picketed, Deef found captains Karnes and William Smith. He talked them into creating a diversion while he and the rest of his men mounted up and took off fast to cover the six miles to the bridge. When they arrived at the bridge, they tried to set fire to it, but the water had been high enough to almost cover it. It was too soaked to do anything but smolder. Deef had brought a couple of axes, and those with tomahawks also got busy chopping. They finally dropped the bridge into the water, but it was after noon.

"Then Old Deef decided he'd pull one of his jokes on us newbies, just to see if we were payin' attention. About a mile from camp, Deef pulled us up in a deep, dry hollow," said Joe.

"I'm gonna ride ahead and see if any Mexican soldiers are about. You youngsters just wait here for me."

"After a few minutes here, he comes back, his horse runnin' full on. He slides the poor mare to a stop and hollers: 'The prairie up there is full o' Mexicans on horseback. My orders are to return to camp, and I will do so or die tryin'. Prepare your weapons and follow me single file through this here holler to where it comes out into Buffalo Bayou.'

"Then he wheeled the mare and takes off on a run whippin' the poor beast side to side with his reins. He's gettin' away from us so we all spur our horses, scared shitless. We finally get up onto the prairie, and there wasn't a Mesican anywhere to be seen. Old Deef practically fell off his mare laughin'."

"What happened then?" asked Jack.

Jacob looked at Joe. "You tell it."

"All right. About that time, we were still a ways away, but we heard the damn fight start. Deef couldn't hear it and was still laughin', but I shouted in his face that they'd started without us."

"'The hell you say,' shouts Deef, then he wheels his horse and we all took off at a dead run so as not to miss out."

Joe continued his narrative. "By the time Deef got us to the battleground, Houston's gray horse was shot out from under him. Somebody grabbed a small horse that was running free and gave it to him. He rode all over the battlefield shouting orders, his feet dangling because his legs were too long for the stirrups.

"We followed Deef into the fray, then Jacob earned his keep. Deef tried to get his mare to jump over some Mexican breastworks, but the mare shied and he went over her head. He grabbed one of his belt pistols and aimed at the head of a Mexican soldier. The cap went off, but the load didn't. Deef threw the pistol at the Mexican, grabbed the man's rifle, and clubbed him over the head with it. Then a Mexican officer came running at Deef with his sword in hand. Jacob ran the officer down with his horse, knocking him to the ground. Deef grabbed the officer's sword and ran him through. About that time, all the Mexicans broke and started running. It was a turkey shoot for the next couple of hours.

"We killed every Mexican we could find. Deef grabbed a hold of a Mexican cavalry mount, hollering for us to stick close. After the Alamo and Goliad, Deef wasn't in the mood to take prisoners, but eventually his blood cooled some. He took us back toward the battlefield, recruiting straggler Texas soldiers as we went. He stationed all us around a big grove of live oak to keep any Mexicans hiding in there from sneaking off during the night."

"Damn, I'm sure sorry I missed that fight," said Bigfoot.

Joe wasn't done. "I heard later we only lost seven men that day, but another four were wounded so bad they died later," he said. "We had thirty wounded who eventually recovered. The Mesicans had at least six hundred killed, more than seven hundred captured, and more than two hundred of those captured were wounded."

Young men searching for adventure and danger continued to arrive in San Antonio early in 1839. Most knew about the atrocities perpetrated on the settlers of the Texas frontier by the Comanche because stories of attacks were sensationalized in local newspapers and embellished by gossip. These same sources generated an equal number of stories about the young leader of a group of elite fighters who were taking retribution. There were plenty of Comanche raids, and they were increasing in frequency. The Republic was broke, but Jack Hays was recruiting men for his survey crews. Those he recruited were required to also join the unpaid militia.

When the Republic was able to find the funds, they paid militia volunteers on active duty a dollar a day plus food for themselves and their horses. But funds were rarely available. Sometimes militia wages were promised but not paid. However, there was considerable demand for survey crews who were willing to brave the dangers. Jack Hays had more business than he could handle. He offered wages and sustenance for survey crews and for men to guard those crews. Jack's reputation as a fierce and successful commander spread throughout Texas and beyond. During the previous year, close to a hundred young Rangers were killed, but that did not deter the arrival of more volunteers.

A group of heavily armed young men usually lined up each morning outside the door to Jack's cabin. All were itching to use their weapons to protect the frontier. The word spread that he was forming a new ranging company to protect settlers. The territory we were to protect was more than a hundred miles long, extending from west of San Antonio south to the Rio Grande.

Jack swung the door of his cabin open, and I followed him out.

"All of you here to volunteer?" he asked. "If so, raise your hand."

All of them raised a hand.

"All right, all of you who own a horse worth at least a hundred dollars raise your hand. Be warned that I will judge the worth of your animal myself."

All but four raised a hand.

"Those of you without a good horse are dismissed. Thank you for your interest, but you do not qualify. If any of you have a second horse of equal value, raise your hand."

One man raised a hand. I saw he also had the required weapons and nodded at Jack.

"Good, you stand over there in the shade next to the cabin. Now, anyone who doesn't own a pistol, a rifle, a fighting knife, and a hatchet or tomahawk is dismissed. Those are all requirements. If you own all of those weapons, as well as a shotgun, join our two-horse man next to the cabin. You will have to prove to me that you are adept at using all your weapons. If you are not certain you can do that, you are excused."

The weeding left five young men standing in the shade, big smiles on their faces.

"Don't be too happy. You're not a Ranger yet. Each of you need to show me how good you can ride and how accurate you are with your rifle and pistol, both on foot and at a full gallop. If you pass those tests, you'll get to demonstrate your skills with knife and tomahawk."

Once a recruit was inducted into the brotherhood, Jack's veterans trained him until all his skills met Jack's high standards. Some might be excellent marksmen and horsemen during their training, but when faced with an enemy trying to kill them, those skills could evaporate. Only an actual confrontation with the enemy could settle that question. Some men became less effective the more time they spent exposed danger. They would have to join those being culled.

When not out on patrol or with a survey crew, one of Jack's experienced associates would have the recruits practicing marksmanship, hand-to-hand fighting, and horsemanship. Another skill, imitating the tactics of the Comanche, was to learn to hang from the side of a mount and fire a pistol under the horse's neck with accuracy. All of the Rangers were constantly drilled in the fighting skills and to immediately respond to the commands and instructions of their captain.

They were still a motley looking crew without uniforms. Some of the men decided on wide-brimmed Mexican-style sombreros, a few wore coonskin caps, but most sported round-crowned leather or felt hats with drooping brims. Their pants and coats were of foxed cloth, wool, canvas, or buckskin. Their shirts were usually homespun cotton or wool. Some fancied Mexican serapes draped over one shoulder. Most had some sort of rain gear or a covering that would serve that purpose. Almost all acquired a buffalo robe at the first opportunity, usually taken from a dead warrior or foraged after the Indians had been driven from their camp.

When not in training camp or on patrol, the heavily armed men, few beyond their early twenties, occupied the bars of San Antonio. They drank whiskey when they had the money and nursed a beer when they didn't. They descended on the cantinas in small groups to drink and talk, gamble, and pick fights.

The number of Anglo residents of San Antonio had grown to nearly forty-five thousand by 1839. There was an ongoing state of war with various bands of Indians and bandits from Mexico. Many of the Mexican bandits were disgruntled veterans of the war with Texas. They were embarrassed and resentful of their defeat and the retreat after San Jacinto. They found refuge south of the Rio Grande from where they were able to cross the border and target remote settlements as well as pack trains bringing supplies and valuable manufactured items to the settlements.

Stories of Jack's fearlessness, decisiveness, leadership skills, and care and nurturing of his men continued to spread. The stories were often embellished and then repeated. Jack was aware of the stories but was not interested in hearing them. I repeated the stories I heard to him whenever

I could, just to watch him squirm with discomfort. He continued to be unsophisticated, easygoing, good-natured, and unflappable.

Even men who had earned respect for remarkable past deeds deferred to him. Despite his shyness, slight build, limited stature, and youth, he gained a reputation for gallantry. He soon became a favorite and sought-after guest at dinners and dances hosted by the married ladies of San Antonio.

One day Jack was inspecting the pistols of two new recruits. He loaded the two pistols and fired them to test their accuracy and heft. After he reloaded the pistols, he spotted a rooster about thirty yards away. The bird was straining his neck to announce his domination over his domain.

"Boys," said Jack, "I believe I'll stop that bird's bragging."

He leveled the pistol in his right hand, seemingly without taking aim, and as the rooster stretched his neck to begin another declaration, he fired. The ball took off the bird's head, the call cut short. This often repeated, and always embellished, story did nothing to lessen Jack's image.

Jack was out of town with one of his survey crews when a bold Comanche warrior rode into San Antonio. The warrior's long braids were enhanced with extensions made from his wife's shorn hair, bright beads festooned the braids. Despite the cold March wind, the warrior's chest was bare. His chest and face were covered in war paint. He rode his prancing pony through the middle of town on Commerce Street. He screamed for anyone with sufficient cojones to come fight his small band of warriors who were waiting just outside of town. Eleven young men, all heavily armed hopefuls, poured out of a cantina and jumped on their horses. Unfortunately, not one of them had any experience fighting Indians, let alone Comanche. The warrior teased them out of town into an ambush set by nearly a hundred warriors. Only three of the boys made it back to town alive, two of them with arrows protruding from their backs.

That June, Jack led a company of men on a two-week excursion into Canyon de Uvalde. Flaco and I were with him. We were pursuing a small band of Comanche who had raided several small settlements. The warriors killed the all men, women, and boys and took two young girls with them. They also absconded with every horse and mule they could round up.

One of our newest recruits rode up next to Jack. "What is it with these Indians and stealing horses, Captain?"

"It is their wealth. They trade horses with the traders at Bent's Fort on the Arkansas River. They want percussion caps, steel knives, hatchets, axes, blankets, ribbons, linens and shrouds, bridles, and things like wire, bells, saddlebags, iron stirrups, and iron pots. They also like mirrors, scissors, glass beads, wampum, tobacco, tinder boxes, tweezers, combs, and dried fruit. If they have Anglo captives and a reward is offered, they will trade those at Bent's too."

"They also trade with the Mexicans, don't they?" asked the youngster.

"Of course. The Mexicans will trade for horses and mules, as well as for captive slaves taken from other tribes. Anglo captives are especially valuable because they can often be ransomed."

Flaco rode up on the opposite side of Jack. "Comanche following off to the right," he said.

"Yes, I know. They've been with us for half the day."

The new recruit jerked his head to the right, wildly trying to see the threat.

"Calm down and look straight ahead. I don't want them to know they're spotted."

"Please warn the men, Flaco, but be quiet about it. Then come back and give me any ideas you have about how to sucker them into an ambush. You drop back to the company, Sean, isn't it?"

When Flaco returned, the two of them discussed the merits of several tricks designed to entice the Comanche warriors to attack the company and fall into an ambush, but Jack's fame had reached these warriors. They were too wary to be taken in, and eventually, they were gone. Two evenings later, Flaco, scouting ahead, found where the Comanche set up camp for the night. We soon surrounded the site, but the warriors were alert, spotted us, and managed to escape. They left the two brutalized girls behind, dead, as well as some of the horses they had stolen.

"Do you think we can catch these bastards, Flaco?"

"No, Jack. They each have at least two or more horses, riding one and leading the others. They will move very fast, changing horses frequently. We won't be able to catch up with them. With extra horses, you and I might catch them, but your men will take too long to change saddles and bridles each time. Also, your people do not have the endurance to keep riding for many days. These Comanche are very accustomed to staying on their ponies for days, moving all the time. No, we will not catch them."

We returned to San Antonio with a few recaptured horses. The animals were returned to their owners or to the heirs of the murdered men. During the remainder of the summer, Jack and his men did reduce the number of Mexican bandits, causing consternation along the frontier.

September was still hot in San Antonio. Jack received a message from Gen. Antonio Canales. The messenger carried a long letter from the general, written in Spanish. Jack, after three years in Texas and daily contact with Tejanos, Texans of Mexican descent, and loyal supporters of the Republic, was reasonably fluent in Spanish. However, he needed to make certain he had interpreted Canales's letter accurately. He walked to the home of his friend, the mayor of San Antonio, Juan Seguin. The mayor was a loyal supporter and very literate.

"My friend, you've got it correct," smiled Seguin. "The general claims he will unite the northern states of Mexico to create a new republic."

"That could be helpful," observed Jack. "To have a buffer state between us and the Mexicans could prove to be significant."

"Indeed so, Jack. I continue to receive information from my friends and family in Mexico. The government there is always open to ideas about how to return to Texas and reclaim their lands."

"Well then, amigo, I ask you to prepare a careful translation of this letter from the general. We will send your translation, along with the original, and a letter I will prepare to President Lamar requesting permission to take my men to support this effort."

Two weeks later, Jack met with the mayor again.

"I have heard from Lamar," reported Jack. "Colonels Sam Jordan and Ruben Ross have been authorized by him to recruit volunteers and join General Canales."

"I agree it would be helpful to us, as we discussed, if the Federalists were able to form a separate republic between us and the Centrists in Mexico City," said Seguin. "I am not certain, however, that Canales is the man to accomplish this."

"Why so?" asked Jack.

"He has no military experience. He is another self-appointed general, a lawyer who writes impressive manifestos and is, by all accounts, charismatic. For some time, he has been leading a group of malcontents, riding the countryside between the Rio Grande and Nueces, creating disturbances but very little else. However, our poet-hero of San Jacinto, President Lamar, seems to believe he can pull this off. Do you know either Jordan or Ross?"

"Yes, I know Ross. He's a good man. I will be happy to serve under him."

"Well, Canales is gathering his army at Lipantitlan on the lower Nueces upstream of San Patricio. Do you know the place?" the mayor questioned.

"I do."

"My understanding is that both Ross and Jordan are on the Nueces, southwest of here and moving toward Lipantitlan."

"I'll gather my men and join them. Flaco's Lipans used to use that area as a campground. Maybe he'll be able to raise some of his Lipan warriors and join us."

The next morning, Jack, Flaco, and the rest of us paraded out of San Antonio to the cheers of the populace, including a significant number of Tejanos.

"I suspect that at least some of these folks are just enthusiastic about this rough crowd getting away from their town for a while," Jack murmured.

Flaco and I just nodded.

We found the two colonels and added our ranks to the 140 men the two had recruited.

"I'm happy to see you, Captain Hays. I'm glad you saw fit to join the fun," announced Colonel Ross. "I understand our president has not seen fit to give you a formal appointment with appropriate compensation, but I understand your men have elected you their captain."

"We're happy to be here, Colonel," Jack responded. "I've told my men of your accomplishments during the war for Texas and as captain of the Gonzales company of frontier Rangers. We are all happy to serve under your command and Colonel Jordan's as well."

Late that same September, the two colonels, with just over 160 men, arrived at Lipantitlan.

Bigfoot Wallace was riding alongside Jack as they approached the earthen embankment that constituted the battlements of Lipantitlan. The dirt was held in place with fence rails on the inside surface.

"Might serve tolerable well as a pigpen, not much of a fort," observed Bigfoot.

"Hope we don't have to fight from it," Jack replied, smiling.

The next day Canales gave the first indication of his leadership skills. His forces included only a few men with military experience, but he was wise enough to rely on them. He split the six hundred men that constituted his army into two divisions and then appointed Col. Antonio Zapata to be in joint command of one of the divisions with Colonel Ross. The second division was to be jointly commanded by Jose Maria Gonzales and Colonel Jordan. Nobody saw fit to inform the general that joint command of forces was a bad idea.

The Texans were soon grumbling. They wanted to fight under the Lone Star flag of their Republic. Canales forbade it. They would all fight under his Federalist flag.

The Federalist forces moved ponderously toward Laredo. They had two-wheeled supply carts rather than wagons. The carts were overloaded and sunk through the top crust of dirt into loose sand, getting stuck as the single axel hung up. Most often the carts had to be unloaded before the straining mules and soldiers pushing from the back could break them free. Progress through the uninhabited region was slow, tedious.

The army wasted more days resting on the north shores of the Rio Grande, while Canales tried to decide if he should attempt a crossing to attack the Centrists forces who were stationed in Guerrero upstream of Laredo. He hesitated because the Centrists were commanded by General Pavon, an experienced soldier.

When the order was finally given, the Texans led the way into the fast-flowing Rio Grande. Their well-trained horses were experienced at fording rivers and did not balk. This was not true of the Federalists' animals, especially the mules pulling carts. When the Federalists tried to follow, almost all their animals balked and then started lunging and bucking. Many riders were dumped into the water. Some carts were overturned and their contents washed downstream. The result was mass confusion and chaos, accompanied by loud shouting and screamed orders that were ignored. We Texans sat on our horses in Mexico, too dumbfounded to even try to help.

Of course, the chaos of the crossing alerted Pavon. He responded by ordering his troops to retreat along the road to Mier, about ninety miles away. When we saw the dust from Pavon's army, Jack's company, followed by the rest of the Texas contingent, gave chase. Only a few of the Federalists managed to join us. Pavon and his army reached Mier and set up their defenses. Jack decided to wait for the rest of Canales's forces. When the

Texans were finally joined by the majority of the Federalists, they initiated contact. Pavon and his army continued their well-executed retreat toward Matamoros, where a sizeable force of Centrists was stationed. The Texans pressed harder, picking off stragglers, but the majority of Canales's army lagged, still encumbered by their bulky supply carts.

The disorganized, half-hearted, chase ended in the rocky hill country downstream from Mier. Pavon finally decided to take a stand along Alcantara Creek where he set up his artillery and waited.

Jack and his men, assigned to the division led by Jordan and Zapata, were the first to arrive. Pavon's nine-pounders barked, but their grapeshot fell harmlessly into the dirt, far short of us. When he heard the sound of the cannon, Canales sent a messenger ordering Jordan and Zapata to stop and wait for him to bring up his army.

Jack was more than frustrated by the order to wait. He got in Jordan's face.

"Colonel, now's the time to take 'em. See that shallow arroyo up there? Those men don't know how to use their artillery. Let me take my men and any others with long rifles that can use them, and we'll pick off the men manning the cannon."

Zapata and Jordan conferred, Zapata agreed with Jordan, and they approved the plan. The two of them decided to join Jack and his men, but just to observe. About fifty Texans dismounted and raced forward to the arroyo. All gained its protection safely, and the sharpshooters began to pick off the artillerymen along with any Mexican soldiers who tried to take their place.

"Where the hell is Canales with the rest of the army? What's Canales waiting for?" Jack questioned Zapata.

"No *cojones*," answered Zapata.

"Hell, let's just take them down ourselves," Jordan replied.

Jack looked back and saw Canales on a hill observing the action with his telescope. "Shit, he sees the situation. Why doesn't he send the rest to join us? We can win this today if he would get off his ass."

"He doesn't have the balls," repeated Zapata. "I'm going."

The three leaders jumped up and charged Pavon's lines. As soon as we saw him running forward, all of Jack's men jumped up and followed, completely confident that he would, with our help, seize the advantage and win the day. The rest of the Texans soon followed our lead. Later, when we were questioned about why Jack inspired such loyalty, we just shrugged and said that we trusted him.

After thirty minutes of aggressive fighting, some hand-to-hand, the Centrists broke ranks, abandoning their positions.

Jack looked back again, still expecting to see the Canales and his Federalists joining the fray.

"The son of a bitch is still standing on the same hill watching us. What the hell is he thinking?"

While Canales prevaricated, Pavon was able to get his supply train moving and even rescued four of his nine-pounders. He moved his army, but he lost two-thirds of his men, killed, wounded, or deserted. He decided to see if he could buy some time and sent one of his captains to the Federalists with a white flag.

Jack stood, incredulous as Zapata welcomed the messenger, an old acquaintance, and then escorted him back to General Canales. Before long, the two returned. They shook hands and embraced, and the captain walked casually back to join Pavon.

"What was that about?" asked Jordan.

"Pavon requested a twelve-hour truce," answered Zapata.

"Don't tell me Canales agreed?" exclaimed Jack.

Zapata shrugged his shoulders and left to direct his troops to set up camp. When they were situated, Canales finally brought up the rest of his army.

Pavon left huge campfires lit and removed what was left of his forces five miles away to a rancho where a labyrinth of stone fences offered good protection.

The next morning, Jack took five of his men and scouted ahead, reporting back to Jordan and Zapata.

"Pavon tricked you," Jack said. "He's gone. Their camp is empty, but they're using the road. What do you suppose the general will want to do now?"

"I'll see if I can wake him up and ask him," replied Zapata.

Thirty minutes later, Zapata returned.

"He is very disappointed that Pavon has so little honor. We are to send scouts to follow and report back."

Jordan looked at Jack and raised his eyebrows. "Hell yes. I'll spread the word. You going to join us, Colonel Zapata?"

"No," answered Zapata. "The general wants the colonel and me to attend a council of war."

"Shit, hombre. You can represent me. I'm going with Captain Hays and his men. Will you send your men with us?" asked the colonel.

"Of course. Go with God."

The Texans and their comrades soon reached the rancho where Pavon was waiting. However, when the general had snuck off the previous day, he neglected to order his water casks filled. He soon realized that his subordinates had not thought to make certain of that task on their own initiative. He knew his remaining men could not fight long without water. He sent out the same captain with a white flag.

"He'll not trick us twice. No truce," Jordan told the messenger. "We'll accept the general's surrender."

After receiving the ultimatum, Pavon came forward and offered Jordan his sword.

"I can't accept it," Jordan told him. "You'll have to give it to General Canales."

Pavon's face looked as though he had just been forced to swallow a handful of donkey shit. He recognized the ineptitude of Canales and the bravery of the men he faced. He thrust his sword into the ground, walked back to his troops, and ordered them to lay down their weapons and surrender.

Centrist soldiers numbering 160 quickly volunteered for the Federalist army. Canales also acquired four cannons, in addition to the two we had previously captured. However, rather than pressing on with his advantage, Canales went back to Mier and spent the next forty days strutting around the town, celebrating his great victory. It was not until late November that he finally decided to start the trek to Matamoros. His army now totaled more than a thousand men, many new recruits wanting to join a winner.

On December 12, Canales arrived outside Matamoros where a general named Canalize was in command of the large garrison. Canales set up his Federalists for a siege beyond the range of General Canalize's cannon. He initiated action by ordering his trumpeters to play as loud as they could through the night. He assumed that with this provocation, General Canalize would respond with a foray of some sort. Nothing happened. After three days, Canales finally agreed to let Zapata and Jordan attack some of the Centrist outposts.

The attack resulted in the death of thirteen of Canalize's soldiers.

All of the remaining soldiers from the outposts retreated to the safety of the fortified town. Canales again did nothing to follow up, despite the entreaties of both Jordan and Ross who were certain they could take the town if allowed to attack.

Ross decided he'd had enough, and so did Jack. All of Jack's Rangers, accompanied by fifty other Texans, returned to San Antonio, leaving Jordan and the remaining Texans to do their best with Canales. Both Jack and Ross considered Canales not only timid and ineffective but lacking the necessary fortitude and aggression to be successful. Ultimately, they were proven to be correct in that assessment.

CHAPTER 7

AFTER THE INEPTITUDE and failures of Canales resulted in the demise of the conceptually idealistic buffer Federalist republic, word reached San Antonio that the Mexican army was once again preparing for an invasion of Texas. The rotund and affable Juan Seguin, mayor of San Antonio, sent for Jack. I went along, curious. Seguin, Jack, and another man were in the cramped front room office of Seguin's four-room frame house. Seguin motioned for us to take two of the three chairs in the room. He and the other man remained standing.

"Jack, this is Jorge Catalan," Seguin noted. "He is my wife's cousin. He lives in Monterey and is a successful businessman there."

We both shook the man's hand before sitting.

"Jorge's business requires frequent travel between San Antonio and Monterey. He keeps his eyes and ears open and can be relied upon. Please tell Señor Hays what you told me earlier, Jorge."

"The gossip is that Laredo will be the staging area for an army of invasion."

"Have you seen any evidence of this?" asked Jack.

"When I came through, I did see some army wagons unloading at a warehouse, but there were not large numbers of soldiers."

"All right, I will need to investigate this. Thank you, Señor Catalan, and you, Juan. If they are mobilizing, I need to know for certain and report to President Lamar."

Two days later, Jack and I left San Antonio with a dozen men. We made our way to Laredo and set up camp where there was good forage for our horses and pack mules, about two miles northwest of the town. That evening Jack called us together in the small thicket of juniper where we were camped. Our hobbled horses and mules were grazing contentedly in the adjacent meadow.

"John and I are going into town to scout around and see what we can discover," Jack announced. "You boys stay put. We might not get back before morning."

Jack and I both borrowed sombreros and serapes from two of our comrades and rode slowly into Laredo. The moon stayed behind a thick cloud covering, and it was dark with slits of light filtering out through the shutters of only the occasional house. The streets were empty, and dust followed the hooves of our horses as they stepped. We came to an intersection where light flooded out onto the street from a cantina. As we rode past, two soldiers came to the open doorway and watched us for a moment. They weren't carrying weapons. They turned and went back inside. We followed every street but saw no sign of a significant encampment of soldiers. We returned to our camp. As the sun came up, Jack called everyone together.

"We're going into town like we own the place. I want you to spread out in pairs. See if you can be obnoxious enough to scare up any soldiers hanging around. If they are present, we need to provoke them to confront us. I also want you to round up any horses and mules you find and bring them back here. John, you're with me."

Before noon, we were back in camp. All together, we appropriated more than thirty head of horses and mules. Some of the horses still wore the saddles they had on when taken. No one in Laredo made any effort to stop us.

"We'll stay here tonight. Build up your fires, so they know where we are. We'll stand two-hour shifts on guard, but out beyond the light from the fires. I want to know if they have the cojones to do anything about us taking their animals."

The night passed without incident. The next morning, Jack wrote a note addressed to the alcalde of Laredo. He affixed the note to the saddle on the best horse in the bunch and sent it back to town.

The note read: "As Texans, we have frequently been subjected to horse thieves coming across the Rio Grande and stealing our animals. We have demonstrated to you that we are capable of this outrage as well, but as honorable men, we have no desire to take what is not ours. Be forewarned that we do not fear you. We will defend our Republic."

After about an hour, Jack turned all the animals loose and sent them on their way back to Laredo, and we turned toward home.

The rumors of an invasion aimed at San Antonio persisted. Hays, accompanied this time by Bigfoot, Perry Alsbury, me, and nine new recruits, returned to Laredo. This time we set up camp on a hill overlooking the town. The following morning, we watched as a forty-two-man company of Mexican cavalry, accompanied by one civilian, exited Laredo and headed toward us. Jack moved us off the hill to the open plain he had selected the previous day as being a good place for a fight. He positioned us for defense and then motioned to Bigfoot Wallace and me.

"Bigfoot, let's you and John and me go see if these hombres want to parley before they fight."

We rode toward the Mexicans who had stopped. The Mexican captain sent the civilian, carrying a white flag, to meet us.

"You are the same man who stole our horses. You are just bandits and very few in number," the man said to open the conversation.

"And who the hell are you?" asked Jack.

"I am Jose Delgado, the alcalde of Laredo. It was to me you sent your insulting note. You see, you are already outnumbered four-to-one. We will shortly be joined by many more soldiers. I demand that you and your men surrender at once. Otherwise, you will be slaughtered like the pigs you are."

"Bigfoot, do you find this man's tone and insolence insulting?" Jack questioned.

"Oh, yeah," he agreed.

"How do Texans respond to this kind of behavior?"

Bigfoot pressed his horse alongside the horse of the mayor and then slapped him on the head so hard the man fell to the ground. I saw the Mexican captain stand in his stirrups and scream enraged invective. He unsheathed his sword, waved it in circles over his head, and ordered his men to attack.

We wheeled our horses and rejoined the rest of our men. When the Mexicans were about 130 yards away, they halted, dismounted, and fired their smooth-bore muskets at us, but at that range, they hit nothing. Then a number of them fired their pistols, the balls rising puffs of dirt more than fifty yards in front of us. The Mexicans retreated to a safer distance, respecting our rifles, to reload their weapons.

Jack stood in his stirrups. "Let's charge but stop about two hundred yards away, dismount, try to pick some of them off, and then remount and retreat."

Three Mexican soldiers fell from their saddles.

The two sides repeated the charade twice. None of us were hit, but several more Mexicans were wounded by our long rifles.

"This time when they dismount to fire, we will immediately return their fire, but only with our rifles. Do not use your pistols, and stay mounted. As soon as we discharge our rifles, we'll charge them, before they can get remounted."

The maneuver worked perfectly. Jack led the charge, aiming his horse at the Mexican captain. When only a few yards away, he killed the man with a single pistol shot to the head. The terrified, still unmounted, Mexican cavalrymen dropped their bridle reins and tried to run for cover. Jack galloped ahead, joined by Bigfoot and me. We soon turned the terrified soldiers and kept them milling until the rest of our men came up.

"Don't hurt them, boys," Jack directed. "There's no need for a slaughter. I see our friend the alcalde has skedaddled back to town. I guess he was pullin' our leg about more soldiers bein' on the way."

At that moment, one of the new men leaned over in his saddle and fired his pistol into the ground, close enough to the rear end of one of the Mexicans to powder-burn his buttocks. Soon, others copied him.

"Enough," shouted Jack. "These hombres are shitting in their pants. Back off."

We all backed our horses away. The terrified Mexicans stood with their arms raised high. Eight Mexicans lay dead from the action; several more were wounded. Perry Alsbury was holding his left shoulder where a musket ball had passed through, leaving a clean wound.

After telling them not to be afraid and to lower their arms, Jack continued in Spanish. "I've got no use for prisoners. I expect you to tell your compadres that Texans only want to be left in peace. We harbor no ill will against the Mexican people, only against your leaders who want to enslave us. Go, return to your people, and tell them how kindly you were treated."

We again returned to San Antonio.

Juan Seguin's spies reported that the Mexican government and military were now quite aware of Captain Hays and his successes against them. They were sending Gen. Rafael Vasquez with a 450-man army to San Antonio to slaughter all defenders, and there was a reward offered for Jack's head.

When General Vasquez was eighty miles from San Antonio, we learned that he decided to try a subterfuge. He set up a permanent camp and sent a spy into San Antonio. The spy was supplied with a considerable amount of silver to purchase trade goods, wagons, and mules. He was then instructed to petition Hays for an escort to accompany him to the Rio Grande where he had anxious purchasers waiting for the goods. He was to explain to Jack that he was extremely fearful of the banditos who preyed upon traders such as himself.

The trader/spy offered good wages for the escort services, so Jack recruited men to accompany and protect the wagon train. Everything was set to depart San Antonio within a couple of days, but that evening, an older Mexican appeared at the door to Jack's cabin.

"Capitan," the gray-bearded man addressed Jack, "I was one of those men you set free outside Laredo when you could have killed us all. I have information for you."

"Come inside, señor. I remember your face. You are a sergeant, am I correct?"

"No longer, Capitan. My enlistment ended, and I now own a small cantina in Laredo. The government has sent General Vasquez, along with over four hundred soldiers, to take back San Antonio and to murder you and your men. One of the soldiers from my old platoon told me that the general has sent a spy to you, posing as a trader. He has set a trap."

The next morning Jack sent for the spy.

"We will be ready to leave in two more days. I have received word that Captain Caldwell is on the way from Gonzales with a hundred men to scout along the Rio Grande looking for trouble. I will only have forty men with me, so I need to wait until Captain Caldwell arrives. I need to meet with him before we go with you. If you will excuse me please, I have many details to attend to before we can leave."

As Jack anticipated, the spy surreptitiously left San Antonio to report to his master. Jack and his forty men followed. The spy led them to Vasquez's camp.

Ben McCulloch, Bigfoot Wallace, and I were in the company. Jack called a council of war.

"Bigfoot, I want you to take twelve men off to the east of the camp. Ben, you pick twelve to go with you west. John and I will bring the rest in from the north. We'll leave the road back to Laredo open for them. We'll let them fall asleep for a couple of hours then give them a surprise. When I fire my pistol, that will be the signal to charge in. What do you think?"

"Sounds like a damn good plan to me," said McCulloch.

Bigfoot and I nodded.

We waited for five hours after sunset, and then the three groups divided and took up positions around the Mexican camp. Jack guided his horse toward a group of tents.

"I expect the officers are in the tents," he whispered to me and then quickly fired his rifle and both pistols, killing three sleepy sentries.

Next, chaos took over. We all fired at any target that presented. Officers poured out of their tents trying to strap on their swords. Jack pulled his horse up while trying to reload his weapons, but the shouting and mass confusion caused the animal to prance, anxious to join the battle. Jack dismounted, held his reins in his teeth, and reloaded his weapons. Vazquez was an experienced general. He had the foresight to order that his officers always have a saddled horse available. Once mounted, some of them were able to marshal a contingent of the well-trained regulars and execute an organized retreat.

Bigfoot and I managed to capture a grizzled major. He told us that his general had spent the previous evening with his senior officers reorganizing his plans for the ambush to account for 140 Texans based on the spy's report. He calculated that they had at least two days to prepare the ambush.

We harassed the retreating Mexican forces all the way back to the Rio Grande valley. On the second day, Jack watched from a hilltop as Vazquez deployed skirmishers on his flanks.

"He's still worried about our made-up reinforcements from Gonzales," Jack laughed.

Much later, we learned that the general didn't learn about Jack's subterfuge until he was back in Mexico. He suffered unkind digs about his defeat by so few Texans for many years.

Jack and all of his men returned to San Antonio, unscathed and, once again, triumphant.

In July 1840, an estimated five hundred Comanche, organized and led by the infamous and highly successful war chief Buffalo Hump invaded Texas territory. Buffalo Hump gathered warriors from several Comanche bands from beyond the Edwards Plateau in west Texas. His Comanche were joined by warriors from several other subservient tribes. The raid proved to be the largest organized invasion of white-held territory up to that time.

Buffalo Hump led his warriors around San Antonio to the south. They penetrated to Victoria, eighty miles southeast of San Antonio. From there, they moved on to Lynnville on the Gulf coast, completely destroying the village, which never recovered. During this sweep, the Comanche and their allies appropriated horses, mules, and cattle; burned property; murdered more than thirty people; and took many captives. Then they turned around to return to their villages far to the west of Austin. They had a huge herd of stolen horses and mules, many looted firearms, and considerable ammunition. They also appropriated mirrors, liquor, cloth, and a mélange of confiscated clothing and held more than forty human captives they intended to sell as slaves to the Mexicans or keep themselves.

Maj. Gen. Felix Huston was in command of the Texas Militia. Word was spread for the militia to mobilize and gather in Austin. Huston's orders were to intercept and exact retribution before Buffalo Hump, his Comanche, and his allies could disperse into the vast areas they controlled.

Ed Burleson arrived with his company of men from Bastrop. Mathew "Old Paint" Caldwell, the most experienced Indian fighter in all of Texas, led the militia contingent from Gonzales. Ben McCulloch, after helping Jack defeat Vazquez, returned to Gonzales and organized his own ranging company. He and his men joined Old Paint. Jack gathered his men, and we made our way to Austin. Other militia and volunteers arrived singly and in small groups ready to fight.

"Black" Adam Zumwalt led a group of volunteers from the Lavaca River area. His was the first group to encounter the Comanche Army at Mercado Creek, about twelve miles east of Victoria. Buffalo Hump was more interested in getting away with the huge herd of captured horses and mules, the stolen booty, and their captives than in a fight. The Indians were using the appropriated cattle for food, but the cattle could not travel fast.

Buffalo Hump moved on with most of the warriors, leaving the cattle with a small group at Mercado Creek. If the white men ignored them to pursue the main body, those warriors were to bring the cattle along. If attacked, they were instructed to offer token resistance and then abandon the cattle and scatter. A small skirmish ensued. Zumwalt lost one man in the short fight and then retreated to a campsite he could defend. Once situated, he sent to Victoria for provisions and ammunition. During the night, the Comanche departed. When he learned the Indians were gone, Zumwalt and his men made their way to Austin.

Once everyone was together in Austin, the militia captains held a meeting and voted that Mathew Caldwell should lead the two-hundred-man force. General Huston, a forty-year-old lawyer, was known to be hot-tempered, extremely volatile, and aggressive. He had fought a duel with Albert Johnson, wounding him in the hip, after President Sam Houston appointed Johnson senior brigadier general and commander of the Republic's army over Huston. Most importantly, Huston had no experience fighting Indians, especially the Comanche. Old Paint Caldwell had skirmished many times against Buffalo Hump and other war chiefs. He understood the Comanche way of fighting.

"I'm honored, boys," said Caldwell, "but I'm a soldier, and I obey orders. Huston is in command, and that's that. I will do my best to consult with him and offer him advice, but he's the one responsible. I won't be part to any kind of mutiny."

That night the officers and General Huston were all gathered around a campfire speculating about where they would most likely find the Comanche. After the meeting concluded, Huston dispatched scouting parties in several directions in an attempt to locate the enemy. Then he retired to his tent. A small group of officers remained, sipping boiled coffee while sitting on the ground around the campfire. I sidled up on the fringe of the gathering behind Jack just to listen to the chatter.

"So," Jack spoke up. "I'm interested in nicknames. I know how you got yours, Captain Caldwell. You've got those weird white patches in your black beard."

"Just so," laughed Caldwell.

"You all know about my compadre Bill Bigfoot Wallace. He's got the biggest feet of any man I've ever known. How about you, Captain Zumwalt? Black Adam, what's that about?"

Zumwalt removed his hat and rubbed his hand over his thick black hair.

"I've got a cousin, also given the name Adam, who has bright red hair. He's Red Adam Zumwalt, and I'm Black Adam Zumwalt."

"Shit," said Ben McCulloch, "that's boring as hell. You need a better story than that."

The militia forces first encountered the Indians at Good's Crossing on Plum Creek, about twenty-seven miles south of Austin.

One of the many war chiefs who joined Buffalo Hump's party was enamored by the gaudy. He rode an elegant, well-bred Appaloosa stallion with a fancy tooled and ornamented Mexican saddle cinched to his back and a silver decorated bridle. He had attached a ten-foot red ribbon to the stallion's tail. The chief wore a pair of polished calf-length boots, a black silk top hat, and a fancy broadcloth swallowtail coat that he put on backward, its polished brass buttons fastened along his spine. He wore only a breechcloth and carried an open umbrella in his left hand. He sang his war song so loudly his voice carried above the firing of rifles and pistols, the shouting of the combatants, and the cries of the wounded.

The Texans tried desperately to kill the obnoxious war chief, but he managed to somehow dodge or use his shield to deflect all the rifle balls sent in his direction. His umbrella was eventually carried away, along with his top hat. He had a hurried conversation with Buffalo Hump and then organized a long line of warriors to lead against us. The warriors used their horses as shields, hanging from the off side while unloosing large numbers of arrows. Buffalo Hump, meanwhile, ordered the rest of his warriors to drive off their huge herd of captured animals and escape with as much loot as they could.

Some of the militia and all of the ranging companies included expert marksmen, but their well-aimed shots were having almost no effect.

"Hold on, boys," shouted Jack. "They are able to deflect your balls with those rawhide shields. You won't be able to penetrate them. The next time they charge, hold your fire until they have loosed all their arrows. When they wheel away, take your shots before they can cover their backs with those shields."

The dandy and several of his followers hit the ground, mortally wounded, after the next charge. The battle then turned into a running fight. The mounted Texans, following the lead of the ranging companies and their captains, chased the Indians for more than twelve miles. Several times Buffalo Hump organized groups of warriors to turn and face the Texans, delaying them as long as possible. Some warriors were more than willing to give their lives so their companions could get away. This tactic enabled a great many warriors to escape with most of their plunder including a great many of the stolen animals. The Indians inflicted grievous wounds on the captives they did not kill outright, knowing this would force many of the Texans to stop and try to help the unfortunates. This tactic depleted the numbers fighting the Indians. At dusk, the Texans were exhausted, but Buffalo Hump pushed his men on, escaping.

"Without the captives to slow them, those Comanche will be able to alternately fast walk, trot, and lope their animals, changing mounts frequently. They can keep that up for days if they have to," explained Old Paint to General Huston. "Our men can't do what those savages have been trained to do since they were pups. There's no sense in trying to catch them now. By morning, they'll be long gone."

In his report, General Huston claimed to have killed eighty Indians, but only twelve bodies were found. He explained that the Comanche tradition was to gather the corpses of their fallen comrades. Huston reported that none of his volunteers were killed and only a small number were wounded. He did make special mention, in his report, of the steadfast leadership and fighting skills of Jack Hays.

The next morning, Jack, along with General Huston, Old Paint, McCulloch, Burleson, Black Adam, and Bigfoot were looking over the smallish herd of recaptured horses.

"See that sorrel mare there? She's got no brand that I can see," said Jack. "My gelding has suffered some arrow wounds. It'll take him some time to heal. Anybody reckon there'll be an objection to me taking that animal?"

"Hays, after yesterday's exploits I reckon whoever the original owner of that animal was, if he's still alive, will not object," answered Huston.

"Did you see the animal Buffalo Hump was mounted on, Jack?" asked Old Paint.

"I did. Was the black around the eyes painted on?"

"Nope. That animal is what the Comanche call a War Bonnet. They breed not only for the characteristics of a good war or hunting pony but for color. They love their colors. They have what they call red paints, actually brown and white combinations; black paints; Appaloosas, of course; and both red and black Medicine Hats. The Medicine Hats can be most any color but have dark bands around their heads, dark ears, and a blaze in the shape of a teardrop shield on their chest. The War Bonnets are Medicine Hats but with black around both eyes. They like them best 'cause from a distance they look like a skull or death's head. The temperament of a War Bonnet pony more resembles a wolf than a dog. They're tough, mean, always ready to kick or bite, but the Comanche consider them the best for both hunting or war. Most all the horses they steal are for trade. They don't value any animal outside their color preferences."

Not only General Huston's report but many other accounts by men who were engaged in the Battle of Plum Creek mentioned Jack's leadership and valor. Jack was ordered to report to President Lamar in Austin. I went along.

"I am Jack Hays. I was told to report to the president."

The clerk jumped to his feet. "Yes, sir, Mr. Hays. The president has been expecting you. Just a moment."

He opened the door he was standing in front of. "Mr. Hays is here, Mr. President."

A moment later, the poet hero of San Jacinto rushed into the anteroom, his right hand extended and a big smile on his face. He looked at us with his brow furrowed.

"This is Jack Hays," I said and put my hand on Jack's back to force him forward.

They shook hands, and then Lamar pulled Jack into his office and took a couple of pieces of paper off the corner of his desk. He handed one of them to Jack. "This is your official commission as a captain of militia." He handed over the second document. "This authorizes you to officially enlist a company of Rangers. We are well aware of your exploits, Captain

Hays, and we need you to act for us in an official capacity. Are you willing to take on the responsibility?"

"Yes, sir."

"Good. Get on with it, young man, and continue to make us proud."

CHAPTER 8

NEWLY COMMISSIONED CAPT. John Coffee Hays started recruiting his company of spies as soon as he returned to San Antonio. Each man agreed to serve for six months. Most were men who had ridden with him previously. Ben McCulloch, Bigfoot Wallace, and I were among the first to sign up. In addition to his long-standing requirements for a good horse, rifle, pistol, knife, tomahawk or hatchet, a saddle and saddlebags, a halter for all horses they owned, and a Mexican blanket or buffalo robe, the new recruits were required to have a Mexican rawhide riata for roping, hair ropes, called *cabestros*, used to stake their horse or horses out to graze, as well as soft cotton rope hobbles.

When out scouting for Indians or banditos an activity we called *ranging*, the company traveled with pack mules, but each man carried a supply of spare ammunition, some salt, and parched corn, and most took along tobacco and coffee in their saddlebags. Long ranging expeditions frequently forced the men, in addition to hunting game, to obtain additional supplies from enemies killed or driven from their camps.

Jack preferred campsites that were within sight of a known Indian pathway. The influx of settlers proceeded at an ever-faster rate. Our captain made certain his men were positioned to observe the incursions of Indian raiding parties or Mexican bandits to better protect the new settlers. He often detailed one or two men to keep watch over a well-used trail while the rest were ranging.

Anyone observing us gathered around a campfire would see that the young adventurers were tough, rough-speaking men, immune to hardship, and always ready for a fight. However, they were not uneducated. Many were well read and could recite, from memory, poetry, as well as the writings and musings of philosophers and historians. During this time, we recruited four men who were lawyers, a dentist, and a medical doctor. More importantly, we counted among us several wonderful storytellers, the best of whom were not loath to embellish the facts.

Soon after Jack's first official company was formed, one of his men, who had been dispatched to watch a trail, raced to tell him that a large number of Comanche had managed to sneak into some settlements west of San Antonio. He observed them driving a large herd of horses and mules along the trail back toward their own lands.

Within an hour, we were riding hard to catch up. Jack, riding his new sorrel mare, was fifty yards ahead of us when he spotted the Comanche starting to make a careful crossing of the Guadalupe River. They did not want to lose any of their purloined animals, so they were gradually easing the herd into the swiftly flowing water.

Jack dismounted and waited for us to catch up to him, signaling us to be as quiet as possible.

"Get down, make certain your saddle girths are tight, and check your weapons. When we charge, most of those warriors will likely form a line to protect the ones trying to get away with the herd. When we go in, we'll form a triangle. I'll take the point. We'll charge directly at their line. Wait until you're close enough not to miss before you discharge your weapons."

He mounted, but as the rest of us began remounting, the Comanche spotted the movement. Their war chief responded just as Jack anticipated, forming his warriors into a long line facing us. A dozen other warriors forced the stolen herd into the river, two riders flanking on each side, one out ahead to encourage the herd to follow, and the others shouting and whooping, their ropes flicking the rumps of the animals at the rear of the herd to encourage them forward.

"Let's go, boys," shouted Jack and spurred his horse into a run.

We fanned out into a triangle behind him and rode hard and fast directly at the line of Comanche warriors. Our charge carried us through the shower of arrows, most not well aimed, and shot from too far away to be effective. When we were within a few feet of the warriors, our horses still running at full speed, we discharged our rifles. Momentum carried us through the line of wounded and dead Indians falling from their animals. Their ponies were pushed aside by the force and speed of our horses. Once through the line, we wheeled about, holstered our rifles, and pulled our pistols. Then we followed Jack back through the line of warriors in the same triangle formation.

The much-practiced skill of firing weapons accurately from the back of a running horse paid devastating dividends. Riderless Indian ponies, their eyes wide with panic, stampeded, causing those warriors still mounted to struggle before being able to bring their animals under control. Jack again turned his horse around. We followed and rushed again at the warrior line. Those men with two pistols shoved the spent one back into their belts and pulled the second. Those with only one pistol used them as clubs or pulled out their tomahawks. Jack carried a shotgun as well as his rifle and two pistols. He unsheathed the shotgun.

The war chief of the raiding party wore an elaborately decorated buffalo headpiece and was riding a black-and-white paint stallion. Both he and the horse were covered in war paint and ribbons. The chief rushed all along the back of his line, shouting orders and trying to reposition his men and give them heart. Jack guided his horse directly toward the chief, put his reins in his teeth, and pulled his second pistol. The chief saw Jack coming at him, jerked his horse around, and charged at Jack with his shield protecting his body, his eyes focused on Jack just above the top of the shield. The chief's ten-foot lance, held in his right hand and steadied by his armpit, was positioned for a fatal thrust. When twenty feet separated them, Jack brought both the pistol and the shotgun up and fired. His pistol ball hit the Comanche between the eyes, and the shotgun blast took away the top of his head. The man tumbled back directly over the rump of the paint stallion, dead long before he hit the ground. The warriors observed their leader hit the ground, with the top of his head gone, and scattered.

We pursued, killing several more warriors. When our horses started struggling to catch a breath, Jack called a halt. "That's enough. Let's round up the abandoned herd of stolen animals and all the Comanche ponies we can."

We forced all of the animals back across the river and headed east to the settlements. Jack threw his lariat over the head of the paint the war chief was riding and then noticed it was branded with Juan Sequin's brand.

"Must have taken him from the mayor's rancho south of town," Jack mused.

Responding to the increasing pressure of settlers constantly pushing westward, the Comanche decided to combine their scattered bands. They changed from their previous, constantly changing extended family campsites to large, partially fortified, semipermanent encampments on the upper reaches of the Nueces, San Antonio, San Sabo, and Colorado rivers. From these locations, they sent out raiding parties. The encampments provided them a fast and easy retreat to semifortified strongholds. When Jack learned of these changes, he decided it was essential for the safety of the frontier that he identify and destroy some of those strongholds.

Flaco brought along a contingent of Lipan Apache and joined the thirty-five volunteers Jack recruited for the assault on one of the Comanche strongholds. We rode west to the Frio River and then upstream to the Sabinal River. The course of the Sabinal was paralleled by a well-known Comanche trail. It was clearly marked on an early Spanish map Jack carried next to his recently sprouting chest hair. The trail followed the sparkling waters of the Sabinal through flat and then rolling terrain interspersed with fractures, faults, and folds. The landscape we rode through was covered by a sand and clay loam that supported hardwood trees and good pasture lands.

Before we reached the source of the Sabinal, our Lipan scouts reported sighting a large Comanche camp.

Jack halted us. "We'll stay here until just before dawn. Make certain all your equipment and weapons are ready for a fight. Keep your horses saddled and bridled, and keep hold on your reins. We don't want any horses wandering off—and no smoking, no noise. The Comanche have big eyes and bigger ears."

As the sky just began to lighten, as silently as possible, we led our horses toward the sleeping camp. When it was in sight, Jack mounted his horse. We did likewise. He looked back to see all his men mounted and then removed a pistol from his belt, waved it in a circle over his head, pointed it at the camp, and spurred his mare forward.

The sound of many running hooves was enough to bring completely naked warriors out of their dwellings, weapons in hand. A few warriors were shot, others were ridden over, and most took cover behind whatever was closest and began to use their bows. It didn't take long for the war chiefs to determine their attackers were few in number. Shouting orders, they rallied their warriors and organized a counterattack. The camp was soon engulfed in confusion. Women and children scurried out of the camp, seeking places to hide. The sound of twanging bow strings was accompanied by the muffled grunts of thrusted spears finding a target, rifles and pistols discharging, and lead balls and arrows thudding into the fighters, trees, or the ground. Shouts of anger, cries of pain, and commands yelled in four languages, English, Spanish, Apache, and Comanche, filled the still, dawn air. The noise and confusion caused horses to panic, rearing, snorting, and whinnying. Two horses bucked off their riders.

We were soon surrounded on three sides. Jack directed us to go in the only direction possible, a thicket containing large trees, heavy brush, and several large boulders. Then he ordered us to dismount.

"Jack, Tom, Steven, and Samuel, you hold all the horses, don't let 'em scatter. The rest of you men find cover and form a circle protecting the horses, we'll need 'em."

The Comanche were certain of their ability to overwhelm the few men so foolish to attack their camp. They charged, in mass, loosed all the arrows they carried, and then retreated to gather more arrows. We all took careful aim with our rifles as the warriors attacked, almost always hitting the warriors we aimed at. The Comanche were not deterred. They were still confident they could decimate us, although they soon recognized Captain "Yack." They knew him.

After a half dozen charges and retreats, Jack ordered us to chase down the warriors as soon as they turned to go back out of range. Using our pistols and rifles, we were able to fell many more warriors, including two war chiefs. Seeing two of their chiefs down disheartened the warriors. They withdrew to a nearby mountain where they dug shallow trenches and waited for the expected attack. We put our long rifles to good use, taking our time. We waited, protected behind good cover, until a warrior exposed himself. When one of us fired, the effect was usually lethal. After two hours, unable to get close enough with their bows and arrows, the Comanche climbed farther up the mountain and scattered.

We returned to the destroyed campground and counted the bodies of sixteen warriors. One of us, Benjamin Prim Jr., suffered an arrow wound to his right thigh. He was held down by four men while Jack dug out the arrowhead. Flaco prepared a poultice, pounding a particular plant root into a mush and then heating it over a campfire before applying to the wound.

"This very good; pull out bad medicine from wound. Also, can use leaves for smoking or tea. Smoking not as good as you tobacco."

"Flaco, I think your English is getting worse. We need to spend more time together." Jack smiled and patted his friend on the shoulder.

"You know this plant?" asked Flaco.

"Yeah, it grows almost everywhere. We call it hogweed. What name do you use?"

"Apache name you no be able say, mean yellow flower. When in flower, you take for you woman. She will like."

"That's good to know, if I ever have a woman."

"You no have woman?" Flaco stared at Jack, his forehead wrinkled, his eyebrows pulled down, clearly incredulous. "You brave and famous warrior. All know of Captain Yack. Why you no have woman?"

"I guess I haven't found anyone I fancy. Besides, I'm likely to get killed one of these days. Don't need to leave a poor widow."

"Flaco get you pretty Apache girl. Many be happy be woman of Captain Yack, be proud."

Bigfoot Wallace was standing behind the two men while they attended to Ben Prim.

"Shit, Jack. You best take Flaco up on that offer. Probably be lots of handsome 'Pache girls to choose from."

Jack looked over his left shoulder at Bigfoot. "Can't you find something useful to do instead of giving me shit?"

Bigfoot walked away laughing. He shouted at a group of men grooming their horses. "Flaco's setting Jack up with a choice of 'Pache girls. Can't wait for that wedding."

Two mornings later we located the tracks of another band of Comanche, headed northwest.

"Maybe twenty-five. Each has extra pony," observed Flaco. "No more than five hours they pass here."

"All right, men. Let's see if we can catch up to these savages," said Jack, spurring his mare into a lope.

Late that afternoon, Flaco stopped and pointed to a thin stream of smoke coming from a cedar brake about a mile distant.

"See it," said Jack. "We'll wait here until they're settled in for the night. You men can eat cold, no fires. We don't want them to know we're here."

Two of Jack's Tejano volunteers couldn't forego their cigarillos after eating. One of them tossed the still-burning butt away, but it landed in a pile of dead leaves, resulting in a smoky fire. The two men soon stamped out the fire, but Jack, incensed, rushed over from where he had been stretched out on the ground. He swung the coiled lariat he held in the direction of the two men but did not strike them.

"Goddamn, don't you two know enough to snub your smokes into bare ground? Shit. All you men mount up. We're going to find out if those Comanche discovered us."

By the time we all gathered our gear, saddled our horses, and rushed to the thicket, the Indians were long gone. Smoke filtered up from the embers of four campfires.

"They no wait now," said Flaco. "No catch them."

Early July 1841, Jack was camped with forty men on Leon Creek, only seven miles west of San Antonio. We occupied one of Deef Smith's old campgrounds. Jack finished drilling the men late in the afternoon and then told us we would be leaving early the next morning to follow the Medina River upstream for a day.

"We'll camp for the night before going through Bandera Pass. We're going to scout the Guadalupe Valley for any sign of Comanche raiders."

The company consisted of his best and most experienced men. When we camped alongside the Medina the following evening, we were spotted by a large war party of Comanche. The war chief surmised we intended to go through the hundred-yard wide, five-hundred-yard long pass the next day. The seventy-five-foot high slopes of the pass were steep, covered with large boulders and brush that offered excellent concealment. An ambush was prepared.

Just before noon we rode into the pass. The Comanche waited patiently until all of us were in, and then both sides erupted with flight after flight of arrows, accompanied by earsplitting war whoops. Many of our horses panicked, rearing and bucking, and many were hit with arrows. Three riders were separated from their mounts.

Jack's calm voice rang out. "Steady, men. Find cover and then dismount and tie up your horses."

We responded immediately, finding trees or stout brush to which we tied our horses. Then we formed a defensive circle, which was routine because of our constant practice of this maneuver.

Warriors charging down the steep slopes were met with a volley of rifle and pistol balls, some men firing while others reloaded. The warriors recoiled, scrambling back up the slopes to find cover. The war chief rallied his warriors. This time they charged and braved the rifle and pistol fire, engaging us in hand-to-hand combat.

Sam Luckey took three arrows to his chest and went down, his head bouncing off a rock. Ben Wallace took a musket ball into his left shoulder fired by the war chief, but Ben was able to get off a shot from his pistol, hitting the chief in the abdomen. They both drew their knives and came together, each striking repeatedly, hitting flesh but missing anything vital. They rolled over and over on the ground until Ben found an opening. He drove his knife between the fourth and fifth ribs on the chief's left side, ripping open the warrior's heart. Ben staggered to his feet, knife still in his hand, covered with blood, looking about wildly for his dropped pistol.

Throughout the fight, Flaco stuck close to Jack, fighting back-to-back. Several times Flaco intercepted a warrior intent on bringing down the infamous Captain Yack. Jack, using a pistol in his left hand as a club and a tomahawk in his right, took on three warriors, each of whom were so intent on taking him down they managed to impede each other. Jack knocked out one with a vicious swing of his pistol, while parrying the knife thrust of another with his tomahawk. Flaco sliced the knife arm of the third warrior and then managed to block a tomahawk attack by another man. Jumping to the side, he slid his knife into that attacker's belly. The two resumed their back-to-back stance, ready to take on the next onslaught.

The grunts and shouts of fighting, interspersed with an occasional rifle or pistol shot, continued for about fifteen minutes but seemed, to us involved, more like an hour. The fight covered a twenty-yard area of ground on either side of the trail and a hundred yards along it. Only after both sides were exhausted did the Comanche retreat, taking their wounded and dead with them. We were too tired and injured to pursue.

"Let 'em go, boys," Jack announced. "We've all had enough."

Every man in the company had at least one wound. Five of our men were dead. Five more were too seriously wounded to sit on their horse unaided. Jack kept brushing blood away from his left eye from a severe laceration on his forehead. He had trouble lifting his left arm from a severe gash in his left bicep, his sleeve bright red with blood. His right sleeve and shirtfront were also covered with blood, but from the warriors he had wounded.

Flaco slapped his friend on the back. "You have new name now, my friend. I name you Red Wing."

While the Comanche retreated to where their horses were hidden at the north end of the pass, we exited the south end after a cursory bandaging of wounds to stay the bleeding. The severely wounded rode double, a relatively uninjured man behind each wounded one holding his compadre upright. The dead were draped and then lashed securely over their own saddles.

Arriving in San Antonio, Jack first made certain his wounded men were well cared for. Next, he arranged for the burial of his dead. He finally stumbled to his cabin and cot, exhausted. The next morning, he wrote his report of the incident and sent a separate note describing the battle to Sam Houston. In both reports, he emphasized the important help provided by Flaco and his warriors.

After his reelection as president of the Republic that fall, a reaction to the all-out war policies of President Lamar, Sam Houston remembered Jack's note and appointed Flaco as a captain of scouts, authorizing him to recruit his own company from his tribe. This was the type of Indian policy that most appealed to the adopted Cherokee, Houston.

That August, while Jack was out chasing Comanche, the citizens of Bexar County elected him county surveyor.

Flaco and his men frequently accompanied us on patrol. Whenever an enemy was sighted, Jack charged, Flaco always the first to follow. After one of these reactions, Flaco was heard to murmur, "Me and my brother Red Wing not afraid to go to hell together. Red Wing, he too mucho bravo. He not afraid to go to hell all by self."

That September in 1841, Jack acquired the weapon that would forever change the tide of battle in Texas and beyond.

CHAPTER 9

JACK AND I stood on the porch of S. M. Swenson's home. We were frequent visitors to the home because Mrs. Swenson was determined to introduce us to every single woman she could find. Jack for certain, me because she felt sorry for me, I believe.

Jack knocked, and Swenson welcomed us in.

"Good evening, boys. Come in. You're both looking quite dapper this evening."

"Thank you, sir. These are the only good clothes we own. Mrs. Swenson is such an outstanding cook that we're not likely to miss an invitation for dinner."

Swenson smiled and patted his significant belly. "You can see I don't miss many of her meals. You are safe, though Mrs. Swenson has neglected to round up any females to introduce to you tonight. You both realize, don't you, that she's determined to get you married?"

"Yes, sir, but I'm not ready for a permanent relationship. I hope none of the ladies expected more from me," Jack replied.

"I'm happy to be included and happy to find a wife," I chimed in.

Swenson chuckled. "My wife tells me, Jack, that you are very adept at letting the ladies down gently, and they have no ill feelings about you."

"Happy to hear that."

Swenson came to Texas with significant financial resources, settled in San Antonio, and invested in land and cattle. Dinner conversation was polite, wide ranging, but about nothing in particular. As we finished the chocolate cake and coffee, Mrs. Swenson announced, "Well I know Mr. Swenson has some important business he wants to talk over with you both. You two go into the parlor, and I will oversee the cleanup of the detritus of this dinner."

"Thank you, Mrs. Swenson. The meal was outstanding, as always. I cannot say how much we appreciate your hospitality. We are certainly the envy of every unattached man in San Antonio."

"You and Mr. Caperton are always welcome in this home, Mr. Hays. Do not believe you boys will escape me. I will find that special lady for you both."

"I'm certain you will," smiled Jack.

The three of us retired to the parlor.

"Try one of these cigars, boys, and let me pour you some of this brandy. I just brought it back from New York. I think you will find both very smooth. I've also got something else I managed to acquire while back east. Did I mention at dinner that I invested some money with a gun maker named Colt?"

"No, sir. I would remember if you did," Jack said. "Is that the same Colt who invented the Colt Paterson?"

"The same. He gave me some samples."

"You are shitting me! Where are they?"

Swenson got up from his chair and strolled over to a sideboard. He opened one of the cabinet doors and took out four identical, well-crafted wood boxes, setting them on top of the cabinet.

Jack jumped to his feet and rushed over as Swenson opened one of the boxes. In it resided a Colt Paterson, five-cylinder, .36-caliber revolving pistol.

"There are four of them, and they are yours," said Swenson.

Jack's smile consumed his face.

"I've been dreaming about these pistols ever since I first heard tell of them. Do you know that in '39 the Republic of Texas purchased a hundred and eighty revolving shotguns, an equal number of revolving rifles, and the same number of these pistols?"

"Yes, I know, but they gave them all to the navy for reasons I will never understand."

"Well, for certain, the navy doesn't know shit about taking care of or using the weapons to good effect," said Jack, picking up the pistol and hefting it. "Beautiful ... must weigh about three pounds."

"Two pounds, eight ounces," answered Swenson. "All four of them are the revised Patersons with the loading levers. They don't have to be partially disassembled to reload like the original design.

"Did Colt show you how to load 'em, how to clean and repair 'em?"

"Of course."

"Show us."

"My pleasure. First you draw back the hammer to only half cock. The trigger only comes down at full cock. At half cock you can pull down the loading lever. That frees the cylinder for removal or rotation. Next you push the barrel wedge, here, from right to left until it stops against this retaining screw."

"Let me see." I pushed forward. "Okay, this screw?"

"Yes. Then you have to pull the barrel and the cylinder off the central arbor. If you have another cylinder ready and loaded, you can just switch them. With the hinged loading lever and this capping window—here—you can reload without taking it apart. Do you want to try it?"

"Of course, thanks," we said in unison.

We each went through the cylinder removal and replacement process twice and then handed the pistols back.

"Each pistol comes with this combination tool that includes the combination seating stem/lever, a nipple pick, a nipple wrench, and a screwdriver." He pointed out each of the parts of the combination tool. "You also have this bullet mold, a muzzle cleaning rod, and this combination powder flask and cap holder."

"Anything special about loading it?"

"Not really. You can fill all five chambers of the cylinder at once from the powder flask. That's why it has the five nozzles. You have to leave enough room above the powder to seat the lead ball. You don't need wadding because the balls from this mold are slightly larger than the chambers. When you seat them below the chamber mouth with this tool, enough of the lead is scraped off to wedge the ball in place. Then you replace the cylinder, and with the hammer still at half cock, you can rotate the cylinder and place the percussion caps in the back of each chamber using this special tool."

"It won't take a lot of practice to learn how to load it," observed Jack. "What about repairs, spare parts?"

"You don't think I would present you with these without spare parts, do you?" laughed Swenson. He pulled out another, much larger wood box from the cabinet. "I've got extra cylinders, hammers, arbors with the breach, action covers, wedges, and bolt frames. I've also got separate parts for the bolt frame, bolts, triggers, sears, trigger springs, bolt springs, male springs, hand springs, and a supply of breach screws."

Jack picked the pistol up again. "Can't wait to take one apart and learn to put it back together."

"Well, let's go through it together." Swenson removed a large scrap of blanket from the same cabinet and spread it over the small table in the middle of the parlor floor. "Let's pull these chairs up to the table."

We huddled over the pistols, taking each apart and then reassembling until we were completely satisfied.

"So, S. M., the word is that the navy's afraid of these weapons, especially the rifles. I've heard that all five chambers can sometimes discharge at once," commented Jack.

"That is the knock on them."

"Any way to prevent that from happening?"

"Not that I know of."

"I think me and the boys need to do some experimenting. Maybe trying less powder, maybe a bit of bear grease to help hold the ball in place and to lubricate when it is discharged."

"Worth trying, Jack. I suspect having five shots without having to reload will be worth the risk."

"Absolutely. These are amazing. S. M., I can't thank you enough. I'm going to take two of these for myself. I'll give one to John and the other to Bigfoot Wallace. I hope you will help me do everything possible to acquire at least one of these for every man in my company."

"For certain. How about another sip of brandy?"

"Gracias Senor. Tu eres muy amable!"

The next day, Jack instructed Bigfoot on how to clean, load, and care for his pistol. The three of us spent several hours practicing with them, both on foot and from horseback. Once we all felt proficient at exchanging the cylinders while on foot, we practiced while on our horses, standing, then at a walk, and finally while trotting and loping. We did not ignore taking the time to practice firing the pistols. We soon determined that the pistols were just as accurate, if not more so, than our single-shot muzzle-loading pistols, even though the barrels were shorter.

A few weeks later, Jack and I were surveying a tract of land on a tributary of the Pedernales. Our camp was on the bank of Crabapple Creek, near the base of a local landmark known as Enchanted Rock. On the third morning, Jack sat cleaning his guns. When he finished, he stood, pushed his two Colts into his belt, sheathed his knife, and picked up his rifle.

"I reckon the climb to the top of that rock won't be easy, but I'll wager there is an unbelievable view of the whole country from the top. Any of you boys want to join me?"

There were ten men in the party, including Jack. Five of us were Rangers, including his friend Ben McCulloch, who had just been commissioned as a lieutenant. The four other men comprised the survey crew, but all were familiar with the use of firearms. I shook my head and looked at the others. Not even Ben seemed disposed to a tough climb up the steep rock.

"Hell, Jack, you go have some fun, if that's what you call it. Reckon me and the boys 'll get a little surveyin' done," answered Ben.

Jack rode his mare all around the base of the large rock that topped the hill and then tethered her. The north side of the rock was too steep to attempt to climb with his leather-soled boots. The other sides were less steep, and there were washes extending from the top of the rock down to its base. Jack made his way up the least steep of the washes to the summit where he discovered a relatively flat area, roughly thirty-five feet in diameter. In the center of the flat area was a crater about seven feet deep with smooth sides sloping to the bottom. He sat on the lip of the crater for some time, contemplating the view and wondering why Flaco told him the place was enchanted. He finally shook his head and started down the way he came up.

He paused a moment when he spotted movement below. He squatted down and soon was able to identify a dozen Indians, spread out below him. They were sneaking up the slope, obviously intent on intercepting him. He knew, even if they didn't know who he was, one man off by himself was too easy a prey not to come after.

Jack scrambled back up the wash and slid down into the shallow crater.

On the north side of the crater was a small cave protected by a boulder in the opening and under an overhanging rock. He squeezed in and then took stock of his weapons. He was appalled to discover he lost his powder flask in the scramble back. It wasn't long before the head of one warrior, then another, popped above the rim of the crater and quickly disappeared. They were Comanche, and now they knew who it was they had trapped.

One of the warriors waved Jack's powder flask above the rim.

"How you be able reload, Devil Yack?" he hollered. "You no have more powder than this, verdad?"

"Come out White Devil. We kill you quick. No torture," screamed another of the warriors.

"You afraid now, Devil Yack? Not so brave?" a third hollered.

All of the taunts were in Spanish. One by one the warriors all started calling him the most insulting names they could think of, hoping he would lose his temper and leave the protection of the cave.

Jack waited, patiently. He put one of his revolvers in his lap and held his rifle ready.

The warriors tried feinting a rush, but Jack waited.

Three of the Comanche circled around and climbed onto the overhanging rock. One at a time they peeked over the edge of the rock, only a few feet away. Jack laid down his rifle and took up the Colt. The next time a head appeared a ball hit the warrior in the forehead. He toppled over the edge of the rock and hit the ground dead at Jack's feet. The other two jumped off the rock, thinking Jack only had his loaded rifle left. He shot both of them with the revolver, killing both.

The other warriors huddled. They could not understand how three of their companions could be killed so quickly with one weapon. One of the youngest warriors decided to take the chance of exposing himself, hoping to gain fame with a quick arrow shot. Jack used his rifle to end the youngster's dreams.

About thirty minutes passed from the time of the first warrior's death. The remaining Comanche decided to all attack at once and kill this man, no matter the cost. They all jumped over the rim of the crater at the same time, sliding down the slope. Jack killed one with a shot to his heart and wounded two more as they scrambled to their feet. He came out of the cave and stood with a revolver in each hand, determined to kill as many as he could.

As soon as we heard the first shot, we all jumped on our horses and started moving carefully toward the rock formation, cautiously making our way to its base. There we found the Comanche ponies tethered. We could hear the warriors talking among themselves near the top of the rock. As silently as we could manage, we made our way up. The sound of Jack's revolvers heralded the final attack. We rushed upward, yelling as loud as we could. The remaining Comanche, not knowing how many Texans were coming to Jack's aid, scattered in several directions.

Thus, was born another Jack Hays legend. His single-handed confrontation at the top of Enchanted Rock.

I managed to get an article in both the *Telegraph* and *Texas Register* newspapers later that year:

"The spy company under Captain Hays has been very efficient and has almost completely broken up the old haunts of the Comanche in the vicinity of Bexar. So great has been the protection and security resulting from the active enterprise of this excellent officer that the settlements are extending on every side around the city, and the country is assuming the appearance of peace and prosperity that characterized it previous to the Revolution."

The encroachment of settlers on Comanche territory continued to grow unabated. The settlers felt more secure with each successful exploit of the ranging companies. The Comanche were even more determined to halt the invasion.

As Jack's reputation and success grew, he became increasingly popular among the upper crust of San Antonio society. He and I and some of the most presentable of his men were frequently the guests of honor at dinners and/or dances sponsored by Mr. and Mrs. W. I. Riddle, Mr. and Mrs. Samuel Mavericks, Mr. and Mrs. Swenson, and Mayor and Mrs. Juan Seguin. Mr. and Mrs. Yturri were occasional hosts, but even more importantly, Mrs. Yturri could be counted upon to open her home as a makeshift hospital. She and her servants nursed wounded members of Jack's company back to health on several occasions.

San Antonio was the town nearest Mexico with a significant Anglo American population. In late winter 1842, the enlistments of Jack's company expired, and he was forced to disband it. The Republic lacked the financial resources to keep his men employed. Jack, however, maintained a loyal cadre of men by using fees from his surveying to pay us. It was fortunate that he did. Santa Anna managed to regain power in Mexico.

He was desperate to reverse the defeat he had suffered at the hands of the Texans at San Jacinto.

The majority of the inhabitants of San Antonio were of Mexican origin. Many of them were Tejanos, loyal to Texas, but a significant number were still loyal to Mexico. We learned that a number of San Antonio loyalists left the city to join a Mexican Army gathering just south of the Rio Grande.

Ben McCulloch assumed command of a company of rangers from Gonzales. Another former lieutenant, A. S. Miller, led another company from the same area. Jack was commissioned as an acting major, but he was rarely paid by the government. He was, ostensibly, in charge of protecting the majority of the southwest frontier. He dispatched McCulloch and Miller, along with their men, to keep watch for an invading force from Mexico. He also sent three of his own men, all faithful Tejanos, as spies to sneak across the border and learn what they could.

On March 4, Jack sent a courier to the capital. He reported that he had not yet heard from his spies, but it was certain that a Mexican Army had crossed the Rio Grande and was on its way to San Antonio. Just before dawn the next day, there was a loud pounding on the door of Jack's cabin. He opened it and invited his three spies inside.

"You boys want some coffee?" he asked in Spanish to calm their obvious agitation.

"No, Jefe," said one of them. "We rode hard to tell you General Vasquez is camped only six miles south. He has at least a thousand men with him."

"All right, Alfredo. Here's what I want you and Jose to do. Choose ten of our men to go with you to the Mexican camp. Sneak in as close as possible and make as an exact count as possible of the number of men and the artillery they have. I also need to know the size of their cannon, how many cavalry horses, and what kinds of weapons the infantry carry. Jesus, I need you to ride to the committee of vigilance at Gonzales. Tell them to raise every man they can and get their butts here as soon as possible. We'll do our best to hold out until they arrive."

After dispatching the men, Jack went to inform Mayor Seguin and the town council of the situation. They immediately asked him to assume command for the defense of the city, and he accepted. He ordered the mobilization of the militia and sent men throughout the town and the country close by, looking for recruits. By that evening, he had 107 men under his command.

As the spy patrol sent to the Mexican camp was returning to San

Antonio, they spotted a single rider carrying a white flag on the road leading into town. They intercepted, blindfolded him, and then brought him to Jack.

Jack addressed him in Spanish. "Señor, I need to send a message about your task to the alcalde and town council to hear what you have to say. I cannot make any decisions without their advice. Would you like a beer while we wait?"

Juan Seguin and all but one of the town council arrived at Jack's cabin.

Jack introduced all of the men to the Mexican, and Colonel Corrasco addressed the town council members.

"I am authorized by Gen. Rafael Vasquez to tell you that if you do not oppose us, he will assume peaceful possession of San Antonio. You will suffer no casualties. I must tell you that the general brings artillery with him, and we expect two thousand reinforcements to our current forces of fifteen hundred men."

"All right, Colonel. I will have my men escort you safely back to your camp," said Jack. "We will seriously consider the offer and our situation and will give General Vasquez our answer by two o'clock this afternoon."

Jack and Juan Seguin mustered all of the volunteers and rangers. The mayor thanked them for being willing to fight for the town.

Jack explained the situation and choices. "We can stay and fight and hope our reinforcements arrive from Gonzales, but it is unlikely there will be more than a hundred or so of 'em. Even with the reinforcements, we will be greatly outnumbered. The Alamo offers less in the way of protection than it did in the fight for independence, and the city has grown without any thought or planning for defense. If we stay and fight, the city will be bombarded with their artillery. We will undoubtedly lose a lot of buildings, and some innocent civilians are likely to be wounded or killed in the fighting. The other choice is to abandon the city and organize a fight when the odds are better. I want you to discuss the choices among yourselves. In half an hour we'll have a vote. The majority will rule."

The men huddled in small groups, argued, and reformed into other groups. Exactly a half hour later, Jack's voice rang out, and the men reformed their ranks.

"All those who want to stay and fight, take a step forward."

Twenty-five of the youngest, most resolute, and foolhardy all of them from Jack's company, stepped forward. Jack smiled.

"Right, step back. All those who want to leave the city until we can muster an army to oppose the Mexicans, step forward."

The remainder of the men all stepped forward.

"All right, the decision is made. I will spread the word that all the civilians who want to leave with us need to gather what they can and meet in the Central Plaza in an hour. We have one artillery piece, so I'll need a team of mules to pull it. John, please see to requisitioning the mule team. I'll send word to General Vasquez that we are leaving the town in his care and accept his word that he will not destroy it. We'll head for Seguin."

Late that same afternoon, Vasquez entered San Antonio with 500 regulars, 250 rancheros, and 30 Caddo Indian volunteers. The remainder of his army stayed in their camp with their supplies and artillery.

Two nights later, we, along with the civilian refugees, made camp on the banks of the Cibolo River. Hays sent a messenger to Austin with dispatches describing the situation.

Our trek the next day brought us opposite Sequin on the Guadalupe River. Our progress was considerably slowed by the arrival of settlers from all along the Guadalupe Valley. They were fleeing east, seeking protection from the Mexican invasion. Late that same evening, captains McCulloch and Miller and their Ranger companies rode into our camp.

The three leaders huddled around the campfire in front of Jack's tent.

"We sent a group of Tejanos into San Antonio last night. When they found us this morning, they reported that Vasquez only stayed two nights in San Antonio. We sent back ten men to follow and find out what he's up to," reported Ben McCulloch.

"Any damage? Did he sack the town?" asked Jack.

"Apparently not," answered Miller. "Some houses were broken into and food and some small items were taken, but everything seems to be intact. No fires were set when they left."

"Well, that's some good news to spread among the refugees. Let's get that word out. Once we get some intelligence on what Vasquez seems to have in mind, maybe we can get these folks back home. Let's send out small groups of scouts to cover all the roads he can use to haul his cannon leading south, west, and north. We need to know for certain where he is and, if possible, what his plans are. Hard to believe he's content to just demonstrate what they are capable of doing."

The next morning, after listening to the reports of the returning scouts, Jack took two dozen of us and pushed hard to reach San Antonio.

We found the town pretty much untouched. Jack stationed us to guard the town, patrolling to prevent looting and waited for the return of the refugees. When they arrived, they reclaimed their houses, businesses, and goods. However, for the next month, very little business was conducted. The Mexican threat was too real. The future of the town was too fragile. Some of the Anglo citizens packed up and moved east. Five days after retaking possession of San Antonio, Jack's scouts returned to report that General Vasquez had crossed back over the Rio Grande, and his troops were disbanding, at least for the time being.

There was no respite, however, for Jack and his Rangers. The Comanche bands, who still totaled about twenty thousand souls, despite a recent outbreak of smallpox, continued to conduct raids on isolated settlements and ranches. The Nocona band of Penateka Comanche, led by the war chief known to the Texans as Buffalo Hump, was a particular problem. He was the same Buffalo Hump who led the Comanche raid that reached the Gulf Coast and the subsequent battle at Plum Creek. He and Jack had faced each other on other occasions as well.

During that same summer, Jack made a trip to the capital, met with President Houston, and was authorized by the Texas Congress to recruit more Rangers. He received a permanent promotion as major of the militia with command of his own company. He also commanded a second company led by Capt. Tony Manchaca. He was authorized to recruit a total of 150 Rangers to patrol the region between San Antonio and the Rio Grande Valley. Unfortunately, the Republic was unable to find the funds to supply, pay, and equip more than eighty men of the force authorized. Jack again dipped into his own funds to recruit, supply, and support the minimum number of men he felt he needed to defend the frontier. His financial resources, however, were limited, and he managed to muster only a total of a hundred men.

Santa Anna was back in total control of Mexico. He was reelected president and was even more determined to regain control of Texas. Late in August, he sent Gen. Adrian Woll, a forty-seven-year-old French-born officer of the Mexican Army of the North, across the Rio Grande to retake San Antonio.

Bigfoot burst through the open doorway into Jack's cabin. "Jack, there are six Mexican spies wandering around San Antonio asking questions about us."

"The hell you say. Take some men and round those birds up. We'll hold them in the jailhouse and find out what the hell they're doing here."

Two hours later, all six Mexican spies were locked up. Jack, Bigfoot, and I took them, one at a time, out in back of the jail. Jack's message to each was the same: "You are here in San Antonio as a spy for Mexico. I have the authority to execute spies."

He pulled his revolver and pointed it at the spy being questioned. "You tell me who is commanding the Army of the North, how many are in that army, where they are now, and how much artillery they have with them. If you don't tell me what I want to know, I will gut shoot you here and now and leave your body to rot here in the sun." He cocked the revolver.

All six spies told everything they knew. Their stories, for the most part, coincided. Jack sent messengers to Sam Houston and to all the nearby towns and settlements. He mobilized all of his militia, telling them to assemble in San Antonio. He took command and prepared to defend the city.

General Woll was a worthy adversary. He circled his army around and through the rough terrain north of San Antonio, evading discovery by our scouts. While Jack and I were out scouting, accompanied by ten Rangers, Woll invaded San Antonio, took many of the volunteer militia prisoners, and occupied the city. When informed of the situation, Jack gathered all of his available troops at Seguin. Sam Houston reacted to the news of San Antonio's capture by putting Old Paint Caldwell, then a colonel, in command of all volunteers. Old Paint and Major Hays merged their forces in Seguin.

Early Sunday morning, September 18, Jack and Old Paint huddled with the officers of their army, which numbered more than two hundred.

"Jack, do you think you and your Rangers can manage to get the Mesicans to send out their cavalry from San Antonio and try to chase you down?" asked the colonel.

"Yes, sir. We can get that done."

"Good, the rest of us will set up along Salado Creek. Your job is to bring 'em to us."

Using the tactics he and Old Paint learned from fighting the Comanche, we taunted the Mexicans until General Woll lost patience. He ordered three units of light cavalry, accompanied by light artillery, to chase us down. Jack instructed us to allow the Mexican cavalry to get close enough to open fire before racing out of range and then to slow down and bring them along again. He was betting, correctly, that the Mexicans were not good enough with their smooth-bore muskets or their rifles while galloping to do much damage. We were able, even when the cavalry commander ordered his men to dismount and take more careful aim, to stay far enough away to keep anyone from being wounded. We continued to remain close enough to tempt the Mexicans and keep them chasing us. We eventually led the Mexicans to where Old Paint had his men dug in, his ambush prepared. Although significantly outnumbered, Old Paint held a strong defensive position. The two forces traded small arms fire and light artillery fire until early afternoon.

Jack huddled again with Caldwell. By then, he successfully obtained revolvers for nine more of his veteran Rangers. All of us were expert at shooting accurately and reloading quickly, both on foot and on horseback.

"Let me and my boys lead a charge, Colonel. These Mexican soldiers are not accustomed to aggressive tactics. You can see how they're content to sit back and just try to pick us off. Plus, they've never had to fight against our revolvers. They will not be prepared for the firepower we can rain on them."

"Maybe you're right, Jack … All right, you get your men ready. I'll organize two waves to follow your lead. Let's give 'em hell. When you're ready, let me know, and we'll be right on your heels."

With Jack in the lead as usual, we charged through the Mexican lines firing. Once through the lines, we turned around, loaded another cylinder, and charged back. By that time, Old Paint had arrived with his men and engaged. The Mexicans wilted under the fierce attack, unable to comprehend how so few men could bring so much firepower. One of our men was killed, and eight were wounded. I took a ball in my left shoulder, but no bones were broken and the ball went all the way through. Jack was unscathed. The Mexicans lost sixty men killed, and many more were wounded. Woll's men retreated to San Antonio.

While we were fighting at Salado Creek, Capt. Nicholas Dawson, along with fifty-four men from La Grange, attempted to join forces with Colonel Caldwell, but they were detected by Woll's scouts. Woll dispatched several hundred mounted men to intercept and capture Dawson's company. Thirty-six Texans were killed, their bodies mutilated. Three of Dawson's men managed to escape, but the other fifteen were taken prisoner and eventually taken to the horrors of the Perote Prison deep in Mexico.

The following morning, the small scout party I was leading found the mutilated bodies of Dawson's men. The scene still comes to me in nightmares—bodies decapitated, genitals cut off, multiple stab wounds, and all left to rot in grotesque positions.

We responded by harassing General Woll's supply lines, picking off his soldiers one by one from long distance. Because he was unable to supply his army, Woll started a retreat from San Antonio. We were charged with keeping the Mexican supply lines disrupted and Woll's army under constant surveillance. Old Paint took advantage of the time to reorganize and resupply his troops. He moved his army up the Medina River on September 21 to rejoin us. Late that night, one of Jack's scouts rode in to camp and found him.

"General Woll has broken camp and is on the move south," Jack reported to Old Paint. "I think we should get across the river and on his tail. We need to harass and hurry 'em on their way."

"I'll get across as quick as I can in the dark, but many of my men lack experience, and getting the cannon across is going to be a pain in the ass," responded Caldwell. "You get your company across and do what you can. I'll join you as fast as I can manage it."

We crossed quickly and rode hard to catch Woll's rear guard the following afternoon. General Woll was an able commander with good intelligence. He knew of Jack and his reputation. He posted a five-hundred-silver-peso bounty for Jack's head and set up an ambush, hiding in a creek bottom. As we approached, they opened fire. One of their musket balls shrieked past Jack's head, knocking Sam Luckey off his horse. Jack immediately spurred his mount forward, the rest of us close behind.

We flushed some of the Mexicans from their hiding places, but Woll had prepared a fallback position. His men retreated in good order to the prepared line of defense. Jack ordered us to dismount and take up positions to prepare for a counterattack. Two rangers lashed Luckey to a travois and took him back to the Medina where they reported to Old Paint, telling him of the fix Jack was in. We were facing overwhelming numbers of enemy and urgently needed reinforcements. Old Paint immediately dispatched a hundred mounted men to join us at our position just north of Hondo Creek. We were still only about fifty miles from San Antonio with both forces on the north side of the Hondo. Woll repositioned his forces to cover crossing the creek. He installed a single cannon, with twenty artillerymen to man it, on a hill on the north side of the creek. The cannon was ordered to protect his army as they crossed.

Jack grabbed the arm of Ben McCulloch. "You up for taking that cannon and turning it on the Mexicans?"

"Let's do it," answered McCulloch.

Both men mounted and raised their revolvers over their heads. "Come on, boys," they shouted. "Let's take that cannon."

We Rangers were joined by many volunteers who quickly mounted, following us as we charged up the hill. The nervous Mexican gunners did not take the slope of the hill into account. Both their first and second loads of grapeshot sailed over our heads. The Colt Patersons created havoc, and soon the cannon was in the hands of the Texans. Three of Caldwell's men were wounded; one of our men took a ball through his right cheekbone. We soon turned the cannon around, loaded it, and started firing at the Mexicans across the Hondo. Within minutes, Woll organized all his remaining artillery. Soon the top of the hill was being pounded. Woll then ordered a counterattack by hundreds of his infantry. Jack ordered the captured cannon to be spiked then we rejoined Colonel Caldwell, who by then had arrived and set up strong defenses. At dusk, the sound of sporadic rifle shots slowed and then stopped. The Texans tended to their wounded, while Woll continued his retreat back to Mexico, taking the prisoners he captured from Dawson's company.

Sam Houston was unable to sit still. He limped back and forth in his office, stomping his good leg, muttering to himself. "I can't believe I didn't execute that son of a bitch Santa Anna. The bastard thinks he can get Texas back. Now Woll is taking Texan prisoners with him back to Mexico. That is not acceptable."

He sent for Brig. Gen. Alexander Somerville.

"General, I have come to regret the day I failed to execute Santa Anna when I had him. In any case, it's too late now. I want you to recruit an army. I advise you to make good use of Maj. Jack Hays and his scouts. He is successful fighting both Comanche and the Mexicans. Please listen to his advice. It is extremely rare for his instincts to be wrong. I want to do everything possible to rescue those prisoners taken by Woll. We need to teach the Mexicans they cannot invade our lands without serious repercussions."

It took Somerville until mid-November to gather about twelve hundred recruits to his camp on the Medina River. He wasted several days awaiting delivery of one particular piece of artillery and then refused to take it after it arrived for reasons he never bothered to explain. Instead of following Jack's advice to take the Laredo road to Mexico, he decided to demonstrate his independence and set out across open country. His army moved slowly, struggling through mud and cold weather. We were acting as scouts, always ahead of the ponderous army. We fumed.

In early December, Jack led us into Laredo. Somerville sent six companies to attack the local garrison, but the Mexican soldiers and many citizens of Laredo crossed the Rio Grande to safety.

Jack moved us out of town to set up a camp where there was good forage. We also needed to rest our horses. Somerville allowed his troops to ransack Laredo for two days. After that, he finally crossed the Rio Grande and marched to Guerrero, about fifty miles south of Laredo. He failed to find a Mexican Army to fight. We were all disgusted when he ordered his army back to Gonzales to be disbanded.

Five of his company commanders, including Jack, wanted to continue without Somerville. They elected Col. William S. Fisher to command and reorganize their forces. Jack's company led Fisher's army to Mier, where we discovered the town devoid of troops.

"Colonel, I don't believe this expedition is going to accomplish much," observed Jack. "My men and our horses are exhausted, and I just received word that the Comanche are taking advantage of our absence. They are raiding settlements in my area of responsibility. I need to get my men back and protect the folks I'm responsible for."

"All right, Major. I understand. You do what you believe you must, but I'll be happy for any of your Rangers who want to stay with us to do so."

"I'll put it to 'em," said Jack. "I've heard from some of my spies that the Mexicans know where we are. General Woll is gathering a large force to oppose you. You'll likely be greatly outnumbered."

"I've heard the same, Major. We'll be ready for them."

Nine of our Rangers, including Bigfoot Wallace, decided to stay with Fisher. Jack and the rest of us made it back in San Antonio in time to greet the new year.

Colonel Fisher and his men engaged the Mexicans on December 25 and 26. They were heavily outnumbered. They did manage to inflict severe casualties on the Mexicans but were eventually forced to surrender.

Bigfoot was among the prisoners who were force marched to Mexico City in early 1843.

The captured Texans were imprisoned at Hacienda del Salado but were able to overpower their guards and flee to the nearby mountains. Unfortunately, 176 of them, including Bigfoot, were recaptured. Santa Anna, true to his nature, decided to make an example. He had the Americans force-marched to a stronger prison at Saltillo and then ordered that every tenth man be executed. As he had done previously, he ordered a wide-mouth jug filled with 159 white beans and 17 black beans. The commander announced that those men who drew a black bean would be shot.

Bigfoot, ever observant, noticed that the black beans were slightly larger than the white beans. When his turn came, he sifted the beans through his fingers until he found a small one. Three of the seventeen prisoners murdered were Rangers.

Following the executions, the remaining prisoners were again force-marched deeper into Mexico to the notorious village of Perote, where an old castle had been converted into what became an infamous prison. Bigfoot organized another escape. Seven of the strongest men agreed to join him, and he guided them back to Texas. During the following eight months, twenty prisoners died of disease and maltreatment in the Perote prison. More than a hundred managed to survive the horrible conditions until they were finally rescued during the Mexican American War.

During the long ride back to San Antonio, we came upon a scene that haunted Jack for a long time. Flaco was out rounding up stray horses with the help of two half Comanche Tejanos and an old, deaf, mute Lipan. They encamped for the night along the San Antonio River, only a few miles from town. During the night, the two half breeds murdered Flaco and the old man as they slept. They absconded with the horses, intending to sell them in Mexico. Two days later, we found the bodies, both with their heads bashed in.

Jack stood over his friend's body, tears running down his face. He bent over, impatiently picking out the maggots squirming in the deep wound in Flaco's head.

"Ben, please take four men with you and follow those tracks. It looks to me there are two riders herding about twenty head of horses. They are headed south, most likely for the border. If you catch up to them, leave them where you shoot them. Just return with the horses."

McCulloch leaned over in his saddle and grabbed Jack's shoulder. "I'll do my best, Jack. I know Flaco was a good friend to you."

When we rode into town, Flaco's enshrouded body was draped over one of the pack mules. Jack gave his friend over to his Lipan Apache family to take care of according to their customs. They invited him to attend the ceremonies where he added his silent tears to their wailing.

CHAPTER 10

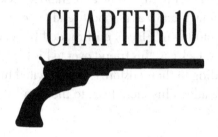

DURING THE CHRISTMAS holiday season, many families traveled to San Antonio to visit relations, renew old friendships, and mingle with the citizens. Among the visitors was the family of Judge Jeremiah H. Calvert who recently moved to Seguin from Florence, Alabama. They were in San Antonio as guests of their old friends, the Swensons. The judge and his wife were accompanied by their three daughters and two sons. Mrs. Swenson, still the matchmaker, invited Jack to dinner during the Calvert's stay.

Mrs. Swenson opened the door to Jack's knock. "Good evening, Jack. Come in. I want to introduce you to Judge Calvert and his family."

"I don't suppose the good judge has daughters of marriageable age by any chance?" asked Jack, raising his eyebrows, stroking his chin, and leering.

"Behave yourself, Jack."

She ushered him into the living room and introduced him to the judge. Jack spent the rest of the evening sneaking surreptitious glances at the oldest daughter, Susan. She was several inches shorter than Jack, slender, beautiful, and vivacious. Her luxurious dark hair fell free, almost reaching the small of her back. Her brown eyes penetrated, as though looking into his soul. She charmed Jack with the graciousness and vitality seemingly bred into Southern women of the time. Jack was hooked but not landed. Susan was only fourteen years old.

Following the Calvert family's return to Seguin, Jack rarely missed the opportunity to make the thirty-mile journey.

"Good afternoon, Judge," said Jack after being shown into the judge's office.

"Hello, Jack. What brings you to my office today?"

"I need your advice about how best to approach the government. They continue to promise but fail to send the financial support I need to keep my ranging company active."

The judge nodded, rubbed his chin, and cleared his throat. "I think one way is to get everyone you know, and everyone who the politicians know, to write letters in your behalf. I am well aware of the esteem and respect you command throughout the western frontier. You need to make certain the politicians are also aware and also understand the importance of the work you and your Rangers do.

"While you were waiting for me to finish the opinion I was writing, I sent word to Mrs. Calvert that you are in town. She replied by telling me to make certain I ask you to join the family for dinner."

"That's very kind of you, sir. I will do as you suggest and am more than pleased for the opportunity to eat another of Mrs. Calvert's meals."

Susan, in collusion with her mother, made certain she was always seated next to Jack at the dinner table. "So, Major Hays, what new adventures have you had since your last visit?" asked Susan.

"Just the usual boring stuff, Miss Calvert. Despite the stories you may have heard about me and my men, those tall tales seem to have a life of their own and minimal basis in fact. Most of the time we are just wandering the countryside. We keep on the lookout for intruders but rarely encounter them. We spend long days in the saddle, no matter the weather, and then make camp where we can find good forage for our animals. We spend considerable time hunting for meat to eat. The hardtack, cornmeal flour, and other provisions the government supplies are pretty meager fare. We certainly do not enjoy anything to compare to this meal provided by your mother. Thank you once again for the invitation, Mrs. Calvert."

He smiled as he bowed his head to Mrs. Calvert and continued. "This is a most excellent roast, Mrs. Calvert. The seasoning is outstanding. I hope you are passing your culinary skills to your daughters."

"My duty is to teach my daughters to be gracious hostesses and good wives."

"If any of this brood come to match their mother, they will make fine wives," laughed the judge.

Susan nudged Jack under the table with her left knee. Surprised, he slowly turned his head toward her and smiled, while lifting another forkful of meat to his mouth. He chewed and swallowed.

"Still tryin' to decide what your mother did to flavor this roast," he murmured to the girl. "Do you know?"

"Are you testing me, Major Hays? Trying to gauge my cooking skills?" She giggled.

Jack blushed. "No, Miss Calvert. I'm sorry if I made you think so. I was just tryin' to make dinner conversation."

I managed to worm all this information from the besotted Jack when he returned to San Antonio.

Susan nudged him again with her knee. "It's rosemary, wild garlic, salt, and black pepper. We coat the roast with some butter and then rub the finely minced herbs into it. Then we sprinkle liberally with salt and pepper and rub it some more. We brown the roast in more butter over high heat, add vegetables, some red wine, and cover and simmer it over a low fire until the meat and vegetables are tender. Don't worry, Major. I can cook."

Both the judge and Mrs. Calvert smiled at the exchange. The two younger sisters giggled, while the two brothers, completely bemused, looked at each other, clueless.

"So, you're on the way to the capital to meet with President Houston. If it is not a secret, what will you be discussing?" asked the judge.

"Yes, sir, I have an appointment with him. We're not done with the troubles with Santa Anna. Some of his agents are fomenting trouble with various Indian tribes. That will be the major topic, as well as a discussion about what the Republic needs to do to help my Rangers protect our citizens. It's always about finances. The Republic seems to be constantly in a dire situation, financially."

"Well, politicians always seem to be able to find the funds for the project they want or they think is important to those who put them in office. I wish you good fortune. I will be happy to send a letter to the governor, my representative, and my senator, and you should ask others of your friends to do the same, as we discussed this afternoon. I'm certain Juan Seguin will be happy to speak up," answered the judge.

Three days later, Jack was shown into Sam Houston's office. The president struggled to his feet and took Jack's right hand in both of his.

"Still having problems with your leg, Mr. President?" Jack asked. "I'm sorry."

"It's the price I pay for being a war hero," said Houston, grimacing at his own poor joke.

"I'm afraid they've got me overscheduled, as usual. Not enough hours in the day and too many folks with too many demands. I can see from your expression you don't have good news for me, Jack. Spit it out."

"We're having some problems with some Mexican residents of San Antonio who are still loyal to Mexico and Santa Anna, but we have a pretty good idea of who they are. Our strategy is to confuse them with bad information. On the other hand, I have, thanks to Juan Seguin, several spies in Mexico whom I trust. I hate to tell you this—I know of your feelings and attachment to the Cherokee Nation—but the United States has been treating that tribe, as they do most others, poorly and unhonorably. We routinely break our promises and continue to take their lands, as you well know. Mexico has been sending agents to the Cherokee tribes now in Arkansas. At least four bands sent representatives to visit General Woll at San Fernando. My information is that those four bands of Cherokee have offered their help for another invasion of Texas. It appears that Manuel Flores, the Indian agent in Arkansas, has been very active in this recruiting process."

"That is troubling news, Jack. You are certain your information is accurate?"

"Yes, sir. My sources have always proven to be reliable. I believe them, and I think the threat to our western frontier is real, maybe even imminent. I know, for certain, Woll has been courting various Comanche bands as well."

"I presume you come to me with a plan, Jack."

"The ranging companies have been quite effective, Mr. President, as you know. The problem is we don't have enough men, and those we do have frequently don't receive supplies, not to mention the pay they are owed. My own company is down to fifteen men. I managed to keep them with me by providing their keep and their wages from my own resources, which, I'm sad to say, are now exhausted. I was forced to release all of them before I left San Antonio for this trip. We need to keep Rangers constantly on patrol if we are to protect ourselves from a successful Mexican invasion."

Jack took a long breath, waiting for some statement from Houston. When the president remained silent, he continued, "We need more regular companies of Rangers with captains who can not only recruit good men but keep them trained and active. The captains must also be able to quickly assimilate volunteer militia when they are activated in the face of an emergency. The militia need to be trained in our methods, so they are ready when needed."

"Mr. Gaston," Houston shouted.

His aide appeared in the doorway to the office. "Yes, sir?"

"Cancel all my appointments for the remainder of the day. I need to compose a special message for Congress, with Major Hays's assistance."

"Yes, sir."

Houston started writing. He paused to read what he had written to Jack, who made a few comments and suggestions. Houston made revisions and continued. After two hours of work, both men were satisfied that the Texas politicians would have a clear concept of what legislation was needed.

"Mr. Gaston," Houston shouted again for his aide.

"Yes, sir, Mr. President?"

"Make two copies of this for my signature, and then see to it that they are delivered directly into the hands of the Speaker of the House and the vice president. This same afternoon, please."

"Yes, sir."

"Now, Jack, I am going to counter your bad news with some good news. I have many reports of your success with those Colt Paterson revolvers you got your hands on. How would you like to supply all your Rangers with them?"

"That would be a dream come true, Mr. President. It would make each of my men the equal of ten enemy in any battle."

"Based on your results, Jack, your Rangers already seem to have that advantage. Anyhow, as an economic necessity, I have made an agreement with the United States to provide protection for our maritime interests. That has enabled me to disband the Texas Navy. I have given our secretary of war the necessary instructions. You need only to go to his office. He will provide you with the necessary documentation to procure the Colts and all the necessary accessories, spare parts, and ammunition."

"That is the best order I've received for a very long time, Mr. President. I don't know how to thank you."

"The thanks I want is for you to keep our southwestern frontier safe, Jack. I'm hoping the revolvers will make that terrible task easier."

"I'm certain they will, sir."

"On your way then, Jack. I'll make certain you are kept informed on how our legislation fares. Godspeed and good hunting, my young friend."

Jack collected the necessary documents from the secretary of war and then traveled to Galveston with me and several old friends, all former Rangers, and two pack mules. We collected the Colt Paterson revolving pistols, extra cylinders, and all the necessary tools and supplies. Jack also requisitioned several revolving-cylinder rifles but decided against the revolving-cylinder shotguns. Those had been proven to be reliably unsafe, exploding at inopportune times.

Upon his return to San Antonio, Jack was immediately confronted by a delegation of citizens, the town council, and Mayor Seguin.

"I have to inform you, Jack," said Seguin, "on the very day you left, the town filled with Mexican thieves and outlaws. They staged a meeting of Mexican loyalists in the main plaza and terrorized both Tejano and Anglo citizens. Just before your return today, they all disappeared."

Jack's response was to put out the word for all of his disbanded Rangers to report for duty. He gave each man two of the Colt revolving-cylinder pistols and began their training in the use and care of these weapons during a twenty-day patrol north and west of San Antonio. We failed to encounter any Indians or Mexican outlaws, but the men became proficient with the revolvers.

On the return to San Antonio, we stopped at Sisters Creek to rest our horses. One of the men spotted a beehive high in a tree bordering the creek. Two of the younger Rangers, Kit Acklin and John Coleman, climbed the tree with their tomahawks, intent upon cutting down the hive and requisitioning the honey. They positioned themselves and began chopping at the limb holding the hive. Coleman happened to look back over the trail we had just come down and gasped.

"Jesus, Kit, lookee there." He pointed. "There's a least two dozen Comanche just sittin' on their ponies watchin' us. Let's get the hell down from here."

"Captain," shouted Kit as he scrambled down. "Comanche up on the hill we come down."

Before the two were back on the ground, Hays and the rest of us retightened the cinches of our saddles, as well as the cinches of the horses Kit and John were riding. We all checked our weapons, mounted, and then waited while Acklin and Coleman ran to their horses, grabbed their reins from the mounted men holding them, and swung into their saddles.

"Ready?" Jack looked around to make certain all his men were mounted. "Follow me."

He urged his horse back up the hill, with us close behind. We were about two hundred yards away when Jack sensed something was very wrong. The warriors sat, nonchalantly, with their legs crossed in front of them, on the backs of their ponies.

"Charge," hollered Jack and spurred his horse forward. When he was only sixty yards away, the warriors had still not moved. Jack leaned back, hauling in the reins of his horse. The animal planted its hind legs under and extended his forelegs, sliding to stop. Behind the waiting warriors, just coming over the top of the hill, were two long lines of mounted Comanche. Hays pointed at a thicket of trees and shrubs off to his left and jerked his horse in that direction.

"Take cover," he shouted.

As we raced for the thicket, the first group of warriors charged after us, shrieking. The other two lines of warriors charged down the hill, fanning out to flank us. As we approached the thicket, a shower of arrows was released from hidden warriors. This time, Jack was at the rear, covering our retreat. He spurred through us with a revolver in each hand, holding his reins in his teeth. Two warriors rose, arrows notched, and Jack fired both pistols. Both warriors grunted and fell. We followed Jack into the thicket, firing at every warrior we could see. The Comanche, not accustomed to fighting on foot, ran for their horses tethered on the opposite side of the thicket.

"Hold up and dismount," shouted Jack. "Kit, John, and Sam, each of you hold five horses. The rest of you take cover but hold your fire until I give the word."

A few minutes later, all three groups of warriors came together and massed to charge the thicket.

"Now," shouted Jack, and well-aimed lead balls knocked warriors from their mounts.

The Comanche, responding to the shouted orders of their war chiefs, divided and rode around the thicket, riding hard in two large circles moving in opposite directions. The war chiefs took their men out of rifle range and planned their next attack.

Before long, the warriors reformed into long lines and slowly advanced until our rifles began to pick them off. There was no confusion this time. The warriors put their horses into a gallop, their lances at the ready. They fully expected their charge to carry them into us before we could reload. They rushed the thicket from every direction. We all stood, holding a revolver in each hand. After firing, we thumbed the hammers back, and the triggers reset, ready to fire another round. With each discharge, a warrior fell from his horse. Those warriors not wounded reached down from their horses, swooped up the wounded, and sheltered them with their shields as they retreated to safety. A few brave, foolhardy souls, were killed after they decided to gain honor, charging at us. The remainder of the warriors retreated to the top of the same hill where the ambush had been set and gathered for another council.

Jack, while reloading his cylinders, took careful note of the gestures of the braves and their war chiefs. He decided they were whipped.

"You men all reload and mount up. After we're all loaded and mounted, we're going to take this fight to 'em. He looked at each of his men as they regained their saddles and nodded their readiness.

"Everybody ready? Let's go directly at 'em."

As we charged up the hill, the Comanche let loose a barrage of arrows. Three of our men were hit. One of their companions rode up next to each of the wounded men and held them in their saddles. Jack and I and our eight remaining men broke through the line of warriors. We turned our horses around and charged back. Each time, our revolvers took a deadly toll. Warriors fell from their animals, dead or wounded. Wounded horses screamed in pain, bucked off their riders, and ran for safety. The Comanche, however, were determined and continued to fight.

Jack shouted at the three of the Rangers holding their mates to keep them from falling. "Take those wounded men back to the thicket. The rest of us will cover you."

All of us unwounded men spread out, retreating slowly and protecting our comrades. As we got close to the thicket, a warrior charged at Sam Walker, trying to skewer him with his lance. Sam swiveled in his saddle and shot the warrior dead, but in doing so, he turned enough for another warrior to drive his lance into his back. John Carlin saw the warrior just as he thrust his lance into Sam and shot the Comanche in the head. I spurred my horse up to Sam, jerked the lance out of his back, and helped him off his horse. Then I dragged him into the minimal protection of the thicket. As another one of our men, Ad Gillespie, approached the thicket, he was hit by an arrow and fell from his horse. One Comanche war chief galloped forward to finish Ad off with his lance. As he raised up to strike, Ad twisted on the ground and sent a revolver ball through the chief's brain. Two of our men ran out of the thicket and pulled Ad into the relative safety of the trees and shrubs. As they did so, several warriors galloped up to attack the three on the ground. Jack and two men charged and drove those warriors back, but they were soon joined by many more Comanche who were focused on retrieving the body of their war chief. More of us joined Jack and continued fighting, but we were soon in danger of being surrounded, cut off from the thicket, and overwhelmed.

"Leave that Injun's body. We'll let 'em have it," Jack shouted. "Take cover in the trees and pick off as many as you can when they come to take the chief away. You men who are protected get your rifles reloaded and help keep 'em away from that body."

Jack dismounted, shoved his pistols back into his belt, and grabbed his revolving-cylinder rifle and his two-barreled shotgun from their saddle scabbards. There were three shots left in his rifle. He knelt to take careful aim as a large group of mounted warriors shielded three warriors who dismounted, lifted their chief's body in front of another, still-mounted warrior, and jumped back on their ponies. Jack and two others fired their rifles. Three more warriors fell wounded while shielding their comrades who had successfully rescued the war chief's body.

The Comanche finally had their fill. They rode away singing death songs and lamenting their wounded.

Jack took a few minutes to check on his wounded men. Three of them were occupied pulling arrows out of themselves and their mates.

"If you boys are right with it, I'm of a mind to chase those Injun's and deal 'em more hurt. I think the fight's out of 'em now.

Walker raised up on one elbow. "Go for it, Jack. Give 'em hell. We'll be all right here."

"All right. You boys game? Reload your weapons and mount up. We'll see how many more we can send to their ancestors."

Jack was joined by all of us who were not wounded. We soon caught up with some wounded Comanche struggling to keep up with the main body. As soon as we were within range, we opened fire, unhorsing several more. The Comanche, lacking the leadership of their war chief, were disheartened. It was clear their hearts were no longer in the fight. They still did their best to carry off their wounded and dead while scattering in all directions. Those warriors brave enough to turn to face us were ineffective. Many of them were wounded by the revolvers. Each of us was able to fire ten rounds and then switch to loaded cylinders to have ten more before having to reload.

The life of a Ranger was hard. Most who enlisted failed to reenlisted. Fifty percent of the Rangers were killed by Indians, Mexican bandits, horse thieves, or Mexican soldiers or, more commonly, succumbed to illness. They lived, except for brief respites, outdoors, camping in the unforgiving heat and humidity of summer or the biting cold wind and sleet of winter. Those Rangers who persevered built a legendary esprit de corps and heroic reputations.

I am called Buffalo Hump by the Texans. I am a war chief of the Penateka. In the year 1800 by the counting of the Anglos, there were an estimated eight thousand Penateka. In 1816, a smallpox epidemic took at least half of our population. In 1839, there was another outbreak of smallpox that further decimated my people, including four of the most successful war chiefs. The Council House Massacre removed a dozen more war chiefs. I managed to escape all of those disasters and became even more powerful and respected. Instead of the normal dozen or two dozen warriors willing to follow me, there are a hundred, sometimes more. I am a shrewd judge of character, I think, and speak fluent Spanish and passable English.

My name is transliterated by the Texans as Po-cha-na-quar-hip. In Comanche, my name means "erection that won't go down." The Anglos will not, or cannot, accept that as a name, no matter that it is a perfectly respectable one for the Comanche. Texans claim Po-cha-na-quar-hip means "buffalo bull's back."

In 1840, when our band was significantly weakened, the Republic of Texas demanded that the Penateka remove themselves from Central Texas, release all our white captives, and stay away from all white settlements. Thirty-three Penateka warriors and leaders arrived at the Council House in San Antonio to negotiate and sign a treaty with the Texans. They brought several captives with them, but one of the returned captives told the Texans that the chiefs had not brought all of their captives. When accused of holding back, we explained that the captives in question were the property of other bands. There was nothing we could do to force the other bands to return them. The Texans didn't believe our explanation. The nonreturn of captives proved to be the excuse the Texans were hoping for. The Council House was surrounded, and almost all the Comanche within were slaughtered. I was one of the few warriors who managed fight my way out and escape.

My response to the Anglo's duplicity was to recruit warriors for the raid that reached as far as the Texas Gulf Coast and ended with the battle at Plum Creek. I got away with only minor wounds from Plum Creek and continued to organize and lead successful raiding parties. Devil Yack Hays and I are enemies. We do our best to kill each other whenever we come in contact.

Toward the end of May 1844, Jack answered a pounding on his door. An obviously distraught recent settler was admitted to his cabin.

"Major Hays, two settlements west of my place have been attacked by Injuns. I fear we are soon to be visited by these savages. They killed and mutilated five men and three women, who I helped bury. What they did to those men and women was inexcusable, too horrific for me to describe. They made off with one young woman and at least seven children."

"Which tribe was it?" asked Jack.

"All the savages are the same. What the hell difference does it make? We need to rid the earth of all of them. You must get rid of these animals and make the frontier safe for honest, hardworking people. We just want the opportunity to make a life for ourselves and our families."

"All right, I'll do what I can to protect your settlement, and the others, but you must understand that you have gone beyond the boundaries that the Republic of Texas agreed to with the tribes. You and the other settlers have usurped lands the Indians consider to be theirs. Our government has affirmed their right to those lands. You have invaded their territory. Despite that, I am sworn to protect you. I will round up all the men I have who are not out patrolling. We'll determine which band of warriors did this and do our best to track them down and rescue the captives. However, it will be wise for you and your folks to abandon your holdings. You should move everyone here to San Antonio until we can find those responsible and provide a level of safety for you to return."

A few days later, we found the tracks of the war party responsible for the attacks. June 8 found us stopped for lunch on Walker's Creek, about four miles east of the Pinta Trace, a well-traveled trail first described in the journals of Marques de Rubi in 1767. That was when his expedition traveled through the Texas hill country.

A gentle but cold spring rain was falling, making the soggy ground even more waterlogged. Water dripped from the huge anaqua tree under which we took temporary shelter. We started two small fires to boil water for coffee, while we chewed on hardtack and beef jerky. Most of the men were sitting on their saddles after staking out their horses to graze.

Jack was uneasy as he strolled around checking on his men. Sam Walker and Robert Gillespie were hunched over one of the fires waiting for the coffee to boil. Jack squatted down across the fire from them.

"Boys, I've got a bad feeling we're being followed. These Comanche aren't doing much to cover their tracks or hightailing it for home the way they normally do. Don't make a fuss, but I would greatly appreciate it, Sam, if you would wander off to the right and you, Bob, off to the left. Circle around to the Trace and backtrack. We need to find out if these Comanche are just playing a game or are on our tail planning some sort of evil."

The two nodded their understanding. Jack got to his feet and walked over to the other fire while checking the load in one of his revolvers. Sam left the fire and disappeared into the brush. After a short wait, Bob Gillespie did the same, going in the opposite direction. Jack made the rounds, telling us of his apprehension and instructing us to check our weapons and bring our horses and the pack mules in closer to the fires.

Thirty minutes later, Sam and Bob slipped quietly back into the clearing.

"You were right, Jack. There's a group of ten Comanche on our trail. They stopped when they spotted us. I reckon they're scouts for a larger party," said Bob. Sam nodded his head in agreement.

"All right, boys," Jack said quietly, "there's Comanche following us. Check your loads once more, saddle your horses, and mount up. We're going to find out what these Injuns have in mind. Sam and Bob only counted ten of 'em, but we suspect there's a passel more of 'em hid out. Ready? Let's go."

Jack led us back along the Pinta Trace at a walk. After a quarter of a mile, we came upon ten Comanche braves aligned across the trail. Both braves and their ponies were covered in war paint. The warriors pretended surprise and ran their ponies into a grove of timber and brush off to the side of the trail.

"Hold up, boys. Let's just sit here a spell. My guess is there's a lot more of 'em in that stand waiting for us, hoping we'll follow 'em in."

We held our ground. Our horses, and especially our mules, became more and more nervous as the minutes stretched out. The Comanche, seeing we were not going to fall into their trap, slowly materialized out of the thicket and formed a battle line. We waited. Eventually, no more warriors joined the line that stretched across the entire meadow through which the trail cut.

"I reckon that's all of 'em," said Jack. "I count seventy-three."

"That's the same as I count," answered Bob Gillespie.

"Well, those are good odds for us, I reckon. You boys all with me?"

We answered with a guttural, "Yup."

Jack touched the flanks of his horse with his spurs, and we advanced at a slow trot toward the line of silent warriors.

The Comanche lined up with a dry-bottomed ravine behind them. The ravine circled in both directions around a large hill, its base covered with a thick stand of trees and brush. As we advanced, the Comanche silently turned, urged their ponies across the ravine, and made their way through the heavy woods and up the steep face of the hill to its flat summit. On top of the grassy high ground, they took up defensive positions and began to taunt us in Spanish and with rude gestures.

"Slow to a walk but keep advancing, boys. Don't shout back at them."

Our silent, measured, advance frustrated the war chief. He rode back and forth in front of his warriors, shouting at us. With each pass, he rode farther down the hill, closer to our still slowly advancing line. He turned his pony back up the hill, stood in his stirrups, and wagged his rear end at us.

"This is where I will put my lance in you Captain Yack," the war chief shouted. "I am Yellow Wolf, and I will have your scalp before the sun sets."

"Let's go teach them a lesson, Jack," said Sam Walker.

"That's exactly what they want, boys. They want us to charge up that hill so they can pick us off. I know this place. The top of that hill is a meadow that stretches out flat for quite some distance. Just be quiet and follow me. We're going to use the ravine to circle round back of 'em."

Jack guided his horse down into the ravine. We were shielded from sight by the thick forest at the base of the hill. We followed him, single file, around the base of the hill, and in the ravine up until we reached the far side of the meadow that communicated directly with the top of the hill where the Comanche were waiting. The Comanche were still staring down the steep slope at the trees from which they expected us to burst at any moment.

We emerged about two hundred yards behind the warriors who were still expecting us to charge out of the woods and up the steep slope.

"Pick a target, fire your rifles, and then follow me," whispered Jack.

We fired, and sixteen Comanche warriors pitched forward with lead balls in their backs. As we charged, the Comanche turned their ponies around to face us. We charged through the line in our V-shaped phalanx. Those of us with revolving rifles fired into the warriors. Those with single-shot rifles used them as clubs.

The well-trained warriors wheeled their ponies to form a half circle and then charged, trying to drive us down the steep slope of the hill. We held our ground. Then the Comanche formed a complete circle and rode around us, firing rifles, muskets, and arrows from under the necks of their galloping ponies while hanging from the off side. On Jack's command, we dismounted, held our reins in our teeth, and took turns firing. We reloaded our rifles while the warriors were still out of pistol range. Indian ponies stumbled and fell, hit by rifle balls, their riders thrown to the ground. Many of the warriors were hit as they scrambled to get away from their downed ponies. Some were wise enough to use the dead animals as shields. There was a lull as the Comanche retreated out of range. Small groups scurried back in attempts to rescue their wounded and retrieve their dead. Many of those warriors paid with their own lives once they were within range of our sharpshooters.

The Comanche gathered, out of range, around Yellow Wolf who exhorted them. They mounted again and charged, abandoning rifles and muskets for their more familiar bows and arrows, lances, and bulletproof shields. Obeying Jack's shouted order, we remounted to meet the charge with our five-shot revolvers. Almost every Ranger, including Jack, suffered arrow and lance wounds, but our revolvers took a massive toll. Twenty-one warriors were killed in that charge; many more were wounded. Again, the warriors retreated. We bound up our wounds, reloaded our revolvers and rifles, dismounted to tighten our cinches, and mounted again.

"They are going to charge again and then quickly retreat. As soon as they turn to get out of range, we give chase. Make every shot count," instructed Jack.

The plan worked. When our revolvers were, empty Jack led us to the highest ground. He watched as Yellow Wolf wove his way among his remaining warriors. I counted just over thirty, including the war chief. Jack glanced over his shoulders and saw that although all of us were still able to sit our horses, four of our men, including Bob Gillespie, had lost so much blood they were having trouble staying erect.

"Anybody have a loaded rifle?" Jack asked.

"I'm still loaded," replied Bigfoot.

"Then slide off that horse and shoot that damned war chief!"

Yellow Wolf sat astride his war pony about two hundred yards in front of us, his shield held in front of his chest for protection. He was shouting at his warriors, about to kick his pony forward. Bigfoot knelt on one knee, took careful aim, and shot him through the head. The back of his head exploded, and he tumbled back over the rump of his horse. Two of his warriors rushed to scoop him off the ground, and the entire war party scattered in three different directions.

Jack held up his hand.

"Hold on, boys. We're damn near out of ammunition, and our horses are spent. I reckon we did some good work here today."

Jack brought us back to San Antonio. During the night of our first camp on the way home, Peter Fohr died from his wounds. After we arrived in San Antonio, Jack made certain our wounded were well cared for and arranged a funeral for Peter. When all his men were taken care of, he returned to his cabin and fell, fully clothed, onto his cot. He was asleep before he could kick off his boots.

The next morning, we were awakened by insistent pounding on the door. Jack shuffled over and opened it to find two of his Tejano spies standing in the doorway, twisting the brims of their sombreros in their hands.

"Major Yack," whispered the oldest, "General Woll has recruited an army and is shortly going to receive regular army reinforcements from the capital."

"How many men does he have?"

"With those coming from Mexico City, perhaps six hundred, maybe more."

"Artillery?"

"Si."

"All right, thank you both. Please return to your families. I will do my best to find a reward for your service."

"All we ask is that you continue to protect our families, Major," responded the younger man. "Adios."

Jack had only forty Rangers fit for duty. Some were out scouting. Most were in camp outside San Antonio. Forty against six hundred trained soldiers, even if only half of them were professionals, were not acceptable odds. He put Ben McCulloch in charge of the Rangers he had on hand with instructions to patrol and keep track of the Mexicans all along the several hundred miles of frontier west of the San Antonio River.

On June 20, General Woll issued a manifesto. In it, he declared that all communications with Texas were ended, and he had recommended to the government in Mexico that war be declared.

Jack hurried to the capital of the Republic to meet with President Houston and report that San Antonio was again threatened by General Woll.

"Sir, I believe your efforts to convince the government of the United States to annex Texas precipitated Woll's decision to take back Texas before having to fight against the entire United States. To be able to protect San Antonio and Corpus Christi from Woll's army, I will need to recruit more Rangers."

Jack returned to San Antonio with a promise of more funding. He divided the men currently available into two platoons. He sent one platoon out to scout for hostile Indians, bandits, or the Mexican invasion force, while the other platoon rested. He often rode out with one platoon and then immediately turned around to lead the other.

A reporter by the name of J. W. Wilbarger accompanied Jack on one of his patrols late that fall and wrote: "I have frequently seen him sitting by the campfire at night in some exposed locality when the rain was falling in torrents or with a cold norther sleet or snow whistling about his ears, apparently as unconscious of all discomfort as if he had been seated in some cozy room of a first-class hotel; and this, perhaps, when he had eaten for supper a handful of pecans or a piece of hardtack."

James Polk was elected president of the United States, and Mexico's envoys in Washington were well aware of the designs of Senator Benson and other of Polk's adherents relative to the concept of Manifest Destiny. The practical goal of that movement required the usurpation of all Mexican territory blocking the politicians' desire to control lands from the Atlantic to the Pacific coasts. The Mexican government decided this was not the time to precipitate the annexation of Texas and a war with the United States. General Woll was instructed to stand down, and Mexico renewed its armistice with Texas. Jack's patrols along the Rio Grande and the reports from his Tejano spies indicated Mexico intended to keep its word.

The Republic of Texas, as always, was in deep debt with little prospect for relief. The Texas Congress again failed to appropriate sufficient funds for Jack to maintain his Ranger companies. Once again, he used his own resources, then obtained credit, but was finally forced to furlough all of us.

Within weeks after his troops were furloughed, bandits and Indian thieves started taking advantage of the Rangers' absence. Horses were stolen from the environs of San Antonio, the Guadalupe settlements, and ranches and farms bordering Seguin. Again, the Texas frontier was lawless. Spokesmen from the various settlements descended with letters and personal visits to the politicians. After redirecting some resources, the Texas government appropriated some funds to rebuild the ranging companies. Several delegations arrived in San Antonio to plead with Jack to reassume his command and reinstate order. At the same time, the government was unable to halt the steady invasion of Comanche territory by ever-increasing numbers of settlers.

The former secretary of state and new president of the Republic of Texas, Anson Jones, recognized the difficulties Hays faced trying to provide protection for the huge frontier. At Jones's urging, the Texas Congress approved a joint resolution to repay the personal funds Jack had expended for the repair of firearms and the shoeing of his company's horses. He was sent $405. The Congress also allocated funds for the recruitment of Rangers. They further ordered that Major Hays was authorized to reorganize Ranger companies in Bexar and two adjacent counties and to assume over-all command of all three companies.

Anson Jones proved to be a strong supporter of the Texas Militia and the ranging companies, but he was motivated by his greater design, which was to keep an independent Republic of Texas. Jack understood this, but his political thinking was more closely aligned with that of Sam Houston, who continued to do everything possible to make Texas a new state of the United States.

I, Buffalo Hump, will tell of what happened. I took advantage of the confusion within the Anglo government. I led fifty warriors as far as Corpus Christi. Devil Yack led a company of his men and intercepted us before we could do more than steal a few horses. I rode toward Devil Yack alone, carrying a white piece of cloth on the end of my lance, my shield was on my back, I wore no war paint.

"My old enemy, now my friend." I addressed Yack in Spanish. "We are not here to kill your people, but we know the Mexicans are your enemies, and they are once again preparing to invade you. We want to fight against the Mexicans with you. We will be your allies, but we need to trade for ammunition with your frontier settlements so we will be able to fight alongside you."

"Buffalo Hump, my worthy enemy. I'm very pleased you and your warriors want peace with us, but I know that your strength is less than half of what it once was. If you go to war with us or with Mexico, you will lose even more warriors. Who then will be left to hunt the buffalo and feed your people?"

"You speak truth, Devil Yack, but your people continue to press into our hunting grounds, and your government does nothing to stop them. You protect those invading our lands. You also protect bands of Indians who are our natural enemies. They come to our lands and kill our buffalo. We must now live by raiding the Mexicans. We are forced away from our normal ways."

"I understand," replied Jack, "and I have had many talks with our leaders about forming a lasting peace with the Comanche. I understand it is necessary to keep the settlers off your lands, but this is difficult to accomplish. They pay no attention to the treaties we sign, and our government is incapable of keeping them away without using force, and even then, it is unlikely to be effective. There are too many land-hungry people who cannot understand the needs of the buffalo or the needs of the buffalo hunters for survival. You know that Sam Houston is a friend of the Comanche and wants a permanent peace with your people. I work with him to achieve this."

"Yes, we know about Houston, who is Cherokee. He says he loves all Comanche, but he also loves our enemies and is no longer your chief."

"That is true, but he still has much influence and is doing his best to make us part of the United States. If you are at war with Mexico, or with us, especially once we are a state, the Comanche will no longer exist. There are too many of us. No matter how many you kill, more will come, and they will bring more and better weapons. You cannot fight us with bows and arrows, lances, bulletproof shields, broken muskets, and captured rifles against cannon. You must know this. Please, go back to your lands and stay at peace."

I nodded my understanding.

"This night we will camp together and make peace between us, between you and me, two warriors who know well the price of war."

The two parties made camp that evening, and some of us made friends of warriors we would have killed on sight that same morning. I sat on the periphery as Jack and Buffalo Hump quietly talked together until dawn. They talked about their families, hopes, desires, and joys. Jack promised that once a lasting peace was secured, he would join the war chief on a buffalo hunt.

The remainder of that year Jack spent considerable time and effort lobbying for the annexation of Texas. His scouts reported that all of the Mexican troops withdrew across the Rio Grande. There now seemed to be tacit recognition of the Rio Grande as the border, not the Nueces, as the Mexicans had previously insisted.

On several occasions, Buffalo Hump, with and without other influential war chiefs, came to San Antonio, arriving with only a handful of warriors and traveling under a white flag. They engaged in conversations with Jack and other leaders on the details of a binding peace treaty. Jack forwarded the substance of these talks to the secretary of state.

That same fall, Jack and I, along with Bigfoot Wallace, Bob Gillespie, Ben McCulloch, and Sam Walker rode to a place near the source of the Pedernales River to meet up with Buffalo Hump and his band for a buffalo hunt. Buffalo Hump sent out scouts to find a buffalo herd. Shortly after the two parties came together, the scouts returned to report the sighting of a herd.

Jack and Buffalo Hump rode side by side on Indian ponies. Buffalo Hump insisted that Jack and all his friends ride the tribe's best hunting ponies. He explained that these animals were trained much differently than their war ponies.

"The pony must be very well trained to hunt buffalo," explained

Buffalo Hump. "If you use a lance, you must drive it between ribs and into the heart with the first thrust. As soon as the buffalo feels the lance, it will turn and try to gore you or your pony. The pony knows to get out of the way fast. It is just as dangerous to use a bow and arrow or a rifle. Once is wounded, the buffalo will do its best to fight. If you or your pony go down, all the buffalo will trample you. They are different than wild horses who will try to avoid you. The buffalo will do their best to kill you. The pony must understand all this and be quick to get away after you shoot."

"What about our pistols?" asked Jack.

"Not powerful enough. The pistol will only make the buffalo very angry. The rifle ball must go between ribs to the heart. A pistol ball will just bounce off a rib. A rifle ball is more likely break through a rib and maybe reach the heart."

Several Comanche hunters rode fast in a big arc to get in front of the buffalo herd and turn it. Once turned, the rest of the Indians rode around a portion of the herd in a diminishing circle until the smaller number started milling. Once this happened, some warriors continued circling, holding the animals, while others dashed into the melee with their lances, bows, and arrows.

"We only kill animals less than three summers, cows or bulls," explained Buffalo Hump. "Follow me."

Jack and the rest of us joined the melee, each of us managed to kill a buffalo with one, well-placed rifle shot. Soon, Buffalo Hump hollered for the circling buffalo to be released.

"This is all we can use," he explained to Jack. "Now we butcher, then the women will come to finish."

Each warrior was responsible for the initial butchering of the animals he killed. Five hunters who failed to bring down an animal, all young teenagers who were charged with riding around the herd to keep it milling, took charge of the animals killed by us. They cut carefully along the spine and then pealed the hide back on both sides. The meat and sinew along the inside of the spine were carefully removed.

"This is the best meat for roasting," Buffalo Hump explained.

"Yes, we know that. We call it the tenderloin," answered Jack.

One of the young warriors looked up at Bigfoot, who was watching closely as he removed the rumen and the rest of the gastrointestinal tract from the animal Bigfoot had brought down.

"If make kill in winter and have frozen hands or feet, put in here." He made a slice into the rumen and demonstrated by pushing his hand inside. "Can also use this as water bag, very good."

It wasn't long until women and children rode up and took charge of the butchering. The hunters wandered off to build cooking fires where they roasted the most prized cuts. These included the tongue, hump, hump ribs, tenderloin, and side ribs. Many were eating the raw liver, using the animal's bile as a sauce. In good humor, they offered this delicacy to us. All but Jack declined. He took a small bite and managed to chew, swallow, and hold it down.

"Guess it's an acquired taste," he announced.

The women finished skinning the animals and then spread the hides, hair-side down, on the ground. Next, they cut the meat from the bone in three- to four-foot strips and piled the strips on the spread-out hide of the dead animal. When the hide was full, they tied it into a bundle. Some of the bundles were loaded on to a travois, and others were just pushed up onto the backs of patient ponies or mules.

"They will hang the meat on racks close to a smoky fire back at our camp," explained Buffalo Hump. "When the meat is dried, they will pack it in a rawhide bag, very tight, then sew the bag closed. It will keep for a long time, if it doesn't get too hot."

Before the hunters stamped out their fires and left to join the rest of the tribe at the main camp, Sam Wallace estimated each man consumed, and held down, at least six pounds of meat. We did our best but were unable to keep up.

Back at the camp, nothing was wasted. We stood watching as marrow bones were cracked and thrown on the fires. When judged done, they were removed and the marrow extracted and used as a sauce for the meat. Hooves and horns were boiled to make glue. Small bones were split, fire hardened, and whittled into needles or awls. Hollow horns were used to carry fire drills, flint, and gunpowder. Sinew from along the spine, fascia under the shoulder blades, and along the hump and abdomen was made into bow strings and thread for sewing and then used in the construction of the best bows. Long tufts of hair were used for thread and to braid into ropes and lariats. Buffalo Hump told us that the bone from the hump was often used to straighten and shave arrows. Scabbards were made from tail skin. Tail bones were used as handles for knives and clubs. Tracheas were dried and used as containers for paints, clay, and makeup. Yellow gall bladder paste was used as war paint. The skin of udders was dried then used for dishes and bowls.

"Pottery is too fragile and heavy. Our lives are spent constantly moving to find food for our horses and to hunt the buffalo," explained Buffalo Hump.

A particular use was made of the unborn fetuses found in three of the cows killed during the hunt. They were boiled in the birth sac.

"This meat is very tender," explained one of the warriors to me. "Tender meat is used to feed babies and old people with no teeth."

I was forced to hide my disgust.

Before we left the location of the kill, Jack noticed that the hearts of all the downed buffalo were replaced inside the rib cage after the pericardial sac was removed. "Why are they leaving the hearts like that?" he asked.

"The heart sac is used to keep special medicine in," explained Buffalo Hump. "The heart is left to show the Creator of all things that our people are not greedy. This ensures the return of the buffalo to this place."

On the ride home, Jack wondered aloud if he could somehow make the constant invasion of new settlers learn about and appreciate the need to retain sufficient open range so the buffalo could continue to exist and provide a livelihood for the remaining Comanche.

"We'll never make farmer out of the Comanche," he told me.

CHAPTER 11

BUFFALO HUMP TOLD me what happened after the Republic of Texas signed a peace treaty with the southern Comanche tribes:

Shortly after the treaty was agreed to and signed by me and other war chiefs, I hosted the Indian Agent Benjamin Sloat in my camp. We held a wide-ranging discussion in my wickiup. It is cramped inside my shelter, and I watched, in amusement, as Sloat gritted his teeth, attempting to block out the strong odors that swirled around his head and invaded his nose.

I told Sloat, "I am going to lead a war party to the Mexican border. I learned that the Mexicans are planning another invasion to reclaim Texas. I must protect my new friends from the Mexicans."

Sloat tried but was unable to dissuade me.

"You must come with us," I told him, speaking Spanish. I think my good friend Captain Yack and his men will join us when we ride past San Antonio."

"I think not," replied Sloat in Spanish. "We are currently negotiating a peace treaty with Mexico. Major Hays will not be authorized to join you."

I switched to English. "Oh, you do not know my friend Devil Captain Yack as I do. You must go with us. You will see. When we camp near to San Antonio, he will join us."

I was able to convince more than seven hundred Comanche warriors to go with me to raid communities in Northern Mexico. We traveled for several days before making camp on both sides of the Frio River, about fifty miles south and west of San Antonio. During the previous two days, while the party rode far to the west of San Antonio, I carefully avoided Sloat. After the various bands of my war party were settled in, I allowed Sloat to find me.

"I thought you told me Major Hays would join us as we went past San Antonio." Sloat did his best to hide his annoyance.

"I am surprised as you that he has not," I answered. "I suppose, since we passed some distance west, his scouts did not report our passing."

"What do you plan to do then?" asked the Indian agent.

"I propose that you and I leave tomorrow morning and ride back to San Antonio. We will meet with Captain Yack. I will convince him to join us with his Rangers."

"All right, let's do that then."

Unbeknownst to the Indian agent, I left instructions for my warriors that as soon as I was out of sight, they should break camp and move as quickly as possible to south of the Nueces River where I would join them. The Indian agent and I arrived in San Antonio after riding hard all day. We found Devil Yack in his cabin at his table. The door to his cabin was open on the pleasant October evening.

"Greetings, my friend Yack," I said.

Jack looked up to us filling his doorway. "Buffalo Hump, Mr. Sloat, what brings you two to my door? Come in, come in."

Jack got to his feet and pushed his chair over to Sloat, indicating with a wave of his hand for the agent to take a seat. After the agent was seated, he motioned me to his cot, while he perched on the edge of the rough table he used as a desk.

"This war chief is leading some seven hundred warriors to raid communities in Mexico. He claims you and your men will join him," explained Shoat.

"I knew you would take the opportunity to strike at them," I said.

Jack smiled ruefully. "So, you managed to get past my scouts undetected with seven hundred warriors? That is very impressive, my friend."

I smiled and shrugged.

"Where are you camped?" asked Jack.

Sloat answered.

"They are spread out on either side of the Frio."

Jack turned again to me. "I suppose you told your warriors to move on as soon as you and Mr. Sloat left camp."

I remained silently stoic.

"Well, Mr. Sloat, you've been had, I'm afraid. My Comanche friend knows very well that Texas has a peace treaty with Mexico, and there is no way I can go with him on a raid. He convinced you to accompany him, knowing that with you along, if his party was discovered, I would be reluctant to attack him for fear of causing you injury. His warriors are no doubt at the Nueces as we speak. I presume he brought an extra horse with him for this ride to meet with me?"

"Yes, how would you know that?" asked Sloat.

"He's Comanche. He will leave here and ride night and day, changing mounts as they tire. It won't take him long to find his war party. I could arrest him and try to hold him here, but I'll bet money none of his warriors have stolen a single horse since they left their home camps."

"They did not raid while I was with them," answered the agent.

"Then I have no grounds to hold him here, and even if I was able to, the other war chiefs know what to do. Even worse, my jailing him will give cause, in their minds, to attack San Antonio when they return with their plunder. That plunder will, no doubt, include firearms and ammunition. You might as well rest up here before you return home, Mr. Sloat. Buffalo Hump has managed to get his war party past us and will avoid us on the way home."

He turned back to me. "You are a very shrewd warrior and leader, my friend. I hope you will restrain your warriors when you return. If any of our settlements are attacked, I will be coming after you."

"Yes, my friend Capt. Devil Yack, I understand. I will do what I can, but as you know, I have no real authority over the warriors who choose to follow me. They can do as they please whenever it suits them. All I can do is point out the consequences of making you angry with us. If we are successful in Mexico and have plenty of horses and plunder, the warriors will be happy to go home quickly to show off and share their new wealth."

Jack stood, nodded, and shook hands with both of us. I departed immediately to catch up with my war party.

Sam Houston and many other leaders, including my friend Jack Hays, lobbied the US Congress. After much argument, that body was finally able to approve the terms under which Texas could apply for annexation to the United States. Work was begun on a state constitution, while arguments and politics shifted to Washington. The Republic of Texas Congress, thinking the US government would soon take over the responsibility of defending Texas, and always searching for ways to cut expenditures, ordered Jack to disband his company of Rangers.

A few weeks later, reality set in with the officers of the Republic. Weeks, possibly months, could pass while politicians argued, but as soon as the ranging companies were disbanded, raids by Indian and Mexican bandits increased. The secretary of state asked Jack to organize and command a new battalion of Rangers. Jack recommended commissions for Ben McCulloch, Bob Gillespie, and Sam Walker as captains. They were the three he considered most qualified to command. Before doing so, he had a talk with me and Bigfoot Wallace.

"John, Bigfoot, Secretary Cooke has instructed me to form a new battalion of Rangers. I plan to recommend Ben, Bob, and Sam as captains. You two are their equals as Rangers and fighters, and I know you are both loyal to me and to Texas, but I need you close to protect my back. It's not that I think either of you are incapable of commanding your own company, just that you are more valuable to me as my lieutenants. Are you comfortable with this?"

Bigfoot responded. "Jack, you and I have been through many battles together. You've saved my ass, and I've saved yours. I am proud and anxious to serve in whatever capacity you think I will be the most use. Besides, I'm not comfortable putting men in a position to be killed or of being responsible for their welfare. For certain, I don't want to worry about the responsibility of making certain they get their rations and pay. Just tell me what you want me to do, and I'll do it."

"I agree with everything Bigfoot said," I chimed in.

"Thanks, both of you. I appreciate your attitude and loyalty. I'm going to have a lot of administrative things to do. I will need you both to break in new recruits, make certain all the men are trained and kept sharp, and make certain my orders are carried out. You will be my right and left hands."

"I prefer to be the left," I smiled.

While Jack and his new captains were recruiting the battalion, Bigfoot and I, along with those experienced Rangers who agreed to serve again, supervised the training of the new recruits.

President Anson Jones traveled to Corpus Christi to meet with Gen. Zachary Taylor who was stationed there by the US government.

We learned that he went there to learn of Taylor's ideas for the defense of the frontier. He told President Jones that he was well informed of Major Hay's successes and needed him to continue to do his job. He said he would write to the adjutant general in Washington to inform him that he needed Major Hays to continue scouting and reporting Mexican activity across the Rio Grande.

In December 1845, Jack was officially authorized to increase the strength of his battalion to sixty-five men. He established a semipermanent camp for his Rangers on the Medina River but maintained his headquarters in San Antonio, where he had recently been elected district surveyor. He couldn't afford to depend on the federal or the Texas governments for his livelihood.

When we were on the Medina, we lived in tents. We enjoyed staggered, short-term visits to San Antonio in small groups. Scouting expeditions, with only sixteen to twenty men gone at any one time, provided a better balance of rest and danger for us.

Dr. Ferdinand Roemer visited San Antonio in February 1846. He was introduced to Jack and me at a party given by the Swensons. The journal he kept about his travels was eventually published. He wrote about Jack's Rangers that discipline was replaced by absolute loyalty to their leader, who set an example for all in enduring personal privations and exertion. He was surprised to find the outward appearance of Jack so little in keeping with his mode of life and the qualities attributed to him. Instead of a fierce, martial, powerful figure, he found a young, slender-built man whose smooth, beardless face, as well as the black dress coat he wore, betrayed in no way his military occupation and inclination. Only in Jack's piercing eyes could one discover his hidden energy and the promise of leadership.

In December 1845, the Congress of the United States declared the Rio Grande to be the southern and western boundaries of Texas, but a Mexican army was being assembled at Matamoros. General Taylor was instructed to take a position on the US side of the Rio Grande in anticipation of the official announcement of the annexation. On February 19, 1846, Texas was declared, from that date forward, a state of the United States of America.

As soon as Jack learned General Taylor was preparing to move his army to the Rio Grande, Jack and I paid the general a visit at his headquarters in Corpus Christi. Jack offered to put his Rangers under the general's command to serve as scouts.

"Thank you for your willingness to serve our country, Major Hays, but I

already have dragoons who are perfectly capable of performing those tasks. I do not believe you or your men will be needed."

I was flabbergasted.

While we were still in Corpus Christi, Jack received word that six hundred Comanche and some allies had raided settlements southwest of San Antonio. Bigfoot and his platoon were following the raiders who were headed north with their loot. We left immediately for the Medina where we arrived well after dark.

"Bigfoot is still tracking them," Ben Wallace told Jack.

"All, right, Ben. I want you to pick out forty of our best men. We'll take them toward Bandera Pass and from there in the direction of Enchanted Rock. I want to leave here at dawn."

"Got it."

Bigfoot rode into Jack's camp as the Rangers were preparing to depart.

"Looks as though they're headed for that small lake at the base of Painted Rock, Jack. If we beat 'em there, we can set up an ambush."

Jack smiled. "I knew I kept you around for something, Bigfoot. Get the men mounted. If we leave here and get humping, maybe we can beat them there."

Jack kept us moving all that day and into the night. At midnight, we stopped and allowed men and horses to rest for two hours. Jack ordered that the horses be given a ration of grain, while we masticated venison jerky. We traveled the rest of the night and the next day with only short stops for water and rest.

At about one o'clock the following morning, we cautiously approached the small body of water, about a hundred yards wide and three hundred long. Painted Rock towered above the west side of the small lake, the water lapping at its base. Along the north shore of the lake, and about a hundred yards from each end, was a grove of willows and thick underbrush. Jack sent Bigfoot with his platoon to make certain the Comanche hadn't arrived ahead of them.

The thicket was clear.

Jack stationed us, hidden from sight, to await the arrival of the war party. Coming from the south, the Indians would have to cross the lake or circle to the east to get around the water to be able to continue their trip north. Jack posted pickets and ordered the rest of us to get some sleep. Just before dawn, the Comanche, spread out in small groups along the trail, unsuspectingly approached the lake, secure in the familiar country. We were in position.

"Now," shouted Jack.

In late fall, early dawn, especially around a body of water, the air is foggy, too foggy for accurate shooting. Only a few warriors were knocked from their ponies. The others wheeled and retreated out of range where they waited for their scattered companions to rush up. Once gathered, they waited until daylight. Their own scouts snuck in close enough to reconnoiter. After the scouts reported the number of Rangers, the war chiefs were delighted. Six hundred against forty was exactly the kind of odds they hoped for.

When they joined the Rangers, all our men were required to have a very good horse. Over the years, by picking carefully through captured Indian ponies and rescued horses whose owners had been killed, we had a large enough herd so each of our men was able to ride one horse and lead another when traveling, another tactic copied from the Comanche. Our men and horses were trained and conditioned to be able to travel fast and for prolonged periods. When he organized this ambush, Jack set up a picket line in the center of the grove. All the horses were tied to that line. He knew the Comanche always lusted after good horses and would try to avoid hitting them. Their hope would be to kill all of us and make off with our horses.

The Comanche formed their lines of attack northeast of where Jack positioned us.

"These warriors are mounted on their best war horses. Most have short bows and quivers full of war arrows. They also carry lances for close-in work. A few have muskets; even fewer have rifles. You all know their rawhide shields will deflect a ball unless it is hit directly at a right angle, and they are very adept at positioning the shields so that doesn't happen. I want each of you to pick a warrior directly opposite you and aim to penetrate his shield or wound him in his leg. If he is within forty or fifty yards and you are certain of your aim, try for a head shot," Jack said.

"Jack," commented Gillespie, "these Injuns are so nicely painted they're too pretty to shoot."

Jack understood that his friend was just trying to divert the apprehensions of the few inexperienced Rangers in the company. Those new recruits were, for the first time, faced with fearsome and overwhelming numbers of savage warriors.

"Yes, indeed, look at that chief riding back and forth in front of the line, haranguing them. Somebody will have to kill that one," added Jack.

The Comanche charged. We held our fire until the screaming horde was within fifty yards and then took turns firing and reloading. By that time, all the officers, and a few of the men, including myself, had revolving rifles. With them, we were able to fire five shots without having to reload unless the rifle jammed, which was not uncommon. The effect was devastating. Volley after volley was sent from the protecting trees.

Many warriors were knocked from their ponies, and the charge faltered. The war chief swung the line to the west, and many of the warriors slid off to the side of their ponies, away from the defenders. They fired arrows from under the necks of their running mounts but found very few targets among us. Those warriors on the east end of the line had to ride past all of us forted-up Rangers. Many ponies and men went down from the withering fire emanating from the thicket of willows. Warriors jumped from wounded and downed ponies, scrambling to get out of rifle range while protecting their backs with their shields.

The war chief gained the relative safety of Painted Rock, and from that location organized another charge, this time from the east. Jack adjusted our positioning, and that charge was also deflected. The war chief regathered his men at the northeast end of the lake and decided to charge directly at the thicket with lances, using their numbers and the bravery of his warriors to overwhelm us. War cries and wild thumping on their excited ponies' sides brought many of the warriors through the rifle fire into close range where they were met by concentrated fire from our revolvers. Many revolvers were discharged close to the ponies' faces, causing them to bolt and turn, exposing their riders. Lances dropped from the hands of mortally wounded warriors. The survivors retreated again behind Painted Rock.

The battle continued all day. Each time the charging warriors were turned away a little faster. When darkness finally descended, the Comanche retreated to the prairie and lit campfires. A few warriors tried to reach the lake for water, but our sharpshooters were quick to discourage them. Most of the braves elected to take turns riding to a stream about twenty-five miles away for water, but they all returned, determined to dislodge us the next day.

Jack changed his guards often during the night, encouraging those relieved to get some sleep. He and Gillespie, McCulloch, Walker, and Bigfoot stayed awake all night, circulating among the sentries to encourage them, helping to maintain a sharp lookout. They also brought water for the horses and for those on guard.

During the night, individual braves and small groups attempted to retrieve their severely wounded and dead comrades. They were usually spotted and fired upon, causing them to retreat.

At dawn, one of the war chiefs divided his remaining warriors into four cohorts and sent them attacking in waves. Jack and his officers kept us firing and reloading in shifts to maintain a steady rate of fire. At midday, four waves of attack followed each other so closely a few warriors in the fourth wave crashed into the edge of the thicket. Jack and Bob Gillespie stood, a revolver in each hand, and shot them down.

Some warriors circled around to the south side of the lake and launched an unsuccessful attack from that direction. Other warriors climbed Painted Rock from its western side and launched arrows from the top. They were too far away for the arrows to be effective, but our sharpshooters toppled several of them into the water.

"That's a tough way to get a drink of water," chuckled Bigfoot after hitting one of them in the chest from two hundred yards away and at least fifty yards above where he knelt.

At dusk, the Comanche again camped out of range and sent parties on the fifty-mile round-trip for water.

Jack and his officers were again awake all night. Our supply of ammunition was shrinking fast, and Jack encouraged us to take more careful aim to make each rifle and pistol ball count. Rifles and pistols were cleaned and reloaded. All spare cylinders were reloaded. Knife edges and hatchets were sharpened. While they worked, the men consumed water, hardtack, and venison jerky. The horses were fed a ration of grain and watered. One of the horses was wounded in the rump by a stray arrow. While the Ranger who owned the horse wrapped his arms around the animal's head and neck and bit down on its ear to distract it, Bigfoot extracted the arrow, dug out the arrowhead, and smeared a poultice on the wound.

One of the Rangers, Emory Gibbons, received a lance wound on his left forearm. Jack cleaned the wound then bound it up with a clean neckerchief.

Before dawn on the third day, another attack was launched, this time from several directions simultaneously. Again, Jack anticipated correctly and had us well positioned to deflect the attack. The retreat was followed by another attack in waves. One particular war chief seemed to be everywhere. Almost every Ranger tried to bring him down, but he was very skillful with his longer-than-normal shield. He deflected every rifle ball sent his way. When the sun was a little more than halfway between the eastern horizon and directly overhead this war chief once again formed his men out of rifle range and rode slowly back and forth in front of them. He had a lot to say.

He suddenly wheeled his horse and charged the grove, screaming. His remaining warriors all urged their ponies to catch up. War whoops filled the still air.

"This looks like a suicide charge," observed Jack. "That's the most determined we've seen 'em. That chief has made up his mind to take us down or die trying. He's lost patience."

"That's still one hell of a lot of Injuns, Jack," muttered Ben McCulloch.

Jack nodded his agreement, knelt on one knee, cocked his rifle, and sighted carefully on the chief, waiting for a shot. The chief looked back to shout encouragement to those following. When he did so, he twisted his body but neglected to move his shield far enough to protect himself. Jack squeezed the trigger. The war chief fell off the side of his pony, hit the ground hard, and remained motionless. The fast-moving warriors closest to him hauled back on their reins, sliding to a stop. They whirled around and surrounded their leader.

"Pour it onto those braves trying to get their chief out of there," shouted Jack.

We fired volley after volley into the milling warriors; three fell mortally wounded, and the others swayed in their saddles as they retreated.

"They're going to come again to rescue that chief's body," observed Jack. "Bigfoot, you think you can get a lariat around him and drag him in here?"

Bigfoot Wallace was already halfway to his horse. He jerked the halter rope loose, leaped onto the animal's back, and charged out of the thicket while loosening his lariat.

"Cover him, boys. Don't allow any of those braves to ride at him," Jack shouted.

Before the dumfounded Comanche warriors could understand what was happening, Bigfoot threw a loop around the dead chief and spurred his horse back to the safety of the woods, dragging the body. The enraged warriors charged but were again met with accurate and devastating fire from the willows. They retreated. A few made a final, half-hearted rush but three of them were unhorsed, and the rest turned. Some of the wounded and a few dead warriors were loaded onto ponies. The entire party rode away to the northwest.

"Hold up, boys. This might be a ruse to get us to follow," Jack noted. "We'll wait a bit."

After waiting until the sun was directly overhead, Jack took myself and six others to follow the tracks.

"Appears they've had enough, boys. Let's get back. We don't have near enough provisions or ammunition to chase 'em down."

The war chief's decorations and weapons were collected and eventually sent to Austin. Most of the Rangers took small souvenirs off the more than one hundred dead warriors, and several took scalps. Jack estimated at least a hundred dead were taken with the retreating band. Many more were seriously wounded.

"I reckon a number of them wounded braves won't make it," observed Bob Gillespie.

"For certain. A bunch of 'em have smashed legs and arms, along with rifle and pistol balls in their bodies," added Ben McCulloch.

CHAPTER 12

WE RETURNED TO the Medina camp, but the term of the men's enlistment was expiring. On March 19, Jack was forced to disband the company. Bob Gillespie was authorized to organize a smaller company from the men discharged by Jack, but they were only to serve for three months.

Jack and I returned to his cabin in San Antonio and he resumed his land surveying business.

Soon after Texas was admitted to the United States, the federal government initiated a series of provocations that made a war with Mexico inevitable. Gen. Zachary Taylor was ordered to take up a defensive position opposite Matamoros. Ordered or not, border crossings by small units on both sides took place all along the Rio Grande. Gen. Mariano Arista, the commander of Mexican forces stationed in Matamoros, sent General Torrejon with sixteen hundred troops across the Rio Grande on April 24, 1846. That same day, Capt. S. B. Thornton's sixty-man company of dragoons, those same dragoons who General Taylor believed could do the job that Jack offered to do, were found and engaged by Torrejon's forces. In the resulting battle, those of Thornton's men who were not killed were wounded and made captives.

Taylor reported to his superiors that hostilities with Mexico had commenced. He sent a message to the governor of Texas, J. P. Henderson, asking that he mobilize the militia and supply two regiments of infantry and two of cavalry.

Jack's cadre of friends, many of his former Rangers, politicians, ordinary citizens, and the multitude of folks he had protected over the years were singly, and in small groups, urging him to organize a regiment as soon as the war with Mexico came about. After word of the debacle with Taylor's company of dragoons reached him, he and Sam Walker rode to Austin to confer with Governor Henderson. The governor authorized Jack to recruit a regiment.

He and Sam left Austin and traveled to Washington-on-the-Brazos, to Brenham, and beyond, visiting all the towns and settlements along the way, gathering former Rangers and new recruits. Every day more men filtered into San Antonio where Bigfoot Wallace and I signed them up. Other recruits joined Jack and Sam on the road. Former Rangers were put to work training new recruits as they traveled. Other individuals and small groups of former Rangers from south Texas learned Major Hays was forming a regiment. They joined him at Seguin. The Mexicans were doing everything possible to sever Taylor's line of communications.

"Sam, I suggest you take all these men and get them to General Taylor," Jack said. "Do what you can to help him. He seems to be struggling. I'll go on to San Antonio and recruit all the men I can."

"All right, Jack. We'll see if we can discourage some Mexicans along the way, but you need to get yourself and a full regiment of men to join us as soon as possible."

The next day, Jack arrived in San Antonio where thirty-five of his former Rangers were awaiting his arrival.

I was waiting for him at his cabin. "More are on the way, Jack. Bigfoot and I have been out hunting down men who served with you. Not a single one of them has refused to join us. A few had to take care of business and arrange for the care of their families, but they'll be here in a few days. But I've got better news for you."

Jack frowned. "What better news?"

"Miss Susan Calvert is in town with her family visiting the Swensons and Riddles. I thought that fact might interest you since you seem to take every opportunity possible to visit Seguin to see her."

"Where is she now?"

"I believe at her cousins, the Riddles."

"You get the recruits settled into our old camp on the Medina," Jack ordered. "See you there."

Susan Calvert was then seventeen years old. The pretty, well-mannered child Jack first met three years before had matured into a winsome, beautiful, gracious, and charming young lady. Jack told me later that he arrived at the home of Mrs. W. I. Riddle, where Susan answered his knock on the front door.

"Well, Major Hays, what a pleasant surprise." She smiled and held the door open. "Won't you come in? I expect you want to pay your respects to Mrs. Riddle. My father is also somewhere about."

"Hello, Susan, don't I, at least, get a hug to go with that smile? I have the impression you are not displeased to see me."

She moved to him with outstretched arms. He wrapped his arms around her and pressed her close.

"Ouch. Jack Hays, if you want to hug me, you must remove your weapons. Those pistols poke and hurt."

"I'm sorry, Susan." He removed his pistols, knife, and tomahawk, placing everything on the bench near the door.

Susan took his hand. "Come along," she ordered. "I think everyone is in the backyard."

After greeting Mr. and Mrs. Riddle, Judge and Mrs. Calvert, and Susan's siblings, Jack asked if he could speak privately with the judge.

"Yes, of course, Major. May we use your parlor, Madam?"

"Yes, by all means." Mrs. Riddle seemed pleased.

Jack followed the judge into the Riddles' parlor, where the judge appropriated an armchair. Jack remained standing.

"Judge Carter, I will come directly to the point. I intend to ask Susan to marry me. I am asking for your blessing."

The judge nodded, took out a cigar from his inside coat pocket, and made a production of clipping off the end, rolling it between his thumb and first finger, and then finally lighting it. He took a deep puff, inhaled, and slowly expelled the smoke.

"Well, Major, I suspect Susan will respond in the affirmative. If she does so, I will be happy to welcome you into our family. However, I understand you are recruiting a regiment to join forces with General Taylor. I also know of your penchant for danger. I welcome your intention to marry Susan, but I ask that you return from war before marrying. She is too young to be a widow."

"I understand, sir. I do have your permission then?"

"Of course."

The judge stood and extended his hand. Jack grasped it and smiled in relief.

"Guess I best go find her. I have a buggy and brought a lunch. I thought she might enjoy a picnic."

"I'm certain she will," smiled the judge.

Jack was not one to share intimate details, so I have to tell his and Susan's story as I imagine it.

A gentle rain fell all the previous night. The road leading out of San Antonio south to a crossing of the San Antonio River was little more than a wagon track of deep ruts and puddles of muddy water. There was no need to hurry. The mare that pulled the rented buggy picked her way at a leisurely walk, avoiding the biggest puddles. Susan chattered. Accustomed to Jack's pensive silences, she flooded him with news and gossip without expecting him to respond. Even with San Antonio and its environs now safe, Jack's eyes were constantly scanning, searching for anything out of the usual, always expecting the unexpected.

They arrived at the river crossing, and Jack flipped the reins, turning and urging the mare along a track that ran parallel to the water. The trail passed through juniper, live oak, willows, and all manner of spring blossoming plants and shrubs. They arrived at a small meadow thick with flowers. Jack stopped the mare in the shade of a huge live oak.

Susan inhaled deeply. "Can you smell all these flowers?" she asked.

"Yep, bluebonnets mostly, but some Indian paintbrush and black-eyed Susan. All right, how about we stop here and have our picnic? Before we do, I'll gather you a bunch of your namesake blooms," Jack responded.

Susan swiveled on the board seat and gave him a hug. "I'll spread the blanket while you gather my bouquet, but before you join me on the blanket, you must take off all those weapons."

While Susan spread the blanket, crushing a profusion of bluebonnets underneath, Jack retrieved the wicker basket containing carne asada wrapped in butcher's paper, fresh tortillas wrapped in a dishtowel, a glass jar of salsa verde, two bottles of beer for him, and two bottles of apple cider for her. He meandered through the meadow selecting black-eyed Susan blooms, while Susan spread out the picnic, tasting a bit of each item as she did. He returned, removed his weapons and his black coat, and laid them on the corner of the blanket, the weapons within easy reach. He stretched out on the blanket close to her and extended his hand, holding the flowers.

"Oh, for me?" she smiled.

"Yes, and I've got something else for you."

He reached thumb and forefinger into an inside pocket of the jacket he had removed. He extracted a small box and handed it to her. She laid down the flowers, took the box, opened it, and started crying.

"What's the matter, Susan?" He sat upright, worried.

"It's an engagement ring."

"Yeah?"

"Are you asking me to marry you?"

"I reckon that's what the ring is for. It's just a small turquoise stone. I couldn't afford anything else. Why are you crying?"

"Oh, Jack, it's beautiful." She slid the ring onto the appropriate finger of her left hand. "It fits perfectly."

"I'm glad. I asked your father this morning, and he agreed, but we have to wait until this war is over to be married."

"Oh, Jack, I would rather be married today, but I will wait for you for as long as it takes, John Coffee Hays."

She scooted to him on her knees, fell on him, and they stretched out on the blanket, entwined. He pushed the hair off her forehead with one hand and rubbed her back with the other. She pushed herself into him, squirming to be even closer, searched for his lips with hers.

The warm spring sun filtered through the fresh green leaves of the live oak that towered over them. The shadows from the leaves lengthened as the sun moved west. The food was forgotten. They finally disengaged, both still fully clothed, both quiet.

"We better get you back to the Riddles. Your folks will start to worry."

"I don't think they worry when I'm with you, Major Hays. You must promise me you will be careful. Don't let any Mexican rifle balls find you."

"I promise, but I'm always careful. Come on, let's get you back."

Three weeks later, Jack traveled to Austin after the state legislature finally gave the governor the authority, power, and financial resources to form the infantry and cavalry units requested by General Taylor. Jack resigned his commission as commander of frontier defense and sent out me, Ben McCulloch, Bigfoot Wallace, and Bob Gillespie to track down all the former Rangers we could find, as well as other men to recruit into the militia regiment.

Jack returned to San Antonio, stealing a few hours whenever possible to spend time with Susan. He welcomed new volunteers at his camp on the Medina, but he was still very selective. One day a young man appeared in front of his tent with a good horse, two muzzle-loading pistols, and a bowie knife. Jack came out of his tent with all his weapons. Including his revolving rifle. Without saying anything, he circled the young man's horse, inspecting it closely, and then picked up each hoof and palpated each leg. "You want to join my regiment?" Jack asked.

"Yes, sir. That is my fondest dream."

"All right, follow me."

Jack walked to the edge of the camp and then pointed at two trees about three hundred yards away. "I want you to put that gelding into an all-out run, pull those pistols on the go, put a ball into that tree on the left as you go past, then wheel that horse as fast and tight as you can, and put a ball into the tree on the right as you pass it. Then pull up in front of me."

The youth did as was instructed but managed to miss both trees with his pistols and almost lost his balance as he turned his horse tight to return.

"Well, you can ride passably, but you can't shoot worth a crap."

"I can hit those trees from here with your rifle, Major."

Jack handed him the rifle. "Let's see what you can do while standing."

The young man put a rifle ball into each tree trunk, but at the edge not the center.

"Well, you're almost a good enough shot standing, and you can ride some. Your horse will pass muster, but I need men who can fight from horseback and stick to the saddle no matter what. I'm sure you're brave enough, but you'll do better in the infantry than in my outfit. If you still want to fight, I'm certain you can find a place in the regular militia. Good luck to you."

Jack turned and walked purposely away.

Men continued to arrive at the Medina camp, some traveling as much as four hundred miles to get there. It wasn't long until Jack had his regiment. He was unanimously elected as colonel of the regiment, Sam

Walker as lieutenant colonel, and another of his former Rangers, Michael Chevaille, as major. Two companies of his regiment, one captained by Sam Walker and the other by Ben McCulloch, had already reported for duty as scouts for General Taylor. Jack sent word that he was on the way with the rest of the regiment. We were known officially as the First Regiment, Texas Mounted Volunteers and unofficially as Hays's Texas Rangers. The regiment's rolls listed seven hundred men.

Before we left San Antonio to join the war, Mrs. Riddle, Mrs. Swenson, and several other ladies of San Antonio, organized a farewell ball for Hays's Rangers. It was a gala affair, and all the rough men were on their best behavior. Susan held on to Jack's arm whenever they weren't dancing. She brimmed with pride at the respect he commanded.

Before reporting to General Taylor, the regiment spent several days in Corpus Christi, and then we traveled on to Point Isabel. Colonel Hays was busy securing equipment and supplies for his regiment. He acquired wagons; mules to pull the wagons; equipage, including tents, cooking, and eating utensils; and ammunition. The tents were a new luxury for most of the hardened Rangers.

Three years earlier, Jack sent Sam Walker, at the time still recuperating from a serious wound caused by a Comanche arrow, to visit with Sam Colt. Jack and Walker had developed several ideas for the improvement of the Colt Paterson five-shot revolver. Walker met with Colt in New York, and the two immediately found common ground. The result of their collaboration was the Colt Walker six-shot revolver, which, after considerable testing and refinement, was purchased by the US Army. Along with cylinders holding six charges instead of five, the refinements included much easier release and replacement of the cylinders, some modifications that prevented multiple ignitions at the same time, a trigger guard, and some other, more subtle changes.

The most important equipment he acquired for every man in the regiment were the new, army-sized, six-cylinder Colt revolvers with extra cylinders for each. He and a few others of us had our revolving-cylinder rifles, and the rest of our men all carried single-shot, muzzle-loading rifles. A few, including Bigfoot, kept their Tennessee long rifles. Before leaving San Antonio, Jack received a special gift from Sam Colt, a pair of elaborately engraved and superbly finished revolvers depicting his victory at Painted Rock.

Hays's Texas Rangers exerted their independence and primary loyalty to their leader by following his example, refusing to accept army uniforms. We were a ragtag-looking outfit who addressed our leader as Jack but maintained exemplary discipline and followed his every order without question. Emulating his old friend Flaco, we vowed we would follow him to hell, if only he would allow us to catch up to him first.

The regiment made its way to Port Brown and from there to Matamoros, arriving on August 2. Shortly after our arrival, General Taylor pinned the eagles of a full colonel onto Jack's plain black greatcoat.

"I am quite surprised and not a little disappointed that you don't have a uniform, Colonel."

"My men refuse to wear them, General. They believe the uniforms make them an easier target. I go along with their thinking on this issue."

"Whatever works for you, Colonel. As long as you maintain discipline and your men follow orders, what they wear doesn't matter to me. Their stubbornness is less costly for the army."

"Yes, sir."

Before the ceremony was completed, Jack removed the coat because of the oppressive humidity and heat. He stood at attention in his shirtsleeves as his regiment passed in review before Taylor and his officers.

After the last of Jack's regiment rode past, General Taylor again turned to Jack and extended a hand holding an envelope.

"All right, Colonel. Here are your written orders. Read them and ask me any questions you have."

Jack took the envelope Taylor held out to him, opened it, and read: "Colonel Hays, you are charged with the communication of the policy of the government, the ascertainment of the operations of the army of the enemy, as well as the feeling of the people, and the cutting off, capturing, or destroying all armed parties. You are to march immediately to San Fernando, one hundred and thirty miles southwest of Matamoros, and from there, in a circuitous route through Linares then China, following the already retreating Mexicans.

"Are your orders clear, Colonel?"

"Yes, sir," Jack responded.

"I require you to secure the China route to make certain the enemy is not lurking to attack my flanks. I will take the army on a more northern route since my scouts tell me the China route lacks enough sustenance for the animals and fresh water for both men and animals."

"Yes, sir. My men are up to the task."

"One more thing, Colonel. I have instructed my assistant quartermaster general, Henry Whiting, to acquire sufficient mules to provide transport for my supplies. You will report to General Whiting and help him decide fair market value for the required animals and method of payment for those you acquire. Do not appropriate the mules, purchase them, but do what you must to acquire them. Do you understand my meaning?"

"Yes, sir."

As Hays's Texas Rangers moved along the route, "Captain Yack," as he was well known to the Mexican inhabitants as well as the Comanche, requested that the alcalde of every town and village they entered come to him. He explained what was required of the village, determined by how many mules were available. Several of his Tejano spies were spread out through the surrounding countryside and made a mule count prior to the regiment entering in force. The owners of the animals seemed to be happy to receive a receipt signed by the colonel for a fair sum to be paid in US dollars when presented to the quartermaster of Taylor's army.

General Whiting's written report indicated that the mules needed could only be acquired from the Mexicans. He instructed Colonel Hays to call on the mayors of each town to assist. He wrote that the call would have been ineffectual had Colonel Hays's regiment not been moving into the quarter. He expected to have the mules required in two to three weeks. The acquisition of the necessary animals would restore the army's means of transportation, on which so much depends.

When our regiment was within six miles of San Fernando, we stopped and made camp. Jack's pickets soon allowed three men into the camp, escorting them to the Colonel's tent.

"Colonel Yack, I am honored to be the alcalde, and these señors are members of the town council of San Fernando. We have been charged to speak to you directly on behalf of the people. We want to inform you that the soldiers who were in our town have departed, and there will be no resistance to your entrance. We beg that you and your men spare the property of our citizens."

"Thank you, Señor Alcalde. I appreciate you coming to give me this message. My men and I are here only to make war on soldiers, not civilians. My men will not molest your citizens in any way unless they are attacked first."

The next morning, the regiment entered the city. As the alcalde had reported, the Mexican soldiers garrisoned there had departed early the previous day. However, most of the businesses in the town closed and shuttered their doors and windows. Most of the homes were boarded up as well. A few people peeped out through shuttered windows as we rode past. Despite Jack's promise, the citizens were clearly worried and afraid of the fearsome Captain Yack stories they had been told. His ruthless reputation for fighting had filtered this far and farther, into Mexico. The authorities of the town welcomed Jack and his regiment by providing lodging and food for the officers, and noncommissioned officers, in several aristocratic Mexican homes. All of the hosts were exceedingly pleasant and accommodating. Servants were dispatched by the wealthier households to assist in feeding the troops.

Three days later, Colonel Hays led his regiment out of San Fernando on the 150-mile trek to China, located a little over midway from Matamoros to Monterrey. The trail, for that's what it was rather than even a wagon track, wound its way through arid plains, hills, and mountains. In the mountains, the track frequently skirted precipitous drops on one side with steep, rock-covered slopes on the opposite. Chaparral and prickly pear encroached on the trail and frequently required that the men ride single file. Jack's scouts fanned out to find watering holes or streams that, more often than not, were far apart and frequently little more than a mud hole or miniscule trickle. But our experienced frontier men knew how to make the most of whatever water was available for men or animals. Two horses succumbed to the harsh conditions, exhausted from the heat and lack of water and food. They were turned loose to fend for themselves, their owners hoping they would recuperate enough during the night to seek out water and sustenance. Two of the more tractable mules were selected to be ridden, their loads distributed to other mules. That same day, two of our most experienced horse breakers had the mules accustomed to saddles and riders. The two Rangers whose horses had to be abandoned were happy to not be on foot. No Mexican troops were sighted.

The regiment arrived in the village known as China. The place had a population of only about two thousand souls, and most of them remained out of sight. Jack set up our camp outside of town and ordered us not to molest the citizens in any way. Some additional spies, relatives of some of his Tejano recruits, were recruited as we traveled into Mexico. The spies reported that the garrison in China withdrew to Monterrey. All the other outlying garrisons were also recalled. Monterrey was being fortified for the inevitable attack.

Jack called Sam Walker to his tent. "Sam, I want you to rest the men here and reprovision. Pay fair prices, but requisition everything you need. Then I want you to go north and set up camp on the San Juan River to wait for me to rejoin you."

He took twenty men with him. We followed the San Juan River to Carmargo, northwest of Matamoros. Matamoros was then, and still is today, only a couple of miles south of the Rio Grande. General Taylor moved his army to Matamoros, awaiting the mules and supplies he needed to move on to Monterrey.

Jack reported to Taylor.

"Colonel, good job. Now I want you to take your men back to China and scout the land to the west and then south of Monterrey. You are to make certain no enemy soldiers are positioned to attack my rear."

"Yes, sir."

We completed the hundred-plus-mile scouting assignment in only two days. Upon our return, we were assigned to lead the army to Monterrey with the companies of Gillespie and McCulloch riding on either side, back and forth the length of the column, to screen the flanks. Seven miles outside of Monterrey, Taylor stopped his army and encamped.

As the sun began to lighten the eastern horizon, General Taylor and his staff, already up and organizing the army since four in the morning, mounted their horses. Bob Gillespie and his company of Rangers left the camp to scout ahead, with the rest of Hays's Rangers close behind. It was about nine in the morning when Jack held us up about three-fourths of a mile outside Monterrey. He sat on the stallion he acquired before leaving San Antonio and viewed the valley of Monterrey. It seemed calm, peaceful, unworried. The steeple of the cathedral poked up through the morning mist.

Taylor and his staff rode up to join Jack. They all took in the view of the valley, redundant in chaparral, corn and sugarcane fields, and groves of fruit trees. The bucolic view contrasted with the neat arrangement of streets and flat-roofed buildings of Monterrey. The calm quiet was shattered by a bugle call. A regiment of Mexican lancers emerged from the edge of town closest to them.

Jack swiveled in his saddle. "With your permission, General."

Taylor nodded.

"Ben, Bob, Sam, and Bigfoot, please form the men in columns of five and prepare to charge."

His voice was raised only slightly louder than his normal speaking voice, but his four longtime comrades responded without pause. Within minutes, the regiment was aligned in our well-practiced attack formation. Jack stood in his stirrups, waved his arm forward, and set out at a brisk trot. We followed.

As the distance between the two advancing regiments closed, the Mexican's wheeled their horses and retreated to a safer distance.

"Hold up," shouted Jack, holding his right arm in the air. "They're trying to lure us into range of their cannon."

As his voice died away in the still air, a cannon boomed, and a ball landed twenty yards in front of Jack. His well-trained stallion didn't flinch. Another boom and a ball whished over our heads. Jack turned his horse without hurrying, and we followed his lead. He broke into a lope with us following until cannonballs and grapeshot fell harmless behind us.

"Did you see where the cannons were located, Bob?" asked Jack.

"I spotted two on top of what they call Independence Hill," answered Gillespie.

"You other men spot any other cannon sites?"

All the men shook their heads, except Bigfoot. "I thought I saw one from behind that ridge."

"You're probably right, but I didn't see anything I thought came from there. All right, I see Taylor is already pulling his army back. Let's catch up and see what he wants to do now."

General Taylor decided to encamp in a large grove of trees just outside the small village of Santo Domingo, only two miles from Monterrey. The site was idyllic. There was fresh, clean water; plenty of wood for cooking fires; and good pasture for the animals close by.

About midway between the camp at Walnut Springs and Monterrey, just off the road, was a substantial but not steep hill. After his men were settled, Jack rode to the top of that hill. Several of us saw him preparing to leave and quickly saddled our horses to accompany him. Our leader wasn't going to find any excitement without us. As Jack sat on his stallion studying Monterrey, some of the younger men decided to show off their horsemanship by challenging the Mexican artillery.

These young, fearless Rangers were exuberant, always challenging each other. They rode as fast as their horses could go in figure-eight patterns, small and large circles, and with sudden changes of direction. Some of them even hugged the walls of the city, safe because the cannon could not be aimed down far enough. The artillerymen manning the cannon could not resist trying to bring the showboating Rangers down. Jack mentally marked the position of each cannon that was fired, while his men continued teasing the enemy until their horses started to tire and they grew tired of the sport. None of the Rangers incurred as much as a scratch.

Jack reached into an inside pocket of his coat, took out paper and a pencil, and made a sketch of the town hugging the north shore of the San Juan River. Monterrey was about a mile long, east to west, and about a half mile wide. It was closed in on the south and east sides by the curving Santa Catarina River. The streets were mostly straight and regular in a north-south or east-west direction. Only a few streets ran off at angles. The foothills of the Sierra Madre encroached on the west side of the city. Taylor brought in his army from the north, where the plains leading to the city were open. The main road from the Rio Grande to Mexico City traversed the southern edge of Monterrey on its way to Saltillo. Marin Road, a major north-south thoroughfare, separated about two-thirds of the town to the west. Independence Hill was included in the western portion. When he finished, Jack marked his sketched map with all the locations from which he observed cannon firing.

Before he went to reconnoiter, Jack sent three Tejano Rangers as spies into the city. They returned to report that General Ampudia's forces numbered more than seven thousand men. The spies also provided information that enabled Jack to modify, and make more accurate, his sketched map. Independence Hill, close by the road to Mexico City, housed a redoubt known to the Mexicans as La Libertad. About three hundred yards south of La Libertad was a large stone building called the Bishop's Palace. It was located midway along the ridge but below La Libertad. La Libertad was on top of the sharp peak of Independence Hill. Its piled rock walls were topped by sandbags and full of artillery and infantry. Six hundred yards south of Independence Hill, on the opposite side of the Mexico City highway and the Santa Catarina River, was Federation Ridge, also well defended, as was Fort El Soldado to the east.

Jack reported to General Taylor and spread out his newly resketched, updated map.

"You are certain of this information, Colonel?"

"Yes, sir. What I was able to observe was confirmed by my spies, and they were able to provide additional information."

"I never expected this level of defense," mused Taylor, removing his campaign cap and running his hand through his thinning hair. "We have 6,230 men, but only half of them are regulars. I'm never certain of the mettle of volunteers. General Ampudia is an experienced soldier. He'll have every building with a flat roof sandbagged. From their fortified positions, his infantry can fire down on our men as they attack. I have nothing with which to batter down barricades or the other defenses he will, no doubt, put up. I don't have nearly enough field artillery to take on defenders who outnumber and outgun us."

Jack frowned. It seemed Taylor was about to give up.

While Taylor ruminated, Jack ambled over to where Gen. W. J. Worth was standing, also with a frown on his face. He took Worth's sleeve and pulled him to the side, where they held a whispered conversation.

"General Taylor," Worth said, walking over to the table where Jack's map was spread. "Colonel Hays and I have a plan. I would like to gain your approval."

"Go ahead."

"What if, with Colonel Hays's help, my division were to circle around Independence Hill, take control of the Mexico City road, then attack the hill from the opposite side. I believe we can take that hill."

"Maybe so, Worth; maybe so. If you think you can do it, go ahead."

Just before noon on Sunday, September 12, 1846, Jack selected 250 of his most experienced men and led General Worth's division of 2,000 south through the foothills and west, out of the sight and range of the Mexicans on Independence Hill. They took control of the Mexico City highway and then turned back north on Marin Road. Surprisingly, the fortified Mexican soldiers did not open fire on them as they moved north. They approached the toe of Independence Hill with the defenders in La Libertad staring down at them. Jack stopped his men as they reached Topo Road and watched as Mexican troops scurried from the Bishop's Palace up the hill to reinforce La Libertad.

Jack and Ben McCulloch dismounted after Jack sent pickets to spread out and warn the column of any impending attack. He and Ben climbed a short way up the hill to reconnoiter and were soon joined by General Worth and his staff.

"Look over to the east, General," said Jack. "Appears General Taylor is moving his troops to threaten the Mexicans from opposite us. I thought maybe he would think to divert some of their attention from us. Maybe he'll even launch an attack."

Worth frowned. "If you say anything, I'll deny it, but I doubt he will actually risk his precious army."

The officers descended from the hill. Jack selected thirty-two of his Rangers and led us back toward the highway to Mexico City to scout any Mexican activity in that direction. Worth's division and the rest of the Rangers followed. As we neared the Mexico City highway, we were ambushed by Mexican infantry secreted on either side of the road. A battery on Independence Hill fired on us, but their cannonballs and grapeshot fell short. While we were fighting off the ambush, Jack sent a messenger back to Worth to report the situation. He looked up to spot a detachment of Mexican cavalry approaching at a fast trot.

"This could get ugly, boys. They could cut us off. Let's get back to Worth," Jack directed.

We made it back to Worth's forces who were scurrying about, fortifying positions on either side of the road. The Mexican Lancers were still coming fast.

"Let's give 'em hell, boys," Jack shouted. He turned his stallion and spurred toward the hard-charging Mexicans. We pulled out our revolvers and crashed into the Mexican lancers, firing right and left. The lancers scattered. None of us were wounded, but the Mexicans retreated, holding their wounded up in their saddles as best they could.

The sun went down beyond the mountains as Jack walked ahead of his horse, holding the reins. He was walking toward a corral adjacent to the Rancho San Jeronimo. As we dismounted and prepared to turn our horses into the corral, Mexican soldiers, hidden on a small hill east of the corral, opened fire.

"If your saddles are off, take what cover you can find," Jack shouted. "The rest of you follow me."

He jumped back on his stallion, unholstered one of his revolvers, and rode hard into the enemy position, several of us following close at his heels, firing at any target that presented. The Mexicans scattered into the increasing darkness. One of our men was wounded, along with several horses. Ben McCulloch discovered one dead Mexican soldier, but several others who were seen to be wounded managed to escape. The clouded sky opened up, and rain pelted us as we returned to the rancho.

The rain increased. None of us had brought along food, coats, or blankets. Our tents, supplies, and equipment were still at Walnut Creek. A few men appropriated pigs and chickens from the rancho, but the fires they lit for cooking drew fire from the cannon on Independence Hill, so they had to be extinguished. Some Rangers, still foraging, found some unshelled corn and munched on that. Most of the men attempted, with minimal success, to sleep curled up in their shirtsleeves on the saturated ground.

General Worth set up his camp out of the range of the Mexican artillery. His men spent a reasonably comfortable night in their tents after a hot meal. We were in our saddles well before dawn. Jack made his way to Worth's tent, avoided the small pond of rainwater in front, and found Worth awake and pouring over a map inside the tent. Moisture of condensation dripped onto his map. Worth brushed some water off the map with the back of his right hand.

"If your men are up to it, Colonel Hays, I need you to make certain we are not attacked from the rear. I will have Captain Smith follow you with his mounted infantry. Secure the highway to Mexico City to protect us."

"Yes, sir. We'll leave immediately."

Jack reached the highway, a well-traveled dirt road with deep wagon ruts, before daylight. We crossed over.

"We'll wait here for sunlight and then reconnoiter," Jack said.

All of the men dismounted, some sat down heavily and fell asleep almost immediately. Others removed saddles and started grooming their horses; others checked their weapons, cleaning and reloading. As dawn broke, I got up from the cold, wet ground. Every bone in my body ached, as did, I'm certain, every man present. Then a picket cried out, "Mesicans comin', Mesicans comin'." I saw a full regiment of Lancers, and they had spotted us.

The Mexican colonel held up his right hand, looked over his shoulder, and shouted for his men to form into attack lines. Each of the men had a pennon attached below the head of his lance. All the pennons were fluttering in the breeze. The Mexicans were obviously accomplished riders, mounted on spirited horses. Although we were just over three hundred yards apart, we couldn't hear anything from their movements or their equipment. Those of us whose horses were saddled tightened our girths and mounted. The rest, many barely awake, jumped to grab their horses and get them saddled.

Jack knew he had to gain some time. "Get the men ready as fast as you can, Ben," he ordered quietly.

He rode slowly, by himself, toward the lancers. He was holding a captured saber, a weapon unfamiliar to him. Halfway to the waiting Mexicans, he stood in his stirrups and bowed to the Mexican colonel. Then he shouted in Spanish.

"Colonel, I presume you are an honorable and chivalrous man. If you are also brave remains to be seen. I challenge you to a duel, man-to-man."

The colonel removed his helmet, bowed at Jack, and began throwing off anything that might encumber him. We moved up closer to our leader. He held up his hand for us to stop.

"He doesn't know shit about how to fight with a saber," murmured Bigfoot.

"We all know that, Bigfoot," I whispered, "but he hasn't removed those fancy six-shot revolvers Colt gave him."

The previous night, Jack had lost his hat. That morning he was wearing a bandanna to keep the hair out of his eyes. He reined his stallion, first in one direction, then another, then in tight circles, making certain the horse was warmed up and ready to respond to his commands.

The Mexican colonel unsheathed his saber and loosened his arm by circling his head with the saber in hand. Jack started his horse toward his opponent at a walk, his horse tossing his head with impatience. The colonel's horse responded by high stepping, pulling against the reins, moving from one foot to another, its hooves hardly touching the ground.

"That's one brave, Mesican," said Bigfoot.

"And a brave horse," I answered. "The son of a bitch doesn't prance; he's dancin'."

When the two men were separated by about forty yards, the Mexican stood in his stirrups, pointed the saber at Jack, and spurred his horse into a dead run. Jack kicked his animal into a gallop and then suddenly reined the horse to the right, dropped the saber, pulled out one of his revolvers, and, swinging over and hanging from the right side of his horse, brought the revolver under the horse's neck. His ball hit the too-brave Mexican colonel in the heart. Jack immediately reined his horse around and, spurring with both heels, raced back toward us, shouting.

"They'll be coming to get revenge for their colonel. Dismount and pick your targets."

As anticipated, the Mexican cavalry were enraged over the dirty trick that cost them their leader. They charged directly at us. Although we were significantly outnumbered, we stood our ground, holding our horses' reins in our teeth. The Lancers pushed through our lines, but our revolvers and rifles took a heavy toll. Once through our line, the Lancers reformed and charged again. Only a few lances found a mark, but more of our pistol and rifle balls hit home. The Mexicans again turned and reformed to charge. The results were similar. Following the decimating third charge, the Mexicans retreated to Monterrey.

We counted nearly eighty Mexicans killed. At least twice that number were wounded. We lost one man, but several others suffered lance wounds, mostly to the shoulders and arms. Two Rangers had profusely bleeding gashes in their scalps.

"I'll never call a Mesican a coward after that display," vowed Bigfoot.

While Jack was attending to our wounded, one of his spies slid to a stop in front of him, his lathered horse snorting and fighting for air.

"There are at least a thousand and a half Mexican soldiers coming up to prevent you from securing this highway," the spy reported.

While the spy was delivering this message, two companies of mounted infantry, commanded by Captain Smith, joined us.

"You and your men are very welcome, Captain," said Jack, reaching across the neck of the captain's horse to shake Smith's hand. Jack now commanded six companies of men, almost a regiment. He ordered one company to hide in a cornfield north of the road and four others to hide in gullies or behind fences on the south side. Every fifth man was ordered to the rear to hold horses.

"Ben, you take your men east on the highway. Show yourselves. If the Mexicans attack, feign a retreat. Make it look real and bring them into this ambush."

"Still thinking like a Comanche, are you, Jack?"

"It could work if their officers have never fought Comanche."

It worked perfectly. As soon as McCulloch's company was sighted, two full regiments of Mexicans charged down the rutted road to capture the greatly outnumbered enemy. Ben turned his men, and they trotted off to the west, but not too fast. The charging Mexican cavalry were armed with shotguns, they called them *escopetas,* as well as sabers and lances. They fired at the retreating Rangers, but their escopetas were inaccurate. None of the Rangers, or their horses, were hit. McCulloch responded to the volley by spurring his horse into a gallop; his men followed as they rode past our hidden fighters. Once the last rank of Mexicans entered into the ambush, Jack jumped to his feet.

"Now!" he shouted.

Rifles and pistols roared. Mexicans tumbled from their saddles. Riderless horses milled and then ran to escape. Other horses, surprised and frightened by the roar of so many guns, shied and bucked off their riders. Screaming wounded, both men and horses, cluttered the road, impeding the escape of those not yet killed or wounded by volley after volley of destruction. Ben McCulloch turned his men back and charged into the fray. Those of us who were hidden abandoned our cover and walked, firing our weapons, into the confused Mexican troops. One of the Mexican commanders finally reestablished order and led his men back to Monterrey with McCulloch and his men at their heels.

More than a hundred Mexican cavalry were either wounded or killed. We lost another man, and seven were wounded.

In the calm after this battle, the sounds of artillery and rifles firing from the northeast suggested General Taylor was attacking Monterrey from that direction. Taylor's units did, in fact, attack the city from several different directions all that day but were turned back each time after suffering heavy losses.

General Worth took control of the highway to Mexico City. He positioned cannon at the junction with Topo Road, where he also set up his headquarters. While Worth was positioning his troops, Hays's Rangers returned to Walnut Creek where they tended to their horses and weapons and then rested, awaiting their next assignment.

Early that afternoon, General Worth sent for Jack who found Worth in his tent, his flag on a pole stuck into the ground to the right of the entrance.

"Colonel, good work this morning. Now I require that your regiment protects my right flank."

"Yes, sir." Jack saluted.

He led us back to the Mexico City highway where we reached the location where Federation Hill ascended from the roadway. He dispersed us in a cornfield on the opposite side of a fence separating the field from the road. On the far side of the field was a row of tall trees. Just as we were settling in, two concealed cannons on Federation Hill opened fire.

Jack called a seventeen-year-old recruit to him. "What is your name again, Ranger?"

"Fred Hutchins, Jack"

"All right, Fred. You see that tall oak off to the right?"

"Yes, sir."

"You think you can climb it and ignore those cannonballs?"

"Yes, sir."

"Then do it. I need to know if the Mexican infantry is getting ready to charge us."

"Yes, sir."

The cannonballs were knocking limbs from the trees and plowing furrows through the corn. Only a few moments after reaching the top of the tree Hutchins shouted down.

"Them cannonballs are comin' closer, Colonel Jack. Can I git down?"

"Stay put," Jack shouted. "Wait for orders."

Just then a messenger from General Worth found Jack. He told Jack that the general needed him to move his regiment to a new position. We were moving out when I tugged on Jack's sleeve.

"You haven't forgot that boy in the tree have you, Jack?"

"Shit ... You and Bigfoot take these men to where they're supposed to be, John."

Jack ran, crouched over, back to the base of the tree. "Where are the Mexicans now, Fred?"

"They're headed back up that hill."

"Well then, maybe you better climb down."

"Can't. I'm supposed to wait for orders."

"Look down, Fred. See who is shouting up at you? I'm ordering you down."

"Yes, sir, Jack. Thank you, sir."

Hutchens scrambled down from the tree as fast as he could. Just as he reached the ground, a load of grapeshot took off the top of the tree. Both men covered their heads with their arms to avoid the falling branches and splinters of wood that showered down on them.

Worth ordered all of his regimental commanders to meet in his tent.

"We have reestablished communications with General Taylor. He insists, and I agree, that the capture of Independence Hill is imperative. I want you three regimental commanders to reconnoiter and make a special study of this section of the hill north of the Bishop's Palace." He pointed to the location on the map spread out on his field desk. The three went to study possible access to the hill.

Our regiment was still without food or additional gear, still in shirtsleeves. We had not eaten for thirty-six hours. Most of us hadn't had more than one or two hours of sleep. We still had some unshelled corn to feed our horses, and some men withheld an ear of the raw corn to munch on themselves.

"If we can take Federation Hill, we will have opened the way to the city. Any of you believe your unit can storm that hill and capture the redoubt on top?" asked Worth.

He looked at each of the regimental commanders. The first two remained motionless, their faces blank. Then his eyes fell on Jack.

"My regiment, with some help at the right time, can take that hill, General," Jack responded with calm certainty.

As darkness closed in that evening, a violent storm again soaked the troops. Worth assigned colonels Childs and Hays to lead 460 men. His orders were for them to move out at three in the morning and storm the hill.

While his exhausted men huddled in the torrential rain, sleeping fitfully, Jack went over and tapped me on the shoulder. I awoke with a start, my rifle in my hand.

"John, go find Sam and tell him I'm going to take Bigfoot and a few others with me on a little jaunt. I want him to make certain the men are ready to join the attack at three in the morning, whether I'm back or not."

"All right, Jack. You certain you don't want me to go with you?"

"No, I need you here." He patted me on the back. "After you find Sam, try to get some sleep."

Jack moved through the camp, touching the men he wanted on the shoulder. He held a finger to his lips and motioned for them to follow him. It was slightly after midnight when he led the men, single file, out of the camp, through our pickets, across muddy cornfields, to the base of Independence Hill. Heavy rain continued to fall as the men crouched, waiting for the Mexican pickets to change. It wasn't long until the sentries were changed, and Jack was able to spot where three of them took up positions. The new pickets made no attempt in the heavy downpour to maintain silence. Jack waited patiently until the new sentries had time to get drowsy.

Jack crept silently, his men, equally silent, behind him. They moved to the back of the closest sentry. Jack and Bigfoot grabbed him, and Bigfoot held a crunched-up bandanna tightly in his mouth. Jack pricked him over his right kidney with his bowie knife and whispered into his ear in Spanish: "Show us where the closest other sentry is. If you make any noise to warn him, this knife will slice through your kidney."

The squad used each captured sentry to identify the location of the next. It wasn't long before they cleared all the pickets from the base of the hill. They hurried, with their prisoners, back to camp. At two forty-five, the sergeants mustered their men. It had turned colder, and the rain continued to pelt us while we shivered.

Jack led one column of men, Childs the other. General Worth stood at the edge of the camp in the rain, his head uncovered, as the two columns walked purposefully and silently past him. As each man passed, the general searched their eyes and nodded his thanks.

General Ampudia considered the only vulnerable approach to the hill to be on the eastern side, a gentle slope up to the Bishop's Palace. That approach was where he concentrated his defenses. We came from the opposite direction, up a steep slope some eight hundred feet. The lack of sentries allowed us to secure the base of the hill, and the heavy rain muffled our noise as we climbed up the mountain. Fissures in the steep rocks provided footholds and handholds as the men helped each other up, using branches and rocks to grab onto.

As dawn came, we were within a hundred yards of the redoubt on the crest of the hill. We continued to climb up, finding shelter among some of the larger rocks. However, we were inevitably spotted. Rifle balls whistled, and rock chips pelted us, cutting through our clothing as we scrambled for cover.

"Hold your fire, fan out, keep cover," Jack shouted, and his commands were repeated.

Finally, when he was satisfied his men had sufficient cover, Jack shouted again. "Give 'em hell!"

Shotguns, rifles, and pistols all rang out as we charged the walls topped with sandbags. Bob Gillespie stood atop two sandbags, ready to jump down inside when a ball thudded into his chest. He staggered and fell to his knees but waved his men forward as they sprang over the wall, three of them vaulting over him, to meet the enemy in hand-to-hand struggle. Hays scrambled to the top of the wall, firing from a revolver in each hand, carefully choosing his targets. In a few moments, the remainder of us were over the wall, and those Mexicans who could still run, did so, sliding and rolling down the gentle slope to the Bishop's Palace.

As the stars and stripes were raised, the Rangers stood with bowed, bared heads. Jack blinked back tears as he pushed the hair from Bob

Gillespie's face. Then he removed Bob's bandanna, placing it over his comrade's face to shield his sightless eyes.

He turned to the silent men gathered around their fallen leader. In an almost inaudible voice, he spoke: "Bob Gillespie was a highly educated, gallant, resourceful, intelligent man, and one of my closest friends. There has never been a time when I could not count on him. I will mourn and remember him as long as I live. I want three volunteers to take his body back to camp. When we return to that place, we will give him the burial a true hero deserves."

The Mexicans were able to take three pieces of artillery with them as they scurried down the hill. The remaining cannons had been spiked. The three taken with them soon began firing on us from the Bishop's Palace. Some of Worth's troops were able to bring up a disassembled howitzer from Worth's camp and reassemble it. Before long, it was answering those men holed with the artillery.

Jack moved his men, along with two companies of infantry, in close to the walls of Bishop's Palace where the Mexican artillery was unable to point down far enough to cause us problems. Our sharpshooters patiently picked off any Mexican soldier who presented a target. This was restful for most of us, but it did not accomplish much.

Jack made a proposal to the other officers. "I will take half my men and conceal them on the right side of the ridge. Sam Walker will conceal the other half on the left side. Captain Blanchard, I would like you to form up your company and act as though you are going to attack the palace. If the Mexicans take the bait, they will form up in front of the palace to attack your company. As soon as they move forward, you retreat back to this spot here." He was drawing a map in the dirt with a stick. "If the Mexicans think we are greatly outnumbered, they will attack. When they have passed by our concealed men, our entire force will raise up, and we'll have them trapped between us."

The plan worked exactly as diagrammed. The Mexicans, caught in the deadly cross fire, tried to get back to the safety of the palace but were prevented from doing so. Those who managed to escape the trap retreated back to Monterrey, and Jack's command took possession of the Bishop's Palace. The remaining defenders of that stronghold panicked, rushing to get to the presumed safety of Monterrey. Four cannons and a significant amount of ammunition were left for us.

Taylor's men cheered when they saw the Stars and Stripes raised over the Bishop's Palace, but Taylor was not ready to press the issue. Worth received no new orders, but he did send some infantry and artillery units to relieve the men who were holding Independence Hill.

At about four o'clock that same afternoon, all us Rangers were back in camp at the junction of the Mexico City highway and Topo Road. Although we still had not eaten, some of the men managed to liberate serapes from fallen Mexican soldiers. They were able to roll up in the serapes and sleep, despite the continuing rain. The next morning, September 23, 1846, Jack took two of his companies and then recruited another unit from Worth's regiment, and the combined forces secured a bridge over the Santa Catarina River, about three miles south along the Mexico City highway. Worth felt the Mexicans might try to bring in supplies on that road. After securing the bridge, Jack received orders to bring his command to a church in the city, close to the Bishop's Palace. Worth moved his artillery to the palace stronghold.

That same morning, we could hear the roar of battle from Taylor's side of Monterrey. Jack told me Worth assumed Taylor finally launched an attack, but I learned later that after his men managed to fight their way to within a block of the main plaza, Taylor decided to pull back. He reasoned that because his men were on duty the previous night, they needed to rest. He told his officers he wanted to plan a concerted attack with General Worth. Worth was unaware of Taylor's thinking and decided to move into the city on his own.

Moving on foot, half of us advanced into the city near the river, while Sam Walker and his men, also on foot, moved parallel to us and into the city. The street Hays followed veered to the right, while Sam's ran straight. Both columns encountered heavy barricades blocking the streets. Flat-roofed houses and buildings on both sides of the streets provided cover for the defenders. Jack halted us and went over to confer with Sam. They each divided their men into six groups. Two groups moved forward while hugging close to the buildings on either side of the street. Two other groups gained access to the rooftops after entering houses. Many of the rooftops were connected, and those that were not were only separated by a few feet. The remaining men were assigned to proceed through or over the high walls that surrounded the yards in back of each building. We advanced in rushes and were able to clear the rooftops, advance through yards, and attack barricades from above, behind, and out front.

Some of the buildings were well defended. Soldiers fired from loopholes in doors and window shutters. We took cover in a building opposite and shot at anything poking through a loophole. Meanwhile, some of us would enter an adjoining building. We punched a hole in the wall between the buildings, took a six-inch artillery shell with a three-second fuse, and dropped it through the hole. The resulting explosion enabled us to make our way through the opening, dispatching any stunned defenders still alive.

At times, we were able to gain the ground floor, but defenders remained upstairs and on the roof. We were all marksmen, some better than others, but all capable. The defenders were soon caught in a devastating cross fire by Rangers on the roof and from the buildings on either side and opposite.

Progress was slow. At twilight, a messenger, accompanied by a relief battalion of infantry, found Colonel Hays. Worth ordered Jack to return to camp and rest his men. Hays left a small contingent of men to show the newcomers how to hold the gains of the day. While traveling the road back to camp, we appropriated several head of cattle and sheep. We were finally able to give attention to the rumblings in our bellies.

When we reached Worth's headquarters, Jack detailed one group of men to care for the horses and another to hurry back to Walnut Springs and bring up our pack mules with our equipment and tents. A third detail butchered the confiscated animals. Soon, meat was roasting over cooking fires. Very few of the men waited long enough for the meat to be more than seared. Many didn't bother to wipe the blood from their beards. After we ate, men started dozing off.

Jack went through the camp rousing the men he needed for picket duty. Jack promised the pickets relief every two hours. In anticipation of an expected counterattack, Jack led twenty men back to the bridge where the highway crossed the Santa Catarina. He also sent scouts ahead on the road. Two hours later, the scouts returned to tell him that about fifty Mexican horsemen were approaching.

Jack set up an ambush, and the Mexicans, unaware, rode into it. Those Mexicans not killed or severely wounded fled. Five Mexican pack mules, loaded with hard bread, were rounded up. When his men were relieved that evening, they took the mules and bread back with them. They ate and fell asleep almost instantaneously, but at three in the morning, we were awakened and instructed to resume the positions in Monterrey from which we had been relieved. As the sun rose, the house-to-house fighting resumed.

By ten that morning, all the Mexican defenders were gone from the principle plaza, all the streets leading into that plaza, and all of the main roads into town. The remaining enemy was trapped, unable to move about and certainly unable to escape. Some were hidden in the cathedral, commanded by a captain who had demonstrated remarkable fortitude and control over his men. Taylor's forces, still on the eastern edge of the city, were heard, and from some vantage points on the rooftops, they could be seen. Without warning, an order directly from Taylor's headquarters was distributed to all commanders to cease fire.

The rain stopped. The sun got hotter as each hour passed. We were less than eighty yards from the cathedral, fuming at not being allowed to secure it. Taylor was negotiating with General Ampudia. At five in the evening, they agreed on an armistice with liberal terms of surrender.

Jack and all of his men were beyond frustrated. We did nothing more than shake our heads. The following day, Hays's Rangers returned to Worth's headquarters camp, saddled our horses, and made a triumphant tour of the city. Jack made certain his wounded were cared for and the horses were fed, watered, and groomed. Horseshoes were reset or replaced as required. When all the animals were taken care of, we ate and then crawled into our tents and blankets and slept the sleep of the righteous.

Taylor lost almost eight hundred men in his ill-timed, ill-conceived, ill-conducted assaults on the east side defenses where the opposing forces were essentially equal. Worth, fighting against significantly larger numbers than were available to him, was infinitely more successful and only lost seventy men.

On September 28, General Worth issued an order that praised Jack and all of us, saying: "I feel assured that every individual in the command unites with me in admiration of Colonel Hays and his noble band of volunteers. Hereafter, they and we are brothers, and we can desire no better security of success than by their association."

Taylor began mustering us out on the last day of September. His supplies and food were running short. He contemplated a prolonged period of inaction while the politicians in Washington debated the next step in the war. Some of us had already overstayed our agreed-to term of enlistment. Taylor knew where he could find us again if he needed us. He gave personal thanks to Jack and his officers and mentioned their achievements in his official correspondence.

While Jack's command was being dispersed, he, his officers, and a few others, including myself, were invited into the home of Don José Maria

Gajar for a celebration dinner. Gajar was a wealthy Spaniard who was forced by Ampudia to give him loans. Gajar was happy to entertain us and showed me what he wrote in his journal on the day of the armistice:

"As they came near, my heart almost failed me; for the Texans, with their coarse hickory shirts and their trousers confined by a leather strap to their hips, their slouched hats, and their sweat and powder-begrimed faces, certainly presented a most brigandish appearance. They came along, yelling like Indians and discharging rifles in the direction of Mexicans on the house tops."

We responded to Gajar's hospitality by obeying Jack's explicit instructions to not liberate any of Don Gajar's property and to not molest anyone in his household. As was always the case, Jack's orders were law.

CHAPTER 13

WE WERE BACK in San Antonio only two days when Jack received a letter from Governor Henderson.

"I'll be damned, John. Look at this." He handed me the letter requesting that he recruit another regiment.

Our accomplishments in Mexico were well reported back in the United States. Individual soldiers from Taylor's army, including many under General Worth's command, wrote letters home describing, in detail, the heroic accomplishments of the quiet, modest, too-young-to-be-believed colonel and his sharpshooting, brave, reckless, and undefeatable Rangers. Many of those letters found their way into local newspapers all over the country, but especially in the South.

The public, spurred on by these reports, clamored to know everything possible about us and our leader.

"Well, I guess my reputation will make it easier to recruit another regiment, but all I want to do is to retire to a private life, marry Susan, and raise a family, John. Do you suppose I will ever get to do that? I'm going to rely on you and Bigfoot to start recruiting men. Mr. Swenson talked to me last night and convinced me that my present notoriety is an opportunity to take advantage of some investment options that Swenson has set the stage for. Sam is going with me. I also intend to hire a contractor and some skilled workers for the home I want to build for Susan."

A few days later, Jack and Sam left San Antonio. Always frugal, Jack hadn't spent much of the salary earned from his many months of service to the government. He also carried a substantial letter of credit from his bank. He stopped in Houston to send a letter to Henderson accepting the commission and describing how he intended to recruit. He also sent a letter to Michael Chevaille, whose organizational skills, attention to detail, and courage as a fighter, he admired. He asked him to agree to join this new regiment and travel to San Antonio to oversee its recruitment.

Major Chevaille cut short his furlough, traveled to San Antonio, and joined Bigfoot and me in our recruitment efforts. The regiment was not to be called up for active service until it was specifically requested by the US Army.

Early in November, Jack and Sam arrived in New Orleans. They read about themselves in the Picayune newspaper. The article made them chuckle, describing how they were warmly greeted by thousands. The article went on to describe how many people were surprised that such brave hearts and the authors of such bold deeds were found in gentlemen so unpretending in appearance and so totally free from the assumption of manner or thought.

"Assumption of manner or thought?" laughed Sam. "Does that mean we don't act as if our shit don't stink?"

Jack smiled. "Something like that I reckon."

General Taylor continued to occupy Monterrey after we were sent home. Then, for reasons unknown, he moved his headquarters back to Matamoros.

While still in New Orleans, Jack received an official communique from Army headquarters in Washington. After he returned to San Antonio, he showed it to me. It said that Santa Anna was again in complete power in Mexico and was preparing his country for a serious war effort.

On November 23, 1846, Gen. Winfield Scott received orders to go to Mexico, take command of all US forces, and organize a Gulf expedition. He was ordered to take Veracruz, use it as a base of operations, and then capture Mexico City. Apparently, those in power in Washington decided that taking Mexico City would settle the issue. The communique also said Taylor was instructed to send every man he could spare to the Gulf Coast. From there, he was to go to Veracruz and assist Scott.

Meanwhile, we were having trouble recruiting. Since the annexation of Texas, one of every six men of legal age had served in the War with Mexico. Not all of them had been in Jack's regiment. Two other militia units had been recruited by other leaders, and they also served under General

Taylor. All of these men had neglected their families and their farms or ranches to do their duty. These experienced fighters were not interested in the indefinite enlistments demanded by the US government. Also, they did not trust, or have much respect for, Taylor as a fighter. More tellingly, they didn't trust Taylor to discharge them once active operations were completed. We were only able to recruit 350 of the 700 men we needed to fill the regiment.

After returning to San Antonio and talking with us, Jack understood that our inability to recruit was primarily due to the indefinite enlistment requirement. Weary and frustrated, he traveled to Austin for a meeting with Governor Henderson.

"Good morning, Colonel Hays. I trust you had an easy ride from San Antonio. I understand the recruiting for your new regiment is not going well."

"Exactly, Governor. The problem is the men don't have much trust in General Taylor, and they are, understandably, reluctant to volunteer for an indefinite term of service to serve under a man they don't trust. I have to tell you I share their concerns."

"Jack, those enlistment instructions are required by the US government. There is nothing I can do to change them. However, I have other news that requires your attention. I recently received information that nearly ten thousand Indians from several different western tribes have been filtering into Texas. My information is that they are scattered along the headwaters of the Colorado. Some war parties have been sighted just eighty miles west of us here in Austin. I have sent an urgent request to the secretary of war, asking permission for you to raise another regiment of mounted militia to specifically protect our frontier."

Jack got up out of the chair he was in and paced the office, rubbing his forehead, deep in thought. "I understand, Governor, but I cannot raise the manpower with the limitations on recruiting Washington puts on us. Trying to rectify the issue by written correspondence back and forth with Washington will make it impossible for me to raise enough troops to join the war in Mexico or protect our frontier until it is much too late."

"I agree, Jack. What do you suggest?"

"I need to get to Washington as soon as possible and meet with President Polk and the War Department. I must explain the problems we face trying to protect our huge western frontier. I don't think they have any concept of how spread out the frontier of Texas is. I must make them understand the distances and types of terrain involved. I will also make it clear to them that the policy of indefinite enlistment is now and will continue to make it impossible to recruit the number of men we need to protect our settlers, let alone raise the number of men they want for the Mexican War."

"I agree. I will supply you with a letter appointing you as my personal representative in this matter. Travel to Washington as soon as possible and make our needs known."

"Thanks, Governor. In the meantime, I will order Sam Walker and his company of Rangers to patrol the country west of here and protect Austin. His instructions will be to engage and run off any Indians they find."

"That will be very reassuring, Colonel. Thank you."

Jack made his way to Washington by steamboat and rail, arriving on March 16. His name and his reputation were well known, and he gained access to President Polk and the War Department the day after his arrival in the city. He made his case to the president and to the secretary of war, Mr. Marcy, in a calm, quiet, but forceful manner. He left no room to doubt his assessment of the situation in Texas or what actions were required.

The following day, a messenger arrived at Jack's hotel with a note from Secretary Marcy. The secretary requested that Colonel Hays report back to the War Department for further instructions.

"Colonel, after our meeting yesterday I received a report from General Taylor that two different bands of Mexican guerrillas have attacked his supply lines. When this report was written, the raids destroyed or took the contents of 150 wagons. One hundred of Taylor's troops and wagoners have been killed. One of the bands is commanded by a Gen. José Urrea, another by Gen. Antonio Canales. The two of them managed to cut communication between Monterrey and Carmargo completely for several weeks. I have also received a special messenger from Col. Samuel Curtis, who is the senior officer on the Rio Grande with headquarters at Carmargo. He requested fifty thousand volunteers."

Jack smiled. "Fifty thousand?"

"Yes."

"If you give me what I need, Mr. Secretary, I can take care of those problems. I have been fighting those two self-appointed generals for years. I know how to deal with them."

On March 20, only four days after his arrival in the capital, the War Department issued an order for Colonel Hays to raise his regiment with the term of enlistment to be either six or twelve months. He was directed to employ as many men as needed to protect the Texas frontier and to use the remainder of his regiment to rid the lower Rio Grande of the Mexican guerrilla bands creating havoc with General Taylor's lines of communication. Taylor found it impossible to send supplies to Monterrey or to send or receive communications from the garrison he left there.

Jack accomplished what he needed to do, but he took some personal time to pay his respects to Sarah Childress Polk, the president's wife. Mrs. Polk was an old and dear friend of Jack's Tennessee family. She sent for him. She knew about Jack's engagement and wanted to know all about Susan and her family.

He arrived again at the White House and was warmly greeted by Mrs. Polk.

"I have received an invitation to attend the wedding of Sen. Thomas Benton's daughter, Eliza, to Bill Jones, an acquaintance of mine from New Orleans, this evening. I don't know either of those folks very well. Do you think I should take the time to attend?" Jack asked Mrs. Polk.

"Absolutely, Jack. The president and I are going to attend, but Mr. Polk must leave directly after the ceremony for a conference he committed to some time ago. You must join us. You can be my escort."

"I will be delighted, madam."

Just before eight in the evening, Jack returned to the White House. The president, Mrs. Polk, and several other guests greeted him warmly. In due course, they all departed for the stately mansion of Senator Benton. After the wedding ceremony, the president, with the new bride on his arm, led the guests to the supper table. He was followed in line by Mrs. Polk on Jack's arm, then the bride's family, followed by the groom and his family.

Jack whispered to Mrs. Polk: "I'm more nervous about this than facing a hundred Comanche."

"Nonsense, young man. None of these people have a weapon." She smiled broadly as she whispered in his ear and then patted his hand.

Jack departed Washington March 26. After arriving in San Antonio, he began enlisting volunteers. Most only wanted to sign on for six months. He dispatched Major Chevaille to take the veteran recruits they mustered and report to General Taylor. Taylor ordered Chevaille to patrol between China and Matamoros. It wasn't long until Urrea and Canales, both unwilling to confront the Rangers, left the area, and the Rangers safely escorted provision trains through the region. Taylor soon reported to the adjutant general that the number of men needed to escort his supply lines could be reduced. He seemed ever mindful of the cost to the government of maintaining militia on active service. That, or the efficiency of Hays's Texas Rangers made him uncomfortable.

For the remainder of 1847, Jack busily deployed his companies of Rangers to patrol the frontier and deal with the everyday concerns of supply, recruitment, training, and organization of his regiment. Susan didn't want to delay their wedding any longer, and neither did Jack. Susan's mother joined forces with her, and the judge relented. The wedding would be held at Judge and Mrs. Calvert's home in Seguin on April 29, 1847.

During his years in Texas, Jack had received several grants of land for his service leading ranging companies. One of these grants was 320 acres located on the Frio River. He gathered all the paperwork for that plot, along with his other land grants, and put the documents in the care of Judge Calvert until the war with Mexico was finished.

Jack sold a section of land, 640 acres, located in Guadalupe County that he had acquired in payment for surveying fees. He also had most of his unspent pay. He set aside funds for construction of a two-story frame house in the two hundred block of South Presa Street in San Antonio. Work on the house was progressing, and Jack kept close watch on the activities there. Along with all his official duties, Jack managed to make frequent trips to Seguin so he and Susan could spend time together, usually taking long buggy rides for picnics in isolated spots where they could be alone.

Early morning April 28 found a large cadre of Jack's friends, including myself, on the road to Seguin. Sam Walker, Ben McCulloch, Bigfoot Wallace, and Mike Chevaille were with us, along with a host of veteran Rangers recently resigned. Also along were a number of individuals from several communities and settlements who felt indebted to Jack for his many contributions to their safety. The weather was calm, sunny, and not too warm. Spring showers had already caused the prairie to burst into a riot of color.

When we arrived, we found the entire population of Seguin and were joined by whole families who knew either Jack and/or Judge Carter. They came from Austin, Houston, San Antonio, and Washington-on-the-Brazos. Many politicians were among those who wanted to join the festivities. The judge was forced to change the venue to the Magnolia Hotel, but the hotel's largest room was not large enough to accommodate everyone. Some folks were left to stand in the lobby, others in the street, all straining to hear through open doors and windows.

Susan's wedding dress was the same one her mother wore for her wedding, originally shipped all the way from Paris. Only slight alterations were necessary for it to fit Susan. Standing in front of a bower of native flowers, the couple recited their vows.

The following day, all of us from San Antonio accompanied the newlyweds on their journey home. Jack drove Mrs. Riddle's buggy with Mrs. Riddle and Susan, his horse tied to the back. Our procession was met at the Salado River crossing by many well-wishers from Salado, including fourteen carriages of ladies.

Major Chevaille arranged a welcome for the newlyweds in San Antonio. Jack and Susan proceeded to the Alamo, where they were saluted with military honors. They walked under the crossed rifles of the regiment and then through the gates of the Alamo. Bells rang from every church in town, as well as the huge alarm bell of the city. Inside the Alamo, the couple found a huge barbeque party already in progress. There was music, dancing, the rapid consumption of two whole roasted steers, and plenty of fixings. Of course, there was also a profusion of toasts to the smiling, laughing bride and her new painfully shy and embarrassed husband.

For the next four days, there was a party every night. Jack and Susan were too polite to refuse attending. During this time, they did manage to steal time away for long buggy rides into the countryside. The owner of the livery stable kept a matched pair of bay geldings to pull the four-wheeled open buggy they used. The couple made a fine display as they trotted out of town, waving and responding to the well-wishes of almost everyone they passed.

The spring wildflowers were in full bloom, their fragrance all but overpowering, as smothering as a heavy blanket. It was a floral potpourri that defied the identification of any single specific flower. The sky was blue, as only the spring Texas sky could be—the color matching that of the profusion of bluebonnets that dominated the countryside. Wispy white cotton clouds drifted across the sky, enhancing the calm that at that particular moment embraced the frontier—a calm that Susan knew, but Jack would never admit, was directly the result of Col. Jack Hays's strength, bravery, dedication, and untiring efforts.

After their picnics, the couple would leisurely begin their return for home. It was Jack's custom to hand the reins to Susan, jump out of the buggy, and run alongside the fast-moving trotters. He was determined to be as fit and ready for battle as any man in his regiment.

On May 14, Hays's regiment of Texas Mounted Volunteers left San Antonio, headed for Monterrey. A vast majority of the men had enlisted for only six months, as Jack had predicted would be their preference. The colonel's intent was to cross the Rio Grande at Laredo, but on the very day they left San Antonio, General Taylor, safe in Matamoros, issued an order that completely ignored the instructions of Governor Henderson and Secretary of War Marcy. His order stated that any man not mustered for the duration of the war, or a minimum of twelve months, should return to his place of enlistment and be discharged.

Taylor sent a messenger to intercept Hays's regiment with this order. The messenger caught up with us at the Nueces River.

Jack read the order and then reread it. He dismounted and walked off into the brush, his hands behind his back, muttering under his breath. Bigfoot Wallace, Ben McCulloch, and I caught up to him.

"What the hell is going on Jack?" asked Ben.

Jack said nothing—just handed us the paper crumpled in his fist. Ben read it, Bigfoot and I looking over his shoulder.

"Well, Old Rough and Ready's living up to his name," said Bigfoot, shaking his head. "Does that asshole ever do anything right"

"Rarely," responded Jack. "Well, let's spread the word. We'll head back home. I hope all of these men get paid, because if they don't, I'm going to raise some kind of hell back in Washington."

The regiment returned to San Antonio. To Jack's relief, the men were paid, albeit not until several weeks after they were formally mustered out. On July 6, Jack received a message from Governor Henderson officially appointing him commander of the Texas frontier. He was ordered to establish a line of defense all along the line that extended from the Arkansas River to the Rio Grande where it emptied into the Gulf of Mexico.

Only two days later, Jack received an order from the secretary of war. It was dated June 2, more than a month late in getting to him. The order directed him to take whatever portion of his command that could be spared from the frontier and report to General Taylor, who was back in Monterrey.

The war with Mexico was heating up again. The press reported on Mexican atrocities—some real, most of them imagined. The effect was to generate overwhelming support for the war, a phenomenon long repeated in the history of man. If the war was lost, Texas was at risk, and the newspapers left no doubt about that. In a matter of days, Jack re-recruited his seven-hundred-man regiment, this time with twelve-month enlistments, and they were mustered into federal service.

Jack's new title was Colonel Commanding the First Texas Mounted Volunteers. He wrote to General Taylor, informing him of his prior obligation to protect the frontier against the recent increase in Indian depredations. He informed Taylor that he would require time to assemble his new command and see to the protection of the frontier.

Taylor received Jack's dispatches on July 21. He sent orders back for Jack to leave whatever forces he deemed necessary for frontier protection and bring the remainder, a minimum of five companies, to meet up with him at Mier. Taylor indicated he had not received any authentic news from US Command in Mexico for more than a month. He was occupied in training his soldiers in camps at Mier and Buena Vista but was more concerned about addressing the rate of illness among his men while they were idle. However, he further reported the guerrillas were, apparently, in good health. The attacks on his supply lines were increasing.

Jack sent a long and detailed report to R. W. Jones, the adjutant general in Washington, describing where strategic posts needed to be located and named the men he believed should command those posts. He added a statement that was extremely unusual for him—criticism of another officer. Before he included the statement, he showed me a draft.

"I regret having to speak in terms of reprehension of an officer ... Ranger companies along our frontier have been kept in a state of almost total uselessness, whilst in the pay of the United States ... during the tenure of the present commander of operations in Northern Mexico."

"Damn, Jack, you are too kind. I think Taylor is useless and would say so," I told him.

When we arrived in northern Mexico, we found a large percentage of Taylor's army was in poor health and not receiving proper care. Jack usurped the responsibility of recruiting and communicating with physicians. He conducted inspections of hospitals and made certain all necessary supplies were delivered. He listened to and responded to all patient complaints and corrected deficiencies of care discovered during his inspections. He also sent an urgent dispatch to the adjutant general, complaining that the federal government was "considerably in arrears" with the payment of his Rangers on active duty.

We were only vaguely aware of how the war with Mexico was progressing. We learned that General Scott captured Veracruz on March

29. Scott met little in the way of direct resistance on the road to Mexico City, which he entered on September 13. Gen. Santa Anna renounced the presidency of Mexico three days later. But all was not well with the US forces.

The previous August, while Scott was still on the way to Mexico City, the Mexican government, at Santa Anna's urging, sent out a call for all loyal Mexicans who resided within eighty miles of any position occupied by the Americans to form guerrilla bands and prevent supplies and communications from reaching those positions and to disrupt communications between Mexico City and Veracruz. The only way Scott was able to get supplies through was to send regiment-sized forces with the wagon trains. He complained to his superiors in Washington that any of his wounded or sick left in villages, towns, or cities along the way between the coast and Mexico City were murdered. He was not even able to protect hospitals in large towns from these attacks. For all practical purposes, regular communication with Veracruz was cut off.

President Polk called Secretary Marcy to his office and started berating him before Marcy could sit down.

"What the hell is happening with Scott in Mexico, Marcy? The reports are most distressing."

"I assume you are referring to General Scott's recent dispatches concerning his problems of communication between Mexico City and Veracruz?"

"Indeed, but I would describe it as more than problems. Our wounded and sick men are being murdered in hospitals, and Scott is powerless to stop it. He says he is unable to bring supplies and medical care through without a whole regiment to protect the wagons? That is not acceptable, Marcy."

"I agree, Mr. President, but the guerrillas are causing problems. They attack and disappear into the rest of the population, who protect and hide them. This is hardly a legitimate form of warfare."

"I was not aware that any form of war was legitimate. You do know that these are the very same tactics our forefathers used during the Revolution?"

"Yes, of course. What I mean is the regular army is not trained and, apparently, is not capable of dealing effectively with these tactics."

"Well, Mr. Secretary, I suggest there is a way to deal with this. Col. John C. Hays has raised a regiment of mounted volunteers from Texas, has he not?"

"I am assured that he has. Yes, sir."

"Well then, he is the most experienced commander in our army at fighting Indians and bandits—a good example of guerrilla warfare. I suggest you order him and his regiment to proceed to Veracruz at his earliest opportunity. Hays will know how to solve this problem for us. Get with it, Mr. Marcy."

CHAPTER 14

PRESIDENT POLK AND Secretary Marcy understood from the beginning that it would be impossible to occupy and control all of Mexico. They ordered Scott to occupy Mexico City, maintain control of Veracruz and its port, and establish and maintain regular communication between Veracruz and Mexico City.

After he occupied Mexico City, General Scott did all he could to assist Polk's envoy, N. P. Trist, to negotiate a satisfactory peace treaty with the new government of Manuel de la Peña y Peña. The negotiations stalled. Gen. Santa Anna, commanding eight thousand troops, besieged Puebla where Col. Thomas Child commanded only four hundred men.

Brig. Gen. Joseph Lane was a political appointee, but a soldier with ability. As soon as he learned of the siege of Puebla, he began marching to that city, intending to relieve Colonel Child. Santa Anna was soon bored with the siege of Puebla. He decided some other task was more important and took twenty-five hundred men with him, leaving Gen. Joaquin Rea to manage the siege. When President Peña y Peña learned Santa Anna had abandoned the siege of Puebla, he removed him as head of the army. Santa Anna understood the resolve and might of the American forces and was happy to turn over his command to Gen. Isidro Reyes and return to his estates and family only seventy miles southeast of Puebla. As General Lane drew closer to Puebla, General Rea retreated to Atlixco, twenty-five miles away, leaving Puebla to the Americans.

Jack's instructions were clear: get himself and his men to the Gulf

Coast with their horses in good shape and wait there for transport to Veracruz. We marched from Mier to Brazos de Santiago in easy stages, so as to not tire men or horses. From there, Jack sent the first detachment of men, horses, and supplies to Veracruz on the ship that was waiting for them. Other detachments were sent as ships arrived with space to carry them. We were all reunited in Veracruz on October 17.

We set up our camp in Vergara, about three miles from Veracruz. Jack, Bigfoot, and I frequently went out to scout the countryside, usually accompanied by ten or twelve men. One day we were heading west, toward Santa Fe, on a road where guerrillas frequently attacked supply wagons. As we approached a bend in the road, Bigfoot pulled up.

"I see some movement in those trees at the start of the bend, Jack. You see it?"

"Yes, indeed I do … You don't suppose there's Mexicans trying to set an ambush, do you?"

"I suspect so."

"All right then, why don't we just sit here a spell and see what happens?"

"Sounds like a plan to me," answered Bigfoot. "You boys might want to dismount and check the loads in your rifles and revolvers. Be ready."

We didn't have to wait long. There was a rush of movement from both sides of the road as nearly two hundred men mounted their horses. They, no doubt, felt secure in the knowledge that they could overwhelm us. They charged. We all waited, still sitting our horses, but every man took careful aim with his rifle. When the charging Mexicans were still over a hundred yards away, Jack hollered, "*Now.*" Thirteen guerrillas fell from their saddles, their riderless horses running into the brush and trees on either side of the road. The Mexicans momentarily stopped but quickly regrouped and spurred their horses forward, thinking to attack before we could reload our rifles. We charged directly at them, firing our six-shot revolvers with deadly accuracy. Sixty more riderless horses fled, and the guerrillas scattered, leaving dead and wounded on the road. We were untouched. We left the dead guerrillas lying in the road and returned to camp. The first band of Mexican guerrillas had experienced the bite of Colonel Hays's Texas Rangers.

One day Ben McCulloch returned from a patrol. Jack asked his adjutant, John Ford, to write up Ben's official report, one of the tasks he was happy to relinquish. I happened to be nearby.

"So, Ben, after you encountered the fifty guerrillas, what happened?" Ford asked him.

"They spotted us and tried to run."

"Fifty of them decided to run from eleven of you?'

"I reckon our reputation proceeds us," McCulloch said with a smirk.

"So it would seem. Then what happened?"

"We chased 'em."

"And?"

"Killed some of 'em."

"Some of them? How many of them?"

"Well, not certain, maybe five or so."

"Five or so? Look here, Ben. We need accurate reports. Jack has to send these official reports to all those stiff-backed generals. The truth now. How many did you kill?"

"No more than twenty-five."

Jack's intent was to establish the lethality and effectiveness of his Rangers, not only for the enemy but for his American commanders. Word of our ruthlessness and ferocity spread quickly. Quite a few of us witnessed or experienced Santa Anna's depredations during the Texas War of Independence. All remembered the Alamo and the massacre at Goliad. Many of our men suffered at the hands of Mexican bandits who came across the border to raid. Those bandits stole animals, and more than a few of the men lost loved ones, a few whole families. Those men were in Mexico for a measure of revenge and were determined to exact it.

Eventually, and inevitably, we were ordered to report to General Scott in Mexico City. At that juncture, because several of our companies were ordered to serve other units as scouts, we were left with only 580 men under Jack's direct command.

Jack's orders were to join a convoy, led by Gen. Robert Patterson, to make the journey to Mexico City. He placed some of us as advanced scouts and the rest to guard the flanks and rear of the long column of marching infantry, a few units of regular cavalry, and many wagons loaded with supplies. The convoy included more than three thousand men.

Jack recruited an English musician by the name of Self, a violin player of some renown in Veracruz. Jack told me he thought it might be good for the men to have some diversion when in camp. I, and most of the others, knew Jack was prone to practical jokes. Self was a tenderfoot. Soon after Self arrived in camp, Jack arranged for some of his men to stage a mock

Indian attack. Self was terrified. Jack tried to atone, but Self sulked, lagging behind the column. He was observed taking frequent mouthfuls from one of several bottles of tequila he managed to acquire along the way. Two nights later, Jack searched for the man, but was unable to find him. The next morning, he took Bigfoot aside.

"We seem to have misplaced our violin player. Why don't you take a few men and backtrack to find him? I presume he will be somewhere along the road, probably drunk."

"When did you last see him, Jack? I can't recall seeing him for a couple of days."

"I saw him day before yesterday and noticed he was still sucking on a bottle. I'm worried he might have fallen far behind and gotten himself into some trouble."

Bigfoot and I took six men with us and rode back along the column until we were well past the rearguard. We didn't find the musician. We continued down the same road for at least three hours, scouring the fields and woods on either side of the road for any sign of the lost violin player. It was dusk when we heard violin music coming from a grove of trees off to the left of where we sat our walking horses. Bigfoot held up his hand.

"Hold up, boys. I don't think he's playin' that fiddle for himself. John and I will go in on foot and see what we have waitin' for us."

We crept as silently through the brush and trees as any Comanche and worked our way in until we spotted a campfire with a dozen heavily armed guerrillas. They were gathered around the musician, who was dancing while he fiddled, his eyes wide open, scanning wildly around at the desperados who encircled him. We made our way back, and Bigfoot whispered instructions to the men with us. Before long, the unsuspecting guerrillas were surrounded. We fired from cover and shot at the guerrillas; two fell dead, and several others were wounded. Those who could run scattered into the woods.

"Let 'em go, boys. They'll spread the word about the devil Rangers bein' invisible at night."

Self, oblivious and still too drunk to notice, continued to fiddle and dance. Bigfoot walked up to him and slapped him on the back of his head.

"Enough, fiddler. You're saved. Act like a Ranger and help these boys gather up the horses them Mesicans left for us. We're gonna take the horses—and you—back up the road to Colonel Jack. For reasons I'll never understand, he's missed your worthless drunken ass."

Two nights later, several of us were under a bridge, sleeping on the ground. I sensed someone on horseback among us. At the same time, John Ford stirred and opened his eyes to see a stranger on horseback. Ford propped himself up on one elbow.

"What is it you want?" he asked.

"How long have you been in service?" asked the mounted man.

"What the hell difference does it make? answered Ford.

"How did you manage to obtain this protected spot?"

"We found it first."

"Who said you could have it?"

"None of your damn business."

"Listen, Soldier. You answer my questions."

"Fuck off."

"I'm wagon master of this convoy. If you assholes get sick, I'll make certain you don't get a ride in any of my wagons. That should teach you to have a smart mouth."

"Fuck off, John replied."

"Whose camp is this, Soldier?"

"It's Col. John C. Hays. That's him over there." He waved his hand at Jack's prone form wrapped in a serape. "If you like, I'll wake him, and you can tell him what you just told me."

The wagon master jerked his horse's head around and put spurs and quirt to the animal, departing the area hastily.

We rode to Puebla where Jack received new orders. The Texas volunteers were to keep the line of communication between Veracruz and Mexico City open. They were to pursue any guerrillas they encountered all the way to their retreats and destroy those safe havens.

When we rode into Puebla, one of Gen. Joe Lane's brigade, Lt. Albert Brackett, was among hundreds of American soldiers who watched us ride down the main street. Brackett befriended me. One evening while drinking cerveza, he confided in me.

"You certainly are an odd-looking set of fellows. It seems to me it is your aim to dress as outlandishly as possible. Bobtailed coats, long-tailed blues, low- and high-crowned hats, some slouched and others Panama, with a sprinkling of black leather caps. These are your uniforms? When you rode into town, you were all thoroughly covered in dust, including your beards. I've never seen a more savage-looking group of cutthroats. Your horses ranged from little mustangs to large American full-bloods and were every shade and color. Each man carried a rifle and two of Colt's revolvers. It seems to me a hundred of you could discharge a thousand shots in two minutes, and with what precision, the Mexicans and Indians alone can tell. I watched closely as you went silently by me and could distinguish no difference between the officers and men. None carried sabers, but all had long knives, hempen ropes or hair lariat, and most also carried a rawhide riata."

Colonel Hays and General Lane formed a friendship based on mutual trust and respect when they served under General Taylor at the battle of Monterrey. While in Puebla, Lane received intelligence that a body of Mexican troops, with several American prisoners, was camped near Izucardo. Lane suggested that Jack do something about the situation.

"I'm going along too, Jack, but I will not interfere. You are in command of this expedition. I'm anxious to see firsthand what it is that you do that is so damned effective and successful."

"Whatever you say, General. I will be more than happy to have your company."

Jack took me and 135 other Rangers with him. Lane ordered Lt. H. B. Field of the Third Artillery to accompany the expedition, with one cannon and thirty-five men. He also ordered Captain Lewis and a company of Louisiana Dragoons to support us.

We rode to Izucardo, through the night, in a cold, pelting rain reaching our destination at sunrise. We paused, hidden in the forest gazing at the enemy camp. It was shrouded in mist with only a few campfires valiantly struggling to provide some warmth to the early risers huddled over them. The officers gathered around Jack who drew a rough map of the camp and surroundings in the ground.

"We're here, hidden in the forest along this road. Their commander's tent is most likely the large one in the middle of the camp. Their animals are in the meadows on either side with forest beyond the meadows and next to the road as it continues. Lieutenant Field, you will initiate our attack by aiming a load of grapeshot at that large tent. Captain Lewis, move your men out and around to the east through the forest. Leave your animals here with men to hold them and don't make any noise as you position yourselves. I want two of the Ranger companies to do the same around to the west. I will lead the rest of the Rangers directly into the camp on the road. Bigfoot, what's your estimate of how many Mexicans are in that camp?"

"Four to six hundred, I'd say, Jack. Six hundred tops. Over to the north edge of the camp there are men with their hands tied behind their backs. They appear to be our American soldiers."

"All right then, let's get going. Pass the word to avoid their prisoners, but I want to strike before they are all up and about."

Fifteen minutes later, the cannon roared, and Jack charged down the road with us directly behind. The speed of our charge, the shouts of "Alamo," and our pistols picking targets overwhelmed the pickets. We spread out as we entered the camp, our horses knocking Mexicans off their feet. I saw the shot from our cannon had shredded the large tent. There were dead soldiers scattered among the remnants of the tent.

The Mexican forces were completely surprised. They panicked and scattered into the forest. Many ran directly into the Dragoons or our men and were killed or wounded. The whole action lasted no more than fifteen minutes. When it was over, I counted seventy-five killed. Among them was Colonel Piedras, the commander, and several of his officers. Twenty Mexicans surrendered. No Americans were killed or wounded. Twenty-one American prisoners were freed.

"Round up horses for our freed men. Make certain they are well armed," instructed Jack. "They will return with us as proud American soldiers." Then he gathered all the officers. "Let's destroy everything else in this camp, except the munitions. We'll pack them into four of those wagons. Make up four-mule hitches to pull the wagons. We'll take 'em back with us, but take care of all the wounded. Let's feed all the men and organize details of Mexican prisoners to bury their dead."

Early the following morning, the expedition left to return to Puebla. Twenty-five Rangers were assigned to an advance guard while a company of Rangers covered the rear of the column. About five miles from Izucardo, the column entered a steep mountain pass. The column strung out with the artillery and loaded wagons, falling farther behind as they struggled up the steep, winding mountain road. General Lane dropped back to encourage the men struggling with the gun, and the loaded wagons to keep up. After some time, Jack rode back along the column to see if he could add his encouragement to that of the General. After he arrived, he dispatched a squad of Rangers from the rear guard to go back along the road to make certain they were not being pursued.

Less than a half hour passed before the hard-riding scouts rejoined the slow-moving wagons and gun.

"At least two hundred Lancers comin' up fast, Colonel Jack," reported the sergeant.

Jack spurred his horse back down the road.

"You Rangers follow me," he shouted, but we were already directly behind him.

Without slowing our pace, we rode directly into the enemy, firing our revolvers with deadly effectiveness. The Mexican Lancers broke ranks and retreated across a wide plain, with thirty-five of us pursuing, Jack, of course in the lead.

Spurring hard, Jack was outdistancing the rest of us, but the Mexican horses were fresher than ours. Jack was still too far away from the enemy for his revolvers to be effective. He holstered the one in his hand and drew his revolving rifle from its scabbard. He swung the rifle over his head, encouraging us to catch up, and then he settled his rifle to his shoulder and fired. A Mexican tumbled from his saddle.

The Lancers raced full tilt across a wide prairie and then rode up into some foothills. By then, their horses were exhausted. Halfway up the hill, their officers ordered them to stop, dismount, and make a stand with their shotguns. The exhausted and terrified soldiers, never accurate with their shotguns, fired wildly as we plunged in among them, able to again use our Colt Walkers that we reloaded while chasing them. However, this time we did not escape unscathed. Bill Williams was shot from his saddle. Another man I didn't recognize was thrown to the ground, and his horse was killed. Several of our men were wounded but stayed in their saddles. The Lancers scattered and fled again, this time over the top of the hill.

Out of the corner of his eye, Jack spotted movement from a ravine near the top of the hill. Fresh Lancers were starting to form up, preparing to charge us, and we were almost out of ammunition.

"Let's get back to the column, boys," Jack shouted. "Make certain you stay with any who are wounded. John, scoop up that man who got his horse shot out from under him. If Bill is dead, we'll have to leave him."

We trotted our horses back down the slope, reloading our weapons.

"I'll provide cover," said Jack. "The rest of you men help the wounded to keep moving."

Jack waited until all of the wounded were being supported and moving down the hill to the prairie. Those of us who were riding double with the most severely wounded reached the level ground of the prairie and quickened our pace. Jack turned his horse, took careful aim with his revolving rifle, and brought down two charging Lancers still more than two hundred yards away. He turned his horse, raced down the hill another four hundred yards, and then turned and brought down two more Mexicans. After reaching the prairie, he galloped his horse a half a mile while placing a full cylinder in his revolving rifle. The next time he stopped and turned to face them, the Lancers reined in and started moving in a zigzag fashion to avoid the deadly fire from the one lone American. Every time Jack turned, he shot another Mexican, and the Lancers' advance was slowed. When we finally entered the pass, Jack spurred his horse to join us and then organized us into a defensive position to prevent the Mexicans from entering the pass. General Lane, hearing the sound of the battle, arrived with a company to the pass entrance where he greeted Jack.

"Welcome back, Colonel. I suggest you send a man to catch up with the column and return with the rest of your Rangers and the Dragoons."

"Sounds like an idea, General." He turned in his saddle and caught my eye. The man I saved was on the ground, and I had remounted. "John, did you hear the General's suggestion?"

"Yep," I told him.

"Well get to it."

Jack and his men held the Mexicans at bay until I returned with reinforcements, whereupon Jack led another charge. The enemy retreated back across the prairie and then dispersed into the mountains. I am pretty certain we killed at least fifty Mexicans that day and wounded many more. We only lost two men, and five were wounded.

In two full days of travel, we covered 125 miles, rescued twenty-one American soldiers, and dispersed more than a thousand Mexican soldiers under the command of General Rea. We managed to drive the Mexican army out of that region.

I learned later that in his report on this mission, General Lane praised Jack and our Rangers but also observed that most military officers, in his experience, think in linear terms, focused on the steady progression of the war and their battle front, with their minds absorbed with their promotions and medals. He observed that Jack approached warfare sideways, as an amateur. Killing the enemy was only part of the process. Colonel Hays relied on surprise and guile to disorient, alarm, and embarrass his foes. His approach was more three-dimensional than linear.

CHAPTER 15

THE RANKS OF Jack Hays's First Texas Mounted Volunteers were predominantly filled by men who had served in various ranging companies since the Republic of Texas was formed. We were purposely colorful, efficient, and a most deadly band of irregular partisans. No such band of warriors had existed, for so long a time, in the United States. We were called into being by the needs of an almost continuous war along an extended frontier by a society that could not afford a regular army. Texans passed in and out of the ranging companies as they were formed and disbanded, but an extremely high proportion of west Texas men served at one time or another. Now we rode into Mexico City.

Jack made friends quickly, and a Colonel Dumont was his most recent. Dumont wrote about our entry into Mexico City:

> Hays's men entered the city of the Aztecs and approached the Halls of Montezuma … the subject of universal curiosity. The sides of the streets were lined with spectators of every hue and grade. Not a word was spoken. They seemed unconscious that they were the observed of all observers. The trees in their own native forests would have attracted as much of their attention as they seemed to bestow upon anything around them.

Our adjutant, Robert Ford, showed me what he wrote in his journal about that parade into the city: "The greatest curiosity prevailed to get a sight of *Los Diablos Tejanos*—The Texas Devils."

Without warning, a Mexican threw a rock into a group of Rangers riding past, knocking the hat off one of them. The hatless Ranger drew his revolver, shot the offender in the head, leaned over the side of his horse, grabbed his hat off the road, and put the hat back on his head while his horse kept pace with all the other animals. Not a word was spoken. No expression registered on any of our faces. A few blocks later, another rock was thrown, another immediate response from a revolver, and another Mexican lay dead on the street. The only other sounds heard were shod hooves striking the paving stones and the creaking of saddle leather.

We were dressed, as always, in anything that came to hand—some with blankets over their shoulders, some in their shirtsleeves, but all of us were well mounted and bristled with weapons. We offered a sight never before seen in the streets of Mexico, and the usually noisy street thugs, known as *léperos*, were as still as death while we passed. Our gallant commander appeared to be the object of peculiar interest, and the better-informed class of Mexicans were particularly anxious to have pointed out to them the man whose name had been the terror of their nation for the past twelve years.

We were all violent men, with short fuses, especially with regard to assaults upon our person. We customarily met any such assault with immediate, excessive violence. Our intent was to discourage any repetition of the offense. Assault upon one's person, for most Texans, extended to his hat or bandanna. You just didn't touch a Texan's hat or bandanna without permission.

The same evening we Tejanos arrived in Mexico City, a group of us were standing in a line to enter a theater. A thief grabbed my bandanna and ran. Before he was more than five strides away, I drew my Colt Walker and shot the thief dead. I walked over to the dead man, retrieved my bandanna, and rejoined my friends.

When General Scott was informed of the killing, he ordered Jack to report to him immediately, along with the man responsible for the shooting, outside the theater.

We marched into the general's opulent office in the Montezuma Castle. Scott sat behind a baroque carved and gilded desk. We halted, stood at attention, and saluted.

"Col. John C. Hays, reporting as ordered, sir."

Jack told me beforehand to keep my mouth shut. He would do all the talking.

"I have learned, Colonel, that since your arrival in this city only yesterday, your men have murdered three Mexican citizens. I will not have it, sir. You are responsible for your men's behavior. I am disgraced by these killings, as is the army of our country. Do you admit to the veracity of these reports?"

"Yes, sir. My men punished three offenders."

"Without due process, Colonel. These are not the actions of civilized men and certainly not of obedient, disciplined soldiers."

"With your permission, General, I would explain the actions of my men."

"I will listen, sir, but I will be hard to convince."

Jack spoke calmly, showing little emotion but great sincerity. We both remained standing at attention.

"All—I repeat, sir, all—of the men in my command have suffered personal loss attributable to Mexican soldiers or Mexican bandits. They have also suffered at the hands of the Comanche and other Indian tribes who maintain commerce with Mexico, trading captives and stolen livestock, particularly horses, to Mexican citizens, for the food and manufactured items they desire. My men have lost brothers and fathers, sisters and mothers, sons and daughters, uncles and aunts, nephews and nieces, cousins and friends. We have all seen settlers and family members cruelly tortured to death. Men, young and old, with their privates cut off or hot coals placed on those regions. Women and girls with their breasts hacked off and their wombs removed, their shrieks of anguish still apparent on their dead faces. At the Alamo, Santa Anna ordered no prisoners were to be taken. At Goliad, four hundred men who surrendered were marched out of the city and slaughtered by the Mexican Army. At Mier and other places where captured Texans were taken, they suffered horribly in Mexican prisons, and most did not survive. I am told that every night a number of your soldiers are stabbed and killed, found dead in the street the next morning. That will not happen to any of my men. Anyone who attacks my men will be immediately shot dead."

Jack took a deep breath. "General, I know you are not accustomed to men as ruthless as mine. However, you can ask any of the officers of your army with whom I have served. They will tell you that my men will follow me to hell and obey my every order, without ever asking a question or doubting my authority. Among the Comanche and the Mexicans, I am known as Devil Jack, and for good reason. In battle, I am determined and ruthless, and my men emulate me. We generate fear in our enemies, and that accounts for much of our success. If you want your communications with Veracruz reestablished and kept open, turn me and my men loose. We will get it done."

I, somehow, managed not to grin as General Scott's demeanor changed from indignation to interest to respect. It was the longest recitation I had ever heard coming from my friend. His words were made more meaningful because they were delivered in a calm, quiet voice that forced the general to lean forward to hear. After Jack finished, the general waited for almost a full minute to make certain Jack was finished. Then he smiled.

"Colonel, you and your man have a seat. Have you acquired a taste for tequila, or are you both Tennessee whiskey men?"

"Thank you, General. A small dose of Tennessee whiskey would not be unwelcome," Jack agreed.

The three of us sipped our whiskeys as the general questioned Jack about his family and especially about his connection to President Jackson, whom he had served under.

I was not tempted to disobey my commander and said nothing.

We left Scott's headquarters with the understanding that Jack would do his best to hold his men's acts of retribution to clear incidents of self-defense.

However, the attacks on other American soldiers in Mexico City did not abate. Any soldier caught drunk or wandering alone was likely to be murdered. It was a rare night when no soldier was attacked and killed. Most mornings up to a half dozen American corpses were found in the streets. The léperos also robbed and assaulted their own people. Their goal was to foment chaos in the city. One of their favorite ploys was to walk the streets in large groups. Whenever such a group encountered an American officer going in the same direction, they would increase their pace and pretend to accidently bump into the officer, pushing him into the gutter as they hurried past. However, when these goons spotted one of us Texans, they soon discovered urgent business in the opposite direction.

Rangers Van Walling and Pete Goss were walking down a street one evening when a band of léperos, standing on a roof where they had accumulated a supply of large rocks, started throwing rocks at them. At the same time, another band of léperos, their knives in their hands, charged at the two Rangers. Walling and Goss pulled their revolvers out and started firing. They soon killed two of the attackers and wounded several others, including two of the men on the roof. The Mexican thugs fled the scene, dragging their dead and wounded with them.

Adam Allsens, a Ranger in Captain Roberts's company, was riding through a barrio known as Cutthroat. He was suddenly surrounded by knife-wielding thugs and was severely slashed, but he managed to spur his horse through the mob. His wounds were so severe one of the doctors treating him remarked he could see Allsens's heart beating through one of the wounds in his chest. Allsens died but was able to provide details about the place where he was attacked and descriptions of some of his attackers.

Nobody from Roberts's company said anything, but it was clearly understood by all the Rangers that vengeance would be extracted.

The following evening Jack was at dinner with a group of senior officers. He told me that one of the officers asked what our response to the brutal murder of one of our own would be. Jack told him he could not arrest men for an act they might or might not be contemplating.

Two nights later, the sound of revolvers being fired came from the offending barrio. The gunshots continued for almost two hours. No police, military or local, were dispatched to discover or stop whatever was happening. The next morning, more than eighty bullet-ridden male bodies were found in the streets of the barrio.

Some of the Rangers devised another strategy to discourage the attacks. They would join a party in progress and pretend to get drunk. They would leave the party stumbling and mumbling. When an assassin approached with his knife ready to do damage, the Ranger would pull his six-shooter and blast the thug into oblivion.

Jack was again ordered to present himself to General Scott. He later told me what transpired.

"The General said there seemed to be increasing numbers of Mexican civilians found dead in the streets each morning. In fact, he said, 'I am told that recently more than eighty corpses were found in one neighborhood.' He asked if I had any information about the situation and added that his military police seem to be in the dark. I told him that I had no direct knowledge of any of my men being involved in these incidents."

Jack said Scott stared at him silently for two full minutes.

"I met his gaze without flinching and said nothing."

Jack was then told that he would shortly receive orders to keep the road to Veracruz clear of the persistent guerrilla attacks on his supply trains. Scott added that he was reasonably certain this will also reduce the numbers of dead Mexicans found each morning.

Scott smiled at Jack, and Jack kept a straight face. "Yes, sir," Jack told him. "My men will be happy to be of use."

Within a few weeks, Jack established outposts along the road between Veracruz and Mexico City. Each outpost was charged with maintaining patrols and eliminating any guerrilla bands they encountered.

One of the most notorious guerrilla leaders was a man known as Padre Jarauta. He was in command of a large band of mounted bandits and Lancers. The Lancers deserted their units to join his cause after their commanders ordered their units to retreat before they even confronted the approaching Americans. It was also rumored that nearly four hundred Mexican infantrymen joined Jarauta's banner.

Our Tejanos spoke Spanish as a first language and were able to mingle freely with the Mexican population as spies. Late one evening three of these men brought word that Padre Jarauta was at San Juan Teotihuacan, not far from Mexico City. Jack immediately mobilized a company of sixty-five Rangers. After riding hard for three hours, we arrived at San Juan and silently entered, arriving at the large main plaza after midnight. The Zócalo was surrounded by stone buildings, but one edifice occupied almost all of one side of the plaza. Jack rode up to a wall of the house, stood on his saddle, and pulled himself up to look into the courtyard. Behind the tall, heavy oak gate of the house was a large stone-paved area with stables taking up one whole side. There were, in fact, enough stables to house all of our horses. Jack scrambled back down and rode over to where Bigfoot Wallace and I waited.

"We'll use this place as our headquarters. Bigfoot, gain entry and talk to the owner. Explain to him that we will not molest his family or people or take anything from them, not even their food. John, you make those orders clear to the men."

Bigfoot, accompanied by three other men, scaled the back wall of the house, awakened a servant, and were led to the master's bedroom. They woke him, and Bigfoot explained the situation. The owner of the house went to the front gate, barefoot and still in his sleeping clothes, and opened the gate.

"Señor Colonel Hays, I know your reputation. You and your men are welcome in my house. The bandit Jarauta taxes me heavily, taking my crops and animals without payment. My house is your house."

"Thank you, señor. What is your name?"

"My name is Don Diego Vicente Garcia de Altoban. I am patron of the hacienda lands extending out from the east side of this village. I am appreciative of your pledge to not do me or my family or any of my people harm. Also, to not take any of my property."

"You can rely on the honesty and obedience of my men. I have given my orders, and they will respect you, your people, and your possessions."

After all our horses were cared for, we ate some of the dried meat we brought along as rations and boiled coffee over small campfires in the courtyard. The owner of the house insisted that we use some of his firewood for our fires. After eating, most of the men curled up on the paving stones and fell asleep.

"John," Jack called out. "Take five men and stand guard just outside the gate. Make certain you and your men are fully armed and ready for anything."

"All right, Jack."

Soon, all was quiet, and then, from three side streets leading into the plaza, twenty mounted men charged across the plaza toward the gate. My small squad repulsed them with rifles and revolvers blazing. Jack pushed open the gate enough to slip out. He immediately saw men on the flat roofs of many of the houses surrounding the plaza, and they were aiming their fire at the gate, albeit with little accuracy. He pointed out to me at least seventy-five more mounted men obviously preparing to storm the house. Several were holding unlit sticks of dynamite. He ordered us all back inside and slammed the gate closed.

"Bigfoot, take a squad of our best sharpshooters to the roof of this house and keep those men on the other roofs pinned down. John, organize two squads of men and have them ready to dash through the gate to meet the next charge." He looked over his shoulder and spotted Ben McCulloch. "Ben, take your best shooters and use the loopholes in that wall to take out those men holding dynamite sticks, preferably as soon as they light them."

We waited only a few minutes.

"All right, men. Here they come," Jack murmured.

The leader of the mounted guerrillas moved forward, but one of his officers spurred his horse forward and rushed past his commander, anxious to be the hero of the day. The gate of the house was flung open, and we ran through, spreading out on either side of the opening where Jack stood, a revolver in each hand, surrounded by ten of us. The hard-riding Mexican officer, while still out of revolver range, was the first to be knocked off his horse by one of the sharpshooters.

When he fell from his saddle, the charging Lancers following him pulled up.

"I think they expect us to run into their lances, boys," Jack shouted. "Take careful aim and take down all you can."

One Mexican officer on the left flank pushed his horse forward. He rode obliquely across, in front of his men, trying to encourage them to continue the charge, but he was also oblique to us. A well-aimed ball from Bigfoot's rifle lifted him over the saddlebow and over the head of his horse. The Mexicans retreated.

"Colonel Jack," one of his spies hissed into his ear, "that one preparing his men to charge us from your left is Padre Jarauta."

"I see him." Jack shouted, "On the left, boys. That's Jarauta who thinks he is going to come at us close to the wall of this house. He intends to separate us from the house and prevent any more of our men from coming out to help. Bigfoot, keep those men on the rooftops down."

Jarauta extended his sword, spurred his horse, and, as Jack predicted, led the charge parallel to and close to the wall of the house. However, Jarauta and his men had never fought experienced, highly trained, and disciplined Rangers or any enemy with the ability to accurately aim twelve balls at them before reloading. As they approached, Jarauta's men were blasted from their saddles, along with those guerrillas brave enough to charge again from across the plaza opposite the gate.

In a few moments, there was mass confusion as falling Mexicans and terrified horses enabled us to stand our ground, bringing down Mexicans until our revolvers were empty. We quickly changed cylinders and continued our deadly fire. Jarauta was knocked from his horse, hit by a ball from the revolver in Jack's left hand, as well as balls from the revolvers of several others. Some of Jarauta's men dismounted and tried to carry their leader to safety, but they were killed or wounded as they struggled to carry him away. More rescuers came and finally dragged him to safety into one of the nearby buildings. Those Mexicans still mounted rode out of the plaza, and those on the rooftops disappeared.

"Ben, bring your men and come with me," shouted Jack.

They brought their horses out into the courtyard, saddled them, and rode out to make certain the Mexicans had, indeed, left the area. Jack and Ben returned as the sun broke over the horizon. They rode into the courtyard, removed their saddles, gave each horse a portion of grain, and began to curry and brush the animals.

"I counted fifteen dead and five wounded so bad they were unable to get themselves out of the courtyard. I reckon many more wounded were able to gather their horses and ride off. None of our men were hurt. That one officer tryin' to rally the troops is in bad shape, unconscious," reported Bigfoot.

"All right, Bigfoot. Please find families in these houses who are willing to take the officer and other wounded in and care for them," Jack said.

"You got it, Jack. We did find Jarauta's horse. The poor animal has got several balls in him and is in bad shape. The saddle is covered with blood, but we couldn't find Jarauta. I reckon they managed to cart him off with the rest of their wounded."

"All right, see to it that the horse is put out of his misery and any others you find that are hurt badly enough you don't think they can recover on their own. Let the men get some rest. We'll head back to Mexico City this afternoon. I imagine Don de Altoban will be happy to see our backsides."

Jack was again summoned to the headquarters of General Scott and took me along. I was, again, instructed to keep my mouth shut.

"I have read the reports of your thirty-hour, one-hundred-plus mile jaunt and success against the guerrilla Padre Jarauta, Colonel. My understanding is that he is badly wounded and, in all probability, will not trouble us in the foreseeable future. Good work. I have another task for you."

"Yes, sir," Jack responded.

"Why is this man always with you?"

"This is Lt. John Caperton, sir. He is one of my oldest friends, and I like to keep him close at all times."

"Whatever. I want you to gather four companies of your Rangers. I am assigning Major Polk, along with two companies of the Third Dragoons, and one company of the Mounted Rifle Regiment, to your command. You do know that Major Polk is the president's brother?"

"Yes, sir."

"Then you understand you are to watch out for his welfare?"

"Yes, sir."

"Good. You are to report to General Lane in Puebla. Your charge is to make all the country around Puebla free of all predatory guerrilla bands. However, Mexico City is full of spies who report our every move to the enemy. I don't want anyone to know of your mission until you have engaged and defeated the guerrillas."

"Yes, sir. I will only share our orders with my senior officers."

"Good. Brigadier General Marshall is on his way here with a wagon train. I expect him sometime tomorrow. I suggest you and your troops depart quietly in the very early hours. You can intercept him and learn what you can of the guerrillas' movements and actions. I will make it widely known that you are supplying an escort for Marshall's wagon train."

"Yes, sir."

As ordered, two hundred of us quietly rode out of Mexico City long before dawn the next day and found General Marshall's wagon train. We learned that a band of guerrillas had been threatening his rear guard for several days. We galloped to the rear of the long wagon train and then continued four miles beyond. But the guerrillas had departed. We moved on to Puebla, where Jack and I reported to General Lane.

"Welcome back, Jack, John. I'm glad you're here. This morning I received intelligence that Santa Anna is in Tehuacán with a hundred regular cavalry, and a significantly larger band of guerrillas. If we can grab him, it will advance our efforts appreciably."

"What's the plan, General?" Jack questioned.

Lane moved to his map table and motioned for us to join him. "I suggest we pretend we are on the way to Veracruz, then feint north at Amazoque ... here. When we reach this ravine"—he pointed at the place on the map with his quirt—"we abruptly change direction, and travel up this ravine into these mountains. There's a trail through them ... here." Again, he pointed. "The trail is about forty-five miles long and joins this road in the valley. If we can stay away from the natives, we may be able to surprise Santa Anna, capture him, and neutralize a large number of guerrilla fighters as well."

Jack stood motionless, studying the map. "Do you know anything about that mountain trail?" he asked.

"Not much. I'm told horses can get through, but nothing with wheels."

"All right, sounds good."

"Good," General Lane noted. "I want to go along like last time, but it's still your show. You will be in charge. Consider me an observer."

Jack smiled. "You mean you'll take orders from me?"

The general and Jack locked eyes; neither blinked. Lane broke first.

"Colonel … that will depend entirely on the orders."

"Thought so."

Both men smiled as General Lane clapped a hand on Jack's shoulder.

"Another thing, Jack. Doctors Brower and Wooster, Colonel Dumont, and Major McCoy are all anxious to accompany us. They want to see your men in action."

"This isn't going to be command by committee, is it?" Jack questioned.

"No, Colonel. I repeat—you are in charge."

First thing the next morning we left Puebla on the road to Veracruz. A flurry of bugle calls, beating drums, and shouted orders heralded our departure. When we reached Amazoque, we turned north. After our scouts reported that nobody was tracking our movements, we changed course again, following another detachment of scouts who had located the ravine. As night fell, the last company of men exited the ravine. A light rain began.

It didn't take long for our scouts to locate the trail leading into the foothills, but the trail soon proved to be more than a little difficult. It was narrow and rocky, and in many places, it skirted a sheer rock wall on one side with a precipitous drop on the other. We were forced to ride single file and often needed to dismount to lead our animals over or around rock slides, huge boulders, and spots where the trail had been partially washed away.

During the long night, it drizzled, then rained, and then rained harder, and then we were pounded by sleet. The sleet storm was followed by more rain. Even as tough and hardened we were, we suffered. Our clothing was saturated. Most of us huddled in our saddles, shivering. Daybreak found us in a long, wide, desolate high mountain valley. The scouts reported that there were two large haciendas at either end of the valley. Jack sent one company ahead to seize control of the far hacienda and led another company to take the one closest.

"I don't want anyone to get out and spread the word," he explained to Lane, who nodded his agreement.

We forced our way into the closest hacienda with pistols drawn. There was no resistance. Before long, Ben returned to tell us the far hacienda was also secured. Jack gathered all the officers.

"I want all our men to stay inside the walls of the haciendas. They are to unsaddle and care for their horses, but no one is to go outside the adobe walls. We'll hole up here and rest till nightfall. Make certain your men get something to eat, and make absolutely certain they don't cause any trouble for the dons or their households."

That night we departed, following a reasonably good road leading toward Tehuacán. We were on the road a little more than nine hours when an ornate coach, pulled by four matching mules in silver ornamented harnesses, was spotted by the advanced scouts under Bigfoot's command. The coach was quickly surrounded. Jack and I spurred forward, followed by Lane and our committee of observers. The scouts disarmed the twelve guards accompanying the coach. Bigfoot was holding the passenger and the driver of the coach at gunpoint, all three of them standing in the road.

As Jack rode up, the elegantly dressed passenger addressed him in Spanish. "Señor, I assume you are in command. My name is Jesus Cordoba Velasquez Luna." He reached slowly to the inside pocket of his coat and, with finger and thumb, removed a document. "I have here a safe-conduct signed by Gen. P. F. Smith, who commands this district."

Although it was slightly past dawn, the sky was heavy with low-hanging clouds, and the light was marginal.

"Bigfoot, put your revolver away and get me a torch," Jack directed.

When the torch was lit, Jack took the document and read it, with General Lane looking over his shoulder.

"What do you think, General?"

"It's General Smith's signature, Jack. I've seen it enough to recognize it. The safe-conduct pass appears to be written by him as well. I think it's the real thing."

"Well, General, I think we need to keep this man in custody until we are in Tehuacán. If we let him go, he's liable to sound a warning."

"It's a risk, Jack, but the document authorizes him to go wherever he pleases in this district."

"Where have you come from, señor, and where are you going?" asked Jack in Spanish.

"I come from Tehuacán and have business in Veracruz."

"And did you meet with Gen. Santa Anna in Tehuacán?"

"Yes, Señor Commander."

"And do you know how many troops the general has in that place?"

"No, señor. I did not count the troops."

"I think it very likely that if we let this man go, he will warn them, General. If he does, Santa Anna will get away from us."

"That may be, Colonel, but we are bound to honor his safe-conduct."

"We have a way to go yet, and if Santa Anna knows we're coming, he'll skedaddle," Jack insisted.

It was clear to me that Lane was losing patience.

"Do you know, Colonel, that according to our military laws, violating a safe-conduct is punishable by the death penalty?" Lane questioned.

"That so, General? Well, I'm willing to chance it. We won't detain this man for very long."

"I would rather you let this man go on his way, Colonel," Lane said.

"If you order me to do that, General, I will, of course, obey your order."

"Very well, Colonel Hays. I order you to let this man back in his carriage and allow him and his escort to proceed on their way."

"You heard the general. All you men move to the side and let this gentleman, his carriage, and his escort pass. After he's past, we're going to proceed as fast as we can down this road. I want to do all we can to get to Santa Anna before he learns we are on the way."

The carriage and its escort left, and we pushed our horses as hard as we could all that day and through the night, stopping to rest for no more than fifteen or twenty minutes every two hours.

As the sun broke through the clouds over the mountains east of us, Jack held up his hand.

"All officers at my side," he ordered, and we gathered around him, still mounted.

"After that forced march, our horses are exhausted. However, I want to rush this town as quickly as possible. If any enemy resistance is encountered, I want every man to fight through it. We know how to do this. Speed, determination, and our skill with firearms will prevail. We must succeed because after this push our horses will be too tired to retreat. Bigfoot, where have your scouts spotted their sentinels?"

Bigfoot pointed out where the known sentinels were located.

"All right, you men rejoin your companies and spread out. When everyone is in position, follow my lead."

The troops were spread on three sides of the town. Jack started forward at a lope, and we took up the charge. When we were within two hundred yards of the town, signal lights were lit by the enemy, and a single rifle ball whistled over Jack's head.

"Polk, take your men and surround this village," Jack shouted. "Do your best to prevent any of their soldiers from escaping. You Rangers follow me."

He spurred his horse into a hard gallop, leading us into the Zócalo. Some of our horses were so exhausted from two days of hard travel and the final charge that they slipped and fell on the cobblestone plaza. There was no resistance. A white flag was flying from a pole extending from the balcony of the largest house facing the plaza.

"You men dismount, spread out, and explore all four streets coming into this plaza. I don't want any surprises. If you encounter any resistance, attack immediately, and I'll send reinforcements."

Jack waited, still mounted. After ten minutes and no gunfire, some Rangers filtered back into the plaza, their arms held wide, indicating no enemy found.

"Sam," Jack said, addressing Sam Walker, "take some men and see if anyone is in this big house. The rest of you break into the other houses if you have to and make certain there are no enemy soldiers or guerrillas hiding out."

Santa Anna had been occupying the large house. The long dining room table still held dishes and some food, and candles were still burning. The inhabitants of the house had fled in considerable haste.

My squad found seventeen trunks, all packed to overflowing, in a room adjoining the patio. They contained dresses—hundreds of them—which General Lane gallantly ordered forwarded to Doña Santa Anna with the expressed hope that when next he found her, he would find her in them. A coat of Santa Anna's, embroidered and embossed with solid gold, was saved to be given to the State of Texas. There was also a resplendent gold bullion sash of immense proportions and weight. This was sent to some other state—I can't remember which one. There was also a life-sized oil portrait of Santa Anna.

Then I drew out of the bottom of a trunk a long, tapering, green, velvet-covered case. I removed a cane of wondrous splendor. Its staff was of polished iron. Its ferrule was of gold, tipped with steel. Its head was an eagle with blazing diamonds, rubies, sapphires, and emeralds and a huge diamond in the eagle's mouth.

My men cried out with one voice. "Give it to Colonel Jack!"

We carried the trophy to the room occupied by the senior officers. General Lane was lying on a small bed in one corner. Jack was resting nearby on a cane chair, and a few other officers were lounging around.

The presentation was made and accepted in a most informal manner, and while all were admiring the imperial bauble, in came the redoubtable Maj. William H. Polk, late minister to Naples, who asked to inspect the cane. While looking at it with beaming admiration, he said, "I should like such a thing as this very much to give to my brother."

Jack replied promptly, "I have no use for such an ornament. Take it, Major, and give it to the president and say it is a present from the Texans."

The following day, we interrogated the local alcalde and some priests. We learned that a messenger had arrived late the previous evening with information that the Americans were on the way. They described the messenger, and we soon realized that he was one of the men who had been escorting Señor Luna. General Lane apologized to Jack and his officers, but I would be quite surprised if he included the information about how our foe learned of our approach in his reports.

The regiment rested for only a day in Tehuacán and then rode north toward Orizaba. We crossed a mountain range and climbed to a pass more than fifteen thousand feet above sea level. The horses staggered with exhaustion, breathing fast and hard, even while walking slowly with their heads down. Some of the men suffered nosebleeds. Most struggled to inhale enough oxygen. A misty rain engulfed us. Visibility was less than twenty feet. Most of us, including Jack, were dressed lightly.

Jack turned in his saddle. "John, you didn't happen to save that fancy coat of Santa Anna's, did you? I believe I might make use of it."

"I believe Captain Daggett has it, Jack. I will be more than happy to requisition it for you."

"No, let Daggett enjoy it. I expect we'll be down out of this mess before too long."

We descended into a valley and made camp outside a small town at the base of the mountain. Two scouts from our advance guard pulled their horses to a stop next to where Jack sat on the ground.

"Colonel Jack, there's an hombre with a wagonload of oranges a few hundred yards down this road. He's willing to sell."

"Take me to him, boys."

Jack negotiated a price and handed over some Mexican silver pesos he had appropriated from the hoard Santa Anna overlooked in his haste to depart. We consumed the entire wagonload of oranges that same evening.

The next day we were three miles from the gates of Orizaba when we were met by a procession of priests leading a throng of citizens. Jack held up his hand to halt the column. The priests walked up to his horse and then knelt in the road, presenting a large silver platter holding the keys to all the government buildings in the town. They pleaded with Jack to spare the lives and property of the citizens, explaining the town only wanted to surrender peacefully.

General Lane rode up. "What do they want, Jack?"

"They want to surrender the town and ask, in return, that lives and property by saved. That silver platter holds all the keys to their government buildings."

Lane took possession of the keys. "Tell them to stand up. They have my word that private and church property will not be taken and that no person will be harmed, as long as they do not attack us first."

Accompanied by the priests and the throng of citizens, we entered Orizaba. We soon found out that the garrison, numbering close to two thousand men, fled the town, leaving a lone brass cannon in the middle of the main street.

Jack and General Lane were riding side by side.

"What do you think just happened here, General?" Jack questioned.

"Jack, I think the same as you. We were duped. The Mexican commander sent out that reception committee to buy time so he could escape. Someday maybe we'll see through these ruses. No matter, though. I'm appointing you military commander of this area."

Lane shouted over his shoulder. "Someone bring Major Polk up here."

When Polk rode up, Lane told him, "Major, I'm making you the governor of this city. Your primary task is to ascertain the relationships between the guerrillas, the citizens, and the officials of this place."

That evening Jack knocked on the door to Lane's quarters.

"Enter."

"General, I just learned that there is a Mexican government warehouse in town that's loaded with tobacco and cigars. Some Mexicans have been removing the product without authority. My men stopped them and are standing guard to prevent anymore pilfering. Sam Walker is pretty knowledgeable about this sort of thing. He estimates that what's in that warehouse is probably worth a quarter of a million, US. My suggestion would be to turn the place and its contents over to the alcalde but insist he provide a receipt with a realistic estimate of the value of the contents."

"That's a good idea, Jack. I've sent to Veracruz for Colonel Bankhead to come here to take permanent possession of this place. He'll be the guardian of that receipt. We won't consider that tobacco as spoils of war, but perhaps you can arrange for the officers to obtain some cigars for their personal use."

"I will make certain Sam takes care of that, General. How many do you reckon your pockets will hold?"

"I suspect an even dozen will suffice. Thank you, Colonel."

The next day, Hays and Lane, accompanied by three companies of Rangers, rode twenty miles to Cóndova and accepted the capitulation of that town. They freed six American prisoners who had been kept there, returning with them to Orizaba the same day.

After we were in Orizaba for a week, Colonel Bankhead arrived with twenty men. Lane left him in charge, and we took a circuitous route back to Puebla. The roads we traveled were new territory for American troops, but along the way, in more than a dozen cities and larger towns, the Mexicans welcomed us in peace, supplying food and drink for animals and men.

Back in Puebla, Hays dispatched a contingent of Rangers and Dragoons to escort wagon trains from Puebla to Mexico City. He and Lane took the rest of the regiment, including me, through Tlaxcala on our way to San Juan de Teotihuacán, only thirty miles or so from Mexico City. Again, Jack pushed us on a long and exhausting forced march through the night. Many of the men slept in their saddles after tying themselves on with their lariats.

At dawn, one of our scouts reported. "Colonel Jack, me and the men just watched an army preparing to abandon San Juan. We grabbed a Mexican sentry. He told us the commander is Col. Manuel Falcón."

"All right. I want two companies of Rangers ready to follow me. Let's see if we can seize this town while the Mexicans are still there."

We raced forward, but Falcón had already departed with most of his men. We killed seventeen Mexican defenders and captured some of Falcón's papers, along with 250 muskets, an equal number of lances, quite a few escopetas, and a large supply of ammunition and uniforms. There were no wagons left in the town to use for transport of the booty, so Jack ordered all of it destroyed. We created a huge, and dangerous, fireworks display. When the fire we set reached the ammunition, the explosions were enormous. Fortunately, no one was injured, although two houses caught fire.

We were gone from Mexico City for a little more than five weeks and completed one of the most rapid and difficult marches of the entire Mexican War. During this campaign, only one private was killed in an accident. Three others were wounded in separate accidents.

CHAPTER 16

A WEEK AFTER returning to Mexico City, General Lane organized another expedition. This time, he assumed command. The aim was to intercept and destroy the guerrilla bands controlling the countryside northeast of the capital. Jack commanded 250 Rangers, Major Polk commanded 130 Dragoons and mounted rifles, and Colonel Dominguez commanded a Lancer company of counterguerrillas.

The route again went through rough, mountainous terrain. It took us three days of hard travel, including riding through the night of the third day, to reach our destination. Lane's information was that the guerrilla leaders Mariano Paredes, J. N. Almonte, and Padre Jarauta, who had miraculously recovered from his wounds, were all three with their troops in Tulancingo.

We were, as usual, leading. When dawn broke, we were within sight of the town but still five miles away. Jack kicked his tired horse into an easy lope, and we followed, but the citizens were inside their homes, and all of the Mexican soldiers were gone. The town was quickly secured, and Jack sent his spies to find out where the guerrillas went. After seeing to his own men, he took inventory of the condition of the other troops.

"General, before we left, I requisitioned two thousand dollars for expenses. My men know how to take care of their horses, and their animals are in excellent condition, but a number of the Dragoons, Lancers, and riflemen were forced to abandon their exhausted or lame animals during our march. Most of them managed to *borrow* horses from the Mexican haciendas along the way, but most of those animals are worthless. Us taking those animals is probably how the guerrillas found out we were on the way. Anyhow, I'm going to need a couple of days to purchase some replacement horses."

"You do what's needed and send out your scouts to locate Jarauta or Paredes," General Lane said.

"Already done, sir."

Two days later, one of our spies returned with information that Jarauta and his men were at Sequalteplan, in the mountains about seventy-five miles north of Tulancingo. Jack and I took the scout to inform General Lane.

"Thank you, young man. Your information is quite welcome," Lane told the Tejano. Then he turned to Jack. "Colonel, I'm sending all the sick men back to Mexico City. As you no doubt know, most of them are from Polk's and Dominguez's commands. I will require a squad of your Rangers to accompany them and make certain they arrive safely."

"Yes, sir. I'll send Bigfoot Wallace with ten men. He'll get them back safe."

"Good. Get the rest of the men ready," the general instructed. "We'll leave at midnight for Sequalteplan. I want you and your Rangers to lead and push hard. I want to be there at sunrise the day after tomorrow."

The column was scattered a long way along the trail when we arrived at the outskirts of Sequalteplan. All of our men soon came up to where Jack and General Lane were waiting with the advanced scouts.

Jack moved his horse forward. "All right, boys, at a trot. Let's see what's waiting for us."

As we entered the outlying roads leading into the town, a Mexican officer stepped through the front door of a house, wiping the sleep from his eyes. In a moment, two of our men were holding him at gunpoint.

Moving at a fast trot, Jack and the rest of us rode toward a large open gate in a wall surrounding a barracks. A guard spotted us and did his best to close the gate, but Jack spurred forward, crashing his horse into the gate. The gate slammed all the way open, flinging the guard to the ground. A dozen of us poured through, following Jack. Once inside the walls, there was not enough room to fight while mounted. At Jack's order, we jumped to the ground to engage the guerrillas who were rushing out of the barracks. All of us stayed calm, taking careful aim before firing. The result was devastating to the surprised guerrilla fighters. They were more accustomed to fighting with overwhelming odds in their favor.

Jack remounted and shouted: "You men clear out these hombres."

I followed him as he rode back through the gate to join the rest of his men, finally joined by Polk's and Dominguez's commands. A group of about sixty guerrillas, led by a colonel, charged from an adjoining barracks.

"Major Chevaille, engage those men and eliminate the threat," Jack directed. Then he called out to the commanders of four other Ranger companies. "You men follow me. We're going to take the Zócalo."

Jack galloped to the main plaza where we were met by rifle fire from several different directions. We spread out and returned fire. Down one of the streets leading into the plaza a large number of Mexican Lancers and infantry rushed from another barracks. Horses were brought up, and the Lancers mounted. At the same time, Jack spotted another smaller contingent of fighters forming into ranks on the opposite side of the plaza. He shouted and waved his arm at a squad of Rangers.

"You men engage that small group of Mexicans," Jack said, pointing at the small group of guerrillas. "The rest of you follow me."

The rest of us knew what Jack would do, and with complete faith, we followed as he charged directly into the larger group of guerrillas, outnumbered by more than two-to-one. The unexpected ferocity and speed of the attack had the desired effect. The Mexicans, already fearful of Devil Jack and his Texans, fired their single-shot muskets randomly and with little effect. We careful aimed, and every shot from our revolvers found its mark.

The Mexicans broke and ran from the plaza, with us in pursuit. One of the more experienced Mexican company commanders was able to rally a few mounted Lancers and provide some resistance, but they were quickly overwhelmed. Some of the Mexican infantry managed to break through locked doors and gates, enabling them to get into houses and courtyards that offered a modicum of protection from which to fight. They were soon flushed out and killed, wounded, or captured by our veterans of house-to-house fighting in Monterrey. The last of the Mexican Lancers made a run for safety.

Jack raised his arm. "Let 'em go, boys. Our horses are too tired to chase 'em. Let's get back to the plaza."

Arriving at the plaza, Jack was sought out by General Lane's adjutant, who had been sent for reinforcements.

"Lane is outnumbered," the adjutant explained. "The Mexicans are ensconced behind barricades and in buildings. The general needs help."

Jack ordered a company of us to run and support Lane. We forced our way through the barricades in the street and through three locked doors into a large building where the Mexicans were sheltering. The speed and fury of our attack was, again, successful. Thirty enemy were killed, and several more were wounded and taken prisoner, but some of the Mexican guerrillas escaped through a rear passageway that we did not know existed. The sound of firearms soon abated and then stopped. Jack dispatched squads to spread out through the town and hunt down any fugitives who remained.

"Bring those prisoners over by the church to me," said Jack.

We interrogated the prisoners and soon learned that Jarauta's headquarters occupied the large church fronting the Zócalo. Jack led a search squad into the church and found evidence that the guerrilla leader had once again managed to escape at the last moment. Papers found scattered in Jarauta's office revealed the guerrilla leader's forces had numbered four hundred Lancers and fifty infantrymen.

That evening Bob Ford reported that the count was 120 Mexicans killed. We suffered five men wounded, three severely, but no dead. Many of our men spent the evening collecting abandoned Mexican lances as souvenirs.

The next morning we left Sequalteplan. When we stopped for the night in a small village, a Mexican, who had been following us for several days, was brought to General Lane to explain himself. I interpreted.

"Señor General, I am not a soldier. I am a man of peace and have not participated in any fighting against you. My two daughters were in Sequalteplan visiting their aunt. The Texans stole their horses."

"Well, sir, it's still light enough out. Come with me to the balcony upstairs. From there, you will be able to see all of our horses in the plaza below. You point out your daughters' horses, and they will be returned to you."

Among the horses standing unsaddled in the plaza, eating their ration of corn, was a very fine chestnut stallion that Major Chevaille had captured in a raid on a small guerrilla camp. Weeks previously, Chevaille presented the animal to General Lane. The Mexican took his time looking over the horses and then pointed at Lane's stallion. "That is one of them."

Lane's nickname among us Rangers was Old Critter Face. He earned it because of his scowl when irritated. When we saw his face, those of us on the balcony, including Jack, started chuckling.

Lane turned to the Mexican, got directly into his face, and screamed at him. "You get your ass off this balcony and out of my sight, you lying son of a bitch, or I will have you dangling by your neck from this railing."

It was not necessary for me to interpret. The Mexican understood the message if not the words.

The next evening, we again made camp early. This time, outside one of the haciendas in the same valley where we had holed up prior to the attack on Tulancingo. Jack did not think it was necessary for him to repeat his previous orders not to take any of the owner's property, assuming his men would apply them to this stay. Some of the younger Rangers decided to requisition fresh meat. A squawking hen betrayed them, just as one of them launched a large rock at a pig, hoping to stun it. The rock ricocheted, hit a boulder, and then bounced off at an angle and hit Old Critter Face on the shin as he strode over to investigate the racket. At that same moment, the don of the hacienda rushed up to complain about his chickens and pigs being taken without payment. The don spoke English.

"General, I am a poor man. Your soldiers are stealing my chickens, my pigs, even some of my sheep and goats. I demand payment."

Lane was leaning over rubbing the bruise on his left shin, his face contorted with rage. "I don't give a shit about your damn animals, or to hear any bullshit about how poor you are. You can go to hell and take your animals with you."

At that moment, Jack strolled up, me following. "What's the matter, General? Are you hurt?"

"Your men are taking this don's animals for fresh food. Deal with him and deal with your men, Colonel." Lane limped away mumbling.

Jack turned and looked at the young Rangers, one of whom was still holding a dead hen by the neck. "You men cease and desist. I don't want any more foraging. What's the count?"

The Ranger holding the hen replied: "I reckon maybe half dozen chickens, no more, and one shoat, Jack."

"All right, that's the end of it." He turned to the hacienda owner, reaching into his pants pocket. The following exchange was in Spanish.

"Señor, here is ten pesos, silver. That will more than pay for the animals that have been taken."

"No, señor. It is not enough. The hens were for eggs, the pig was my best …"

"Stop talking. The price is fair. If you persist, I will turn my men loose. They have been fighting Mexicans for a long time while eating parched corn and dried jerky. They just wanted some fresh food. Do not provoke me, señor. I have a strong suspicion that you sent a warning to the guerrillas in Tulancingo. If you wish to continue complaining, I will interrogate your household and find out if my suspicions are verified."

The don turned and quickly walked back to his house.

When we returned to Mexico City, we again paraded through the streets on our way to General Scott's headquarters. Every Ranger carried a captured Mexican lance. This time, we were returning from a two-week expedition during which time we traveled more than five hundred miles. During the previous six weeks, we rode more than nine hundred miles, many of those miles through dangerous, steep, rough mountains, using barely passable trails. We engaged the enemy and won every engagement.

Mexico was in turmoil. The Mexican government was in disarray and losing the war. The politicians turned again to the charismatic Santa Anna, who was, by then, living in exile in Cuba. The wily character was still able to convince the Mexican people that he was the solution to their problems. He even managed to convince President Polk that he could end the war with terms favorable to the United States. He returned to Mexico and assumed command of the Mexican Army. He managed to win some territory back, but at the battle of Buena Vista, he once again made poor decisions and suffered heavy losses. His response to that debacle was to relinquish command of the army. A month later, he assumed the presidency of Mexico.

During the winter of 1847/48, American and Mexican authorities negotiated for a considerable time before reaching an agreement. The Treaty of Guadalupe Hidalgo was signed February 2, 1848. It established the Rio Grande as the border between the two countries, and Mexico recognized the US annexation of Texas. It agreed to sell all of California, plus all of its territories north and west of the Rio Grande, for the payment of $15 million. This huge tract of land ceded most of what would become the states of New Mexico, Arizona, Southern Colorado, and Southern Utah to the United States. The United States, for its part, agreed to settle all claims of US citizens against Mexico.

After the treaty was ratified, Santa Anna resigned as president and prepared to go into exile again. One rarely talked about aspect of the treaty agreement was that any subsequent revolts by Mexicans would be suppressed by the combined armies of both nations. The guerrilla leaders Paredes and Almonte retired to their home territories and ceased to cause trouble. We removed Padre Jarauta's fangs, and the most daring and energetic guerrilla commander was neutralized. Occasional attacks on supply trains between Veracruz and Mexico City continued but were conducted by lesser leaders with smaller groups of fighters.

Jack was again summoned to General Scott's headquarters to receive new orders. Before he reported, he told me he hoped the orders would muster us out and facilitate our return to Texas.

It didn't happen. We were ordered to move to Veracruz but to proceed slowly in that direction, flushing our all the thieves, bandits, and criminals we could locate. Scott wanted the road between Mexico City and Veracruz kept safe.

The first day of our journey was peaceful, almost idyllic. The rumor spread among the men that we were on the way to Veracruz, and when we arrived, we would be mustered out and sent home. One of our youngest Rangers was a boy of only seventeen. His name was Jack Phillips, known by all of us as Little Jack. He was Jack's hostler; his job was to ride one of Jack's extra horses and lead the others. He was expected to remain close at hand, so Jack could signal him to bring up a fresh horse in a hurry. Little Jack, full of exuberance and anticipation at the thought of going home, persisted in loitering with Jack's horses at the rear of the column. Then, without warning or orders, he would suddenly gallop the length of the column with the excuse that Colonel Jack, who customarily rode ahead with the advance scouts, needed a fresh horse. He did this several times the first day and continued to do so, occasionally, over the following days.

I was riding with Ford and Chevaille, and each time Little Jack raced past us, our horses acted up. Little Jack's exuberant antics were also causing a disturbance among the other horses the length of the column. Each time this happened, the two officers hollered at Little Jack to slow down, but he just laughed; joy bubbled out of him. After Little Jack raced past on the fourth day of the march, Major Chevaille lost his temper.

"I wish the damn guerrillas would catch that boy and teach him a lesson."

That evening Jack called a halt at a particularly scenic spot. His mood was lighthearted, and his mood permeated the camp. He neglected his usual practice of ordering all of his horses brought close to him for the night.

At dawn, the regiment broke camp. That morning, Chevaille, Ford, and I decided to ride with the advance scouts. Jack was back with the rest of the Rangers. Before long, we came upon a mutilated body in the middle of the road. We all dismounted. Ford knelt to determine if there was any life remaining and then stood upright.

"It's Little Jack. I didn't even recognize him at first. He's dead, and the colonel's horses are gone. What the hell was he thinking?"

Chevaille responded. "He wasn't, Bob. Boys his age don't think. He was probably just taking Jack's horses for another run for the joy of it. I swear to you and to God I will never make another wish about a man being taught a lesson as long as I live."

Jack rode up but said nothing about his horses. He sadly ordered Little Jack be buried just off the road and then called for Captain Walker.

"Sam, I want you to remain in this vicinity with two companies. Use your best trackers and scour this place clean of any and all guerrillas. Do not rejoin us until you are certain these murderers are no longer a threat. It will be best if they are all dead. If you are able to recover my horses, I will consider it a favor."

Walker nodded his understanding. Jack moved the rest of the regiment on down the road, while Walker spread his men on either side of the road to find the tracks of the guerrillas.

The regiment continued slowly toward Veracruz. Jack sent out spies to ferret out any local knowledge of guerrilla camps or activity. When any actionable intelligence was received, he sent companies to eliminate the threat.

Bigfoot Wallace delivered the sick and wounded men to Veracruz safely and then turned his squad around and rejoined us.

"Bigfoot, Miguel found me this morning and told me there is a small band of guerrillas holed up in San Carlos," Jack said. "Take some of your men and get rid of them."

"You got it, Jack."

After arriving in Puebla, the regiment tarried for only a day. The next morning, Sam Walker arrived with his men but not with Jack's horses.

"Found 'em, attacked immediately, killed twelve of 'em, but the others scattered. No sign of your animals, Jack. Sorry."

"You think the ones that got away will come back to cause trouble?" Jack questioned.

"Don't think so. There wasn't more than half dozen of 'em, and they took off in six different directions. I think, by the way they skedaddled, they've had enough fighting."

Jack next took us northwest, on the lookout for guerrilla bands operating out of Oriental, Perote, and other villages and towns in the region. We arrived in Tepeyahualco and stayed for a few days while Jack sent out spies to locate any small bands still plaguing the area.

Santa Anna employed his well-honed skills of saving his own skin. He petitioned the authorities of both governments to allow his departure into exile, and both agreed. He and his family were provided with passports, but they had to await the arrival of a vessel to transport them. Col. George Hughes was the governor of the area around Xalapa where Santa Anna was ensconced. Santa Anna corresponded with Hughes and asked that he and his family be allowed to await transportation out of Mexico from his estate located near El Lencero, only a few miles southeast of Xalapa. Hughes replied that whenever the general was ready to move to his estate, he would be given all honors and provided with a safe-conduct and an escort. When his vessel arrived, another escort would be provided to the coast.

We arrived at Xalapa and reported to Colonel Hughes. That's when we learned about Santa Anna's situation. The morning of March 28, Hughes and his staff left Xalapa with three companies of Maryland Mounted Volunteers commanded by Maj. John R. Kenly. They went to the hacienda where Santa Anna was staying to escort him, his family, and his retainers to the general's estate. The procession, aside from Hughes and Kenly and their men, consisted of a platoon of well-mounted and well-equipped Mexican Lancers who rode in front of Santa Anna's ornate carriage. The carriage was pulled by eight matching mules and followed by the rest of a full company of Mexican Lancers.

I found out later that on the way to the estate, the party stopped at the hacienda of Gen. José Durán, where they had been invited to participate in a dinner to honor Santa Anna. General Durán served under Santa Anna during several campaigns, and he felt honored to host this special meal for his commander. After arriving at the Durán hacienda, the parties took time to rest and freshen up and then gathered for dinner at three in the afternoon.

Señora Santa Anna, his second wife, was seated at the head of the table, her husband on her right. She was not yet twenty years old, of average height, and proud of her youthful, full figure. Her hazel eyes sparkled. Her hair was long, almost black, and hung down past her waist. She always protected her fair skin from the sunlight. She was, even at her young age, very poised, dignified, and gracious. Santa Anna was, as always, resplendent in uniform and manner. To his señora's left, sat Colonel Hughes and next to him Santa Anna's daughter by his first wife. The daughter was then fifteen years old and in every respect the exact opposite of her stepmother. The other guests were arranged by rank along both sides of the table, with General Durán and his wife at the far end. Major Kenly was seated to the left of the host.

As the dinner progressed, those officers and men not seated at the table congregated outside on the patio. Servants passed among them with various tidbits and bottles of wine filling their goblets before they were emptied. More American officers arrived and joined the patio throng, most just curious for a glimpse of Santa Anna.

After the dinner had been consumed, Santa Anna passed around a case of fine cigars and invited all the attending officers to join him in a smoke. The rich food, generous portions of the various wines that accompanied each course, as well as the tobacco convinced Santa Anna he was in his rightful place. He was the center of attention—the most important man in the room.

Even before Santa Anna departed Major Kenly was apprehensive about this trip. He knew the Rangers were camped on either side of the road from Xalapa to El Lencero, just down the road from the Durán hacienda. Kenly was also very aware of the antipathy of the Texans to Santa Anna. He worried about the general's safety and sought out Jack."

"Colonel Hays, I know there is a lot of bad blood between many of your Rangers and Santa Anna," Major Kenly began. "I cannot defend or excuse any of his actions, but you are aware he is traveling under a safe-conduct order. Can I be certain none of your men will pose a threat?"

"Major, my men have been made aware of the situation. There will, no doubt, be plenty of malevolent stares, but none of my men will do more than spit at the ground as he passes."

"I can count on that?"

"Yes, Major. You can."

Kenly was still worried. As the officers gathered around to enjoy the cigars and bask in the brilliance of Santa Anna, Kenly glanced at the men gathered on the patio. Then he noticed some new arrivals, among them myself and Jack, both of us without uniforms or insignia." We joined the men on the patio. Jack took a glass of wine from a servant. Kenly excused himself and hurried to greet Jack.

"Colonel, I would like to present you to Gen. Santa Anna."

"I would like that, Major," Jack responded. "Lead on."

As the two approached the still-seated Santa Anna, the group of Mexican and American officers surrounding him fell silent. Some of the Mexicans put a hand on their sword hilt. Santa Anna was munching a mouthful of melon while holding a cigar in his left hand.

Kenly spoke. "General, please permit me to present you to—" At that moment, Santa Anna turned and started to rise. "Colonel Jack Hays," Kenly concluded.

The room went completely silent. Gen. Santa Anna flushed and then slumped back into his chair. After only a moment, he recovered and sat up straight again and resumed chewing the melon in his mouth. His eyes were focused on his dinner plate.

Jack bowed politely, just the hint of a smile at the corner of his lips. He murmured, "General," and then turned and left the room.

I watched as Santa Anna finally swallowed what remained of the thoroughly masticated melon and turned to Kenly. "Major, we are ready to resume our journey as soon as you can muster your escort."

Before coming to the Durán hacienda, Jack left strict orders with all his officers. "You must convince the men that the son of a bitch is in his own country and is traveling under a safe-conduct granted by our commander. If we kill the son of a bitch, the entire civilized world would consider it murder. More importantly, the act would dishonor Texas. Just tell them to keep their mouths shut and their revolvers holstered."

All of the men acknowledged the order.

Kenly, still worried about how we would act, placed a company of his men on either side of Santa Anna's carriage. The entire Mexican escort rode in front of the carriage, and a third company of Maryland Volunteers protected the rear of the procession. As they approached our camp, Kenly positioned himself just ahead of the mules pulling Santa Anna's carriage.

We were aligned, sitting on the stone walls or leaning against them, on both sides of the road. Almost seven hundred Texans sat or stood, quiet and motionless. A few spit saliva enhanced with tobacco juices into the dust of the road as the carriage passed. The Mexicans lost their cool. The carriage driver shouted at his mules, whistled, and whipped them into a run. The Mexican escort was just as anxious to clear the area. Our un-uniformed representatives of the great state of Texas were motionless and silent. There were no salutations, no ungraceful remarks. When the procession was out of sight, we broke ranks and returned to camp.

That April, Gen. W. O. Butler succeeded General Scott. Butler complimented Jack on his control over his men and then assigned him to take a contingent of Rangers and escort Santa Anna to La Antigua on the coast. Once there, the general and his entourage boarded a Spanish ship bound for Venezuela.

CHAPTER 17

WE WERE BACK in camp, close to El Lencero. Every day another unit of the American Army passed by the camp in high spirits on their way to Veracruz to be discharged, loaded onto transport ships, and sent home. We received no such orders.

The hacienda, still owned by Santa Anna, consisted of considerable land on either side of the road to Veracruz. In fact, the Ranger camp was located on a portion of those lands. We were again prey to the general's double-dealing, although, in truth, Jack was unable to prove that what transpired was at Santa Anna's direction. Santa Anna's majordomo, the manager of the estate, was asked by our quartermaster to supply meat for the regiment. He did so, charging premium prices, but the meat frequently went bad before it could be used. The quartermaster, Lieutenant Pancoast, complained, but the majordomo insisted he was providing the best meat available.

One evening Jack and I squatted by a campfire to share a meal with some of the men. He took a bite of meat and immediately spat it into the fire. "What the hell is that supposed to be?"

All of the men grouped around the campfire laughed.

"That's what we've been getting," one of them explained. "We've complained to the lieutenant that the shit is often spoiled before we can cook it, but the Mexican who gets it for us told Pancoast it's the best meat available.

"That's bullshit," Jack exclaimed. "The meat I've been served isn't spoiled, this crap certainly is. You need to cook it with lots of chilies and onions and for a long time. If it's well cooked, you won't get sick, and maybe the chilies will mask that god-awful taste. I'm getting to the bottom of this."

Jack and I went back to his tent, and he sent for Miguel Cervantes, a Tejano friend of long-standing. Cervantes was one of his most effective spies.

"Miguel, I want you to do some sniffing around," Jack directed. "Santa Anna's majordomo has been supplying the men with spoiled meat. Find out what that son of a bitch is up to."

"My pleasure, Jack. I've been choking it down for several days now."

"Damn, why didn't anyone say anything to me about it?"

Miguel shrugged and left. The following evening, he was back.

"Just as you suspected, Jack. The man has been purchasing meat that's been on sale so long it is ready to spoil. Then he's been charging Pancoast top prices for it."

"All right. Thank you, Miguel. Do you think he's been doing this on his own or at Santa Anna's direction?"

"I don't know, but I wouldn't put a trick like that past Santa Anna. If you leave this to me, I will find out and deal with him. As you well know, I lost family at the Alamo, and there's still a score to settle with that snake Santa Anna."

"All right then," Jack agreed. "I'm going to involve Bigfoot in this too. When you brace the man, make certain Bigfoot is with you. He'll know how to make the bastard spill his guts. I'll trust you two to find out if the man is just a crook or if he's acting for Santa Anna."

I knew that Bigfoot's grievances with Santa Anna were far from settled. He was quite happy to take on this chore. I asked if I could go with them when he and Miguel rode to the hacienda. When the majordomo came out of his office to learn what we wanted, the two grabbed him and forced him back. The man was clearly terrified. When Bigfoot pointed his bowie knife at the man's testicles, he acknowledged his misdeeds but denied that Santa Anna had a hand in the swindle. The two confiscated his sizable stash of silver pesos.

"This will be returned to our quartermaster so he can find an honest man to purchase good meat from. If we find you have been lying to us about your general's part in all of this, it will go very badly for you," Miguel told him. "Our commander is very harsh with thieves. You can count yourself very fortunate you are dealing with us and not with Devil Jack … Ah, you know the reputation of our colonel. Good."

That same week Jack took me and twenty Rangers with him to Mexico City. He wanted to make certain the road was still free of bandit activity. It was. In Mexico City, he conferred with General Butler.

"I believe the road to Veracruz is safe now, General," Jack reported. "You can reestablish stagecoach service to Puebla, Veracruz, and other towns along the route. I will confer with the garrison commanders along the way and formulate action plans for them on how to deal with any future guerrilla or bandit attacks."

"Thank you, Colonel. I appreciate your efforts. Anything else?"

"My men have done what they could, General, and they are more than ready to return home."

"That's understandable, Colonel. I will address the issue. Anything else?"

"No, sir."

"Good. Thank you again, Colonel. The efforts of you and your men are appreciated."

"Thank you, sir."

Soon after his return, Jack received the order to march us to Veracruz to be mustered out. A few weeks later, Jack and all his officers, along with those members of his regiment who had not been transported back to Texas previously, boarded the steamboat *Maria Burt*. The ship made its way to Powder Horn, Texas, located on Lavaca Bay. When we disembarked, we were warmly welcomed with speeches and a dinner. Then we were the honored guests at a dance that same evening. This protocol of welcoming speeches, a dinner, and a dance was repeated each evening when we reached a new town. The trip back to San Antonio took five days.

We rode into San Antonio in the early afternoon. Welcoming speeches stole almost an hour. Jack and those of his officers and men with spouses and families were impatient for reunion, but they all managed to keep smiling until the last of the participating orators had finished their remarks, whereupon soldiers and families rushed into warm embraces and kisses. Jack and Susan were besieged by many well-wishers but eventually managed to break away and escape to the house Jack had built for his bride. Neighboring towns helped stage the celebratory ball attended by more than three hundred invited guests, but it didn't begin until nine in that evening.

I wasn't present but have imagined what happened next.

As the sun set, Susan and Jack remained entwined on their bed.

"I missed you so much, my darling," she said, stroking his long, straggly hair and then the smooth skin on his chest, lightly touching the raised scars of the many wounds on his arms and body, "but, dearest, you can do with a bath."

Jack laughed. "So, you managed to not breathe in the stink of war and deprivation until now? I am frankly amazed, Susan. Well, how about we both get into a bath—maybe together. That will save us some time before we have to get ready for tonight's festivities."

"Do we have to go?" Susan pleaded.

"Yes, unfortunately, I think so. We've been fighting for these folks. They want, and need, to thank us. It would be impolite to ignore them."

Susan pouted as she climbed into the warm water to join her husband.

He touched her lower lip and then spread her mouth into a smile with thumb and forefinger. "No more pouting," he said. He then kissed her, first lightly, then with more intensity and passion, and they moved to the bed again.

At a quarter-past eight Jack jumped out of the bed and slapped Susan's bare bottom. "Up, girl. Time to get dressed, or we'll miss the party."

At nine o'clock, the committee on arrangements ushered in all of the distinguished guests to the applause of everyone gathered. The dancing continued until midnight, and then food and drink were provided. After the meal, the music and dancing continued until a little after four in the morning.

Of course, the beautiful and amiable lady of Colonel Hays was the bright and particular star of the evening, the cynosure of all eyes and the constant recipient of the most marked attention. I was not the only one unable to keep my eyes from her.

A week later, Jack was in Austin in a meeting with the governor and other state officials. They all pleaded with him to resume command of the frontier battalion.

He told me that he told them he had enough. His finances were a mess, and he had to travel to Washington to settle his war accounts and formally resign from the US Army. He told them he intended to resume the land surveying business and that he heard talk of establishing an all-weather, overland route to the Pacific. If it were true, it would be a project of great interest to him.

About that same time, John Ford and I were enjoying dinner together, and he read to me this entry from his journal.

> He expressed no feeling of jealousy toward his subordinate officers. He gave them opportunities to distinguish themselves and was outspoken in his commendations of good conduct. He was lenient to the erring, unless the offense had involved a taint of dishonesty; then he was immovably rigid. He was almost idolized by many. He was modest and retiring; an expression of admiration of his acts would cause him to blush like a woman.

> As a commander, he trusted a great deal to the good faith of his officers. He went among his men, patiently heard their complaints, and redressed abuses. He knew how to conduct marches requiring toilsome endurance and to prevent his men from becoming despondent. On the battlefield, he saw everything and readily took advantage of the errors of the enemy. He was cool, self-possessed, and brave; a good shot, and the man who singled him out in a fight came to grief.

> Had the Mexican War lasted longer, another brigadier general would have been appointed. It was understood in the City of Mexico that Colonel Hays had an excellent chance to receive the appointment. A county in Texas was named in honor of him soon after annexation.

After Jack concluded what he needed to do in Washington and returned to San Antonio, I was among the dinner guests of Mr. and Mrs. Elliot, as were Susan and Jack. Another guest that evening was a young attorney recently arrived from Virginia. He was enthusiastic about opportunities in California and was planning to travel there. Jack was intrigued. He questioned the lawyer extensively, until Susan burst into tears.

"What's the matter, Susan? Are you ill? Do we need to call for a doctor?" Jack asked.

"Why are you even thinking about California? I would be here alone, while you face danger on the road and who knows what after you get there. You will have to get established and gain some financial success before you could send for me. Then I will have to travel all that distance, leaving family and friends here. Jack, what is in California that you cannot accomplish here in San Antonio?"

Mrs. Elliot could no longer hold her tongue. "Your wife is correct, Jack Hays. Why do you upset her so with this kind of talk? Come with me, dear. Let's leave these male animals with their wild talk and dreams."

EPILOGUE

The California bug bit, but the people of Texas still expected Jack Hays to rush to save them from every threat, real or imagined. His financial situation was still not secure when the state government contracted with him to lead a survey crew to establish a route from San Antonio to El Paso. He agreed after amending the contract to allow him to hire some of his former Rangers, including myself. We were needed to provide protection from the Comanche, who were once again creating problems for smaller settlements and travelers.

Jack's fortunes took a further upturn in early 1849 when he was appointed Indian agent for the Gila River country in Arizona. Then the California gold rush built momentum. He and I recruited forty men, most of them ex-Rangers, to take a convoy of wagons and pack mules with trade goods to California. We also negotiated a contract to supply beef for a party of US soldiers going from Texas to California. The soldiers had no way to keep meat fresh. We supplied them by driving a herd of cattle to be slaughtered as required. We traveled with our wagons, pack mules, and cattle along the same route we surveyed to El Paso. Then we crossed the mountains to the Gila River where Jack delayed to settle some issues for the tribes. We then followed the Gila to its confluence with the Colorado River and traversed the desert to San Diego. There we discovered that more opportunities were in the San Francisco area. So, we sold our trade goods, our remaining cattle, and our horses and booked passage on the *Freemont*. We arrived in San Francisco fifteen days later.

Another former Ranger, John McMullin, also had shares in this endeavor. At age fifteen, he joined Jack's Ranger company and served with distinction. He eventually rose to the rank of captain and also served with Jack in Mexico. After we arrived in California, McMullin went into the cattle business and eventually became owner of one of the largest cattle ranches in the Stockton area.

However, Jack was unable to escape his reputation. San Francisco County boomed through the gold rush and then the silver rush. It was a wild, wide-open frontier, with no effective law enforcement. The community was badly in need of a firm hand. While we were busy expanding our real estate holdings, surveying, and starting a cattle ranch, Jack was induced to run for county Sheriff, the most influential and powerful position in the county.

The first election for county officials was set for April 1, 1850. There were three candidates for sheriff, two of them self-proclaimed colonels. The first was J. J. Bryant, a famous and wealthy gambler, who also owned a fancy hotel, the Bryant House. He was the chosen candidate of the Democratic Party. The second candidate was J. Towns, who represented the Whig Party. Jack, the only actually commissioned colonel, ran as an independent. On the day of the election, Bryant decorated his hotel, which was located on the plaza where the voting was taking place with bunting. He hired a band that played loudly and with great enthusiasm and set up a bar with free drinks and free food for all voters. Jack countered by riding his stallion into the plaza, putting the animal through a routine of high stepping, fast turns, and rearing on its hind legs to demonstrate his horsemanship. He also sprinkled a group of his ex-Rangers through the crowd. We informed the voters about who Jack was and what he had accomplished. He won by a slender margin, appointed me as his deputy, and soon brought law and order to the county. Most importantly, he demonstrated his legendary honesty and high moral standards in everything he did.

Three years later, Jack resigned as sheriff to accept an appointment as Surveyor General of California. As he continued to build his financial holdings, his business acumen and well-earned reputation for honesty paid dividends. He became one of the most important real estate developers and ranchers in the San Francisco area. In 1852, he recognized the opportunity and was an early investor and founder of Oakland. We and his other partners surveyed the site and laid out the town. He was an active civic leader, increasing his wealth with investments in utility companies, banks, wharves, and railroads, all of which he also promoted. He became a mainstay of the California Democratic Party and, in his later years, was a generous supporter of charities, academic institutions, and education.

Once he was firmly established, he had a house built and sent for Susan. Four of his former Rangers accompanied her to safeguard her journey. He promised to help them all get established in California and did so. Susan's party traveled by ship from Houston to Panama, crossed the isthmus, and then took another ship to San Francisco.

Susan gave birth to a son in 1853. They named him John Caperton Hays. I was and am very honored. To keep his promise to his old Comanche adversary, the boy was nicknamed Buffalo Hump. John Caperton (Buffalo Hump) Hays lived to be fifty-eight, dying in 1911. Another son, Richard, was born in 1855 but only lived seven years. Kitty, Jack and Susan's first daughter, died when only a year old. Their second daughter, Susan Mary, was born in 1858. She was only five years old when she died. Susan Besswick Hays was born in 1859 and was still alive as I record these final thoughts. Harry was born in 1861 and died when he was sixteen years old. Their last child, Elizabeth (Betty) Brenham Hays, was born in 1869.

At the start of the Civil War, both the North and the South had strong adherents in California. Both sides offered Jack a general's commission, but reason prevailed. Despite his many connections to Texas, his true friends urged him not to participate. He remained neutral throughout that terrible time.

Lake Lahontan covered a significant portion of northwestern Nevada many thousands of years ago. The first Native Americans settled on the lakeshore about ten thousand years ago, but the ancestors of the present-day Northern Paiutes probably arrived at the lake about five hundred years prior to the arrival of the Americans. John C. Fremont passed along the eastern shore of the lake in January 1844 and named it Pyramid Lake after camping near a pyramid-shaped rock, of which he wrote, "presented a pretty exact outline of the great pyramid of Cheops."

The Paiute and other tribes in the area united to prevent the further incursions of white settlers eager for land. The inevitable conflict started when the Indians killed the station tenders at Williams Station on the Carson River. The white settlers quickly organized themselves, and more than a hundred men rode to chastise the savages. They were attacked by a strong force of Indians near the mouth of the Trukee River. This became known as the first Battle of Pyramid Lake. Over two-thirds of the whites were killed. Panic spread over all the region, including northern California. The settlers feared there would be a generalized Indian uprising.

Jack was soon contacted and authorized by the state of California to organize a regiment of six hundred volunteers to deal with the situation. The regiment rendezvoused in Virginia City, Nevada. Jack insisted, as a condition of his taking command, that all officers and men place themselves under his complete control. Once the regiment was organized, he and I and the rest of the ex-Rangers we recruited spent several days drilling and training the men. We didn't depart until Jack was satisfied that we had instilled enough military discipline for the men to receive and carry out his orders without confusion. Those who would not, or could not, meet Jack's requirements went home. We left Virginia City on May 24 1860. We continued to drill and train his troops as we traveled.

The Second Battle of Pyramid Lake took place on June 2, 1860. The Indians fought fiercely, but we prevailed.

After 1870, Jack and Susan moved to their ranch in Alameda County, and he semiretired. He suffered from rheumatism, and his general health gradually declined. He died on San Jacinto Day 1883 at the age of sixty-six. John Coffee Hays spent only thirteen years of his life in Texas but should be remembered as, perhaps, the most storied Texas Ranger in history.

The following references were used to supply details for this novel:

James Kimmins Greer, *Texas Ranger, Jack Hays in the Frontier Southwest*.

Elmer Kelton, *Lone Star Rising, the Texas Rangers Trilogy*.

Joseph Wheelan, *Invading Mexico, America's Continental Dream and the Mexican War*.

Harry McCorry Henderson, *Colonel Jack Hays, Texas Ranger*.

Gene Shelton, *Captain Jack, The Story of John Coffee Hays*.

S. C. Gwynne, *Empire of the Summer Moon, Quanah Parker and the Rise and Fall of the Comanches, the Most Powerful Indian Tribe in American History*.

Stephen L. Moore, *Texas Rising, The Epic True Story of the Lone Star Republic and the Rise of the Texas Rangers, 1836–1846*.

Jane Strain Kent, *Adam Zumwalt Jr., 1795–1872, Dewitt Colony Minuteman, Rancher and Farmer*.

Wikipedia, *Battle of Plum Creek*.

Ibid., *Battle of Pyramid Lake*.

Ibid., *Battle of Salado Creek*.

Ibid., *Benjamin McCulloch*.

Ibid., *Colt-Paterson*.

Ibid., *Colt-Walker*.

Ibid., *John Henry Moore*.

Ibid., *John Salmon Ford*

Ibid., *Lipan Apache People*.

Ibid., *Mathew Caldwell*.

Ibid., *Nueces River*.

Ibid., *Old Three Hundred (Texan Grandees)*.

Ibid., *Percussion Cap*.

Ibid., *Robert Addison Gillespie*.

Ibid., *Sam Houston*.

Ibid., *Samuel Hamilton Walker*.

Ibid., *William A. A. Wallace*.

Ibid., *Young Perry Alsbury*.

Ibid. Sons of Dewitt Colony, Texas, *Capt. "Black" Adam Zumwalt.*

Ibid., *Eyewitness Descriptions, the Council House Fight.*

Ibid., *Mathew Caldwell.*

Ibid., *The Tumlinson Family of Dewitt Colony.*

Ibid., *The Comanche Attack on Linnville, the Battle of Plum Creek.*

Ibid. Texas Historical Association (TSHA), The Handbook of Texas, *Debt of the Republic of Texas.*

Ibid., *Gillespie, Robert Addison.*

Ibid., *Hays, John Coffee.*

Ibid., *Huston, Felix.*

Ibid., *Tumlinson, John Jackson, Jr.*

Ibid. PoliceOne.com, *Police History: The Story of John Coffee Hays, Texas Ranger.*

Texas State Library and Archives Commission, *Republic of Texas Currency.*

Ibid., *Texas Adjutant General's Department, An Inventory of Republic of Texas Military Rolls at the Texas State Archives, 1835–1846.*

Ibid., *An Inventory of Ranger Records at the Texas State Archives, 1839–1975.*

Ibid. FAO Corporate Document Repository, *Elementary Surveying Equipment.*

Ibid., History Channel online, *8 Famous Texas Rangers.*

Ibid., Africa Geography, *Chain Surveying and Its Equipment.*

Ibid., Guns America, News and Reviews, *Cowboy Time Machine: Colt's First Revolver, the Paterson, Yesterday and Today.*

Ibid., *Joint Resolution, 1844 (copy of original document), Reimbursement of Captain John C. Hays for shoeing horses.*

Ibid., *Colt-Paterson Pistol.*

Ibid., *History of Republic of Texas, Chapter Four, Launching a Nation, 1836–48.*

Ibid., *Instruments used in Chain Survey.*

Ibid., *Jack C. Hays.*

Ibid., *John Coffee Hays.*

Ibid., *Loading a Muzzle Loading Percussion Revolver.*

Ibid., *(copy of original document) Muster Roll of Spies for the Protection of Bexar County Called into Service on the First of September, 1841.*

Ibid., *Google Books, Roll Call Bexar Spies.*

Ibid., *Taxes, Republic of Texas.*

Ibid., *Texas 1836 Campaign Map.*

Ibid., *Texas Ranger Hall of Fame and Museum, Ranger History in a Brief Form.*

Printed in the United States
By Bookmasters